MW00583176

High Risk
A Detective Liv DeMarco Thriller

G.K. Parks

This is a work of fiction. Names, characters, places, events, and other concepts are the product of the author's imagination or are used fictitiously. Any resemblance to actual persons, living or dead, places, establishments, events, and locations is entirely coincidental.

No part of this book may be reproduced in any form or by any electronic or mechanical means including information storage and retrieval systems, without express written permission from the author.

Copyright © 2021 G.K. Parks

A Modus Operandi imprint

All rights reserved.

ISBN: 1942710259
ISBN-13: 978-1-942710-25-7

For my mom and dad

ONE

"We need to go." Carter tugged the balaclava off and stuffed it inside the bag. He peered out the rear window at Star Cleaners. What had they done? He swallowed, eyeing the shattered front door. "Come on. Let's get the hell out of here."

"Not yet. We have to wait for him." Diego exhaled and squeezed the steering wheel, sensing waves of anxiety rolling off the man beside him.

Carter's eyes darted back and forth. He could hear sirens. They were getting closer. He checked the mirrors. Were those flashing lights? He thought he saw a reflection on the slick streets. "The cops are coming. Don't you hear that?"

"Hear what?" Diego eyed him curiously. "You feeling okay?"

"No." Carter ran a hand down his face and bit his lip. "No one was supposed to be inside. He said no one would be there. It's a dry cleaner's. Why would anyone be there at this time of night?"

Diego swallowed. So the noise he heard had been

gunfire. "Calm down." He kept one eye trained on the side mirror. "What happened?"

"He's fucking insane. That's what happened." Carter reached into his pocket with shaking hands and pulled out a pre-rolled joint. He held it between his lips while he searched for his lighter. "Diego, man, I'm telling you this was a bad idea. This guy..." He shook his head. "How well do you know him? Shit."

"What?"

"He killed him. Shot him right in the head. Didn't even think twice about it." Locating the lighter, Carter held it to the end of the joint just as the back door opened.

"Put that out," the third man said, tossing a heavy bag across the seats before climbing in beside it. "We don't need to risk leaving evidence behind." He tapped Diego on the shoulder. "Drive."

Diego put the car in gear, glancing at Carter from the corner of his eye, but the man in the passenger seat didn't say or do anything. The unlit joint remained hanging from between his lips while he stared straight ahead, as if he were too afraid to turn around and face the man in the back seat.

After a few blocks, the man in the back tapped Diego again. "Pull over up ahead. There aren't any cameras in that alley. We need to ditch the car. Things didn't go as planned. It's too hot to drive around in this, unless we want to get caught."

"No one wants that." Diego checked the mirrors, but the streets were empty. He stopped in the alley and turned off the engine. "Did we at least get what we were after?"

Carter fidgeted in the seat, anxious to run. The bag at his feet contained only cash. That hadn't been the goal, but Diego wasn't going to argue about receiving a bonus.

The man in the back seat smiled. "We got them." He reached forward and tapped Carter on the shoulder. "Hey, you all right?"

Carter flinched at his touch. "Uh-huh."

"You ain't acting right. Turn around and look at me."

After sucking in another breath, Carter turned in his seat. "What?"

The man studied his face and searched his eyes. "You ever kill anyone before?"

"I didn't kill that guy. You did."

The man snickered and shoved the gun into Carter's hand. "I wouldn't be so sure about that. It was your intel, remember?" Then he gave his nervous accomplice two friendly taps on the cheek. "Don't worry so much. He was a security guard. He had it coming. And if I hadn't intervened, that'd be you lying dead on the floor."

"Security?" Diego asked. "Why would a dry cleaner's hire a guard?"

"Who knows? But someone should have found that out when conducting the research. It would have been nice to know what we were walking into. Maybe things wouldn't have had to get loud and messy. If you don't like killing, try to do better next time." The man stared into Carter's eyes. "You got it?"

"Ye-yeah." Carter swallowed.

The man smiled at him. "Good." He tugged the mask off his face and smoothed his staticky hair as best he could. "Let's wipe the car and torch it. It'll delay the cops when they come looking, and you know they'll come looking."

Because you left a body behind, Carter thought.

"Gas can's in the trunk," Diego said. "I'll find us something else."

"No," the man in the back seat said, "the police

would expect that once they find the car. Let's take the subway instead." He checked his watch. "The trains are running, and the station's not far from here."

"Maybe we should split up," Carter suggested, fingering the strap on the duffel at his feet.

The third man eyed Carter. Normally, they'd split up and meet back at the apartment later, but he couldn't be sure what the Nervous Nelly might do. "No. We're in this. We stick together until we see it through." He tossed a rag into the front seat. "Start wiping. Make sure you don't leave any prints or DNA behind. The fire should cook everything, but let's not take any chances."

"Yeah, okay." Carter opened his door and tossed the duffel out.

The three of them wiped every smooth surface and made sure to empty the interior. Then Diego doused the car in gasoline, and Carter tossed his lighter into the open window. Immediately, flames filled the inside.

"Now's a bad time to grow a conscience," the third man warned as they ducked out of the alley and headed across the street, remaining out of sight of the few street lamps and storefronts with exterior security cameras. "We're in this now. There's no turning back. If you have a problem with the way things work, you should have thought about it before." He shoved Carter against the wall. "Tell me now. Are we going to have a problem?"

Diego stopped, looking uneasy as he watched the exchange.

"No problem here." Carter shoved the third man off of him.

"Good, because we're just getting started."

*   *   *

"What do we have?" I brushed a highlighted tendril behind my ear. I didn't even have time to tie my hair up before we got the call this morning.

The officer rubbed one of his eyes. "See for yourself, Detective."

I peered through the broken glass. Blood spatter covered the left wall and the potted plant. But from here, I couldn't see a body. My partner, Detective Brad Fennel, carefully stepped through the broken front door and went around the counter, stopping at the opening.

"Just one victim?" he asked.

The officer snorted. "Unless you find more."

"Let's hope not." Fennel met my eyes. "Hell of a way to start the day."

"I'm guessing he probably thought the same thing." I nodded to the officer and entered the dry cleaner's. The sign on the back wall offered dry cleaning, laundry, pressing, folding, and free delivery. Pulling on a latex glove, I tugged on the open drawer to the cash register. It was empty. "Money's gone, assuming the owner left anything in the drawer last night."

"We'll have to ask." Fennel stood over the victim. "According to responding officers, the vic's name is Jonathan Gardner."

"Yep," a voice called from behind the curtain that led into the back. A moment later, a crime scene tech popped her head through.

Simmons, I thought, but I couldn't recall her first name.

"Hey, Ellie." Fennel nodded to her. "I haven't seen you in a while."

"I know." She winked at him. "I've missed those big brown eyes of yours." She knelt down beside the body. "We couldn't ID him from his photo on account of most of his face being blown into the wall and that plastic ficus." She pointed to the spatter, which made my partner turn a sickly yellow-green. He swallowed but held it together. "So we ran his fingerprints."

"Does he have a record?" I asked.

"No," she looked up at me, "uh..."

"Liv DeMarco." I jerked my head toward Fennel. "I'm Brown Eyes' partner."

She laughed. "Nice to meet you, Detective DeMarco."

"Yeah, you too." I crouched down next to her. "Has the coroner been here yet?"

"No. They're backed up. So we're not touching the body. But I'm willing to go out on a limb and say cause of death was a gunshot to the face. The bullet went through Mr. Gardner and right into that wall." She pointed up at the hole.

Fennel turned and moved closer to it. It sat level with the tip of his nose. That probably meant Mr. Gardner was just slightly shorter than my partner. So maybe 5'10. Carefully, I picked up the victim's wallet, which had been dropped beside his body. I checked his stats, not surprised to find my guess accurate. I tossed the wallet to my partner and stood up.

"You said he doesn't have a record." Fennel flipped through the contents. Aside from Gardner's license and gym membership, the wallet was empty. "So why are his prints in the system?"

"He works for a security firm. They're all on record." Simmons grabbed the edge of the counter to help herself up. "Moonlight Security." She shifted her gaze from him to me. "You ever heard of them?"

I shook my head and turned to Fennel.

"Yeah, maybe." He closed the empty wallet and handed it to Simmons, who made an evidence bag materialize out of thin air. "So what are we thinking?

Robbery gone wrong?"

She shrugged.

"Who found the body?" I asked.

"Mr. Lee, the dry cleaner." She pointed to the curtain which led to the back. "Sgt. Chambliss is speaking to him now."

"In here?" I asked. Normally, we didn't question suspects in the middle of our crime scene.

"Lee placed the 9-1-1 call from his office phone. I don't think the sergeant's had much luck clearing him out. But we gave the entire place a preliminary sweep. We didn't find a murder weapon or any indication the killer entered the office. According to Mr. Lee, the office door was still locked when he arrived. I don't think anything's missing."

Fennel jerked his chin toward the curtain. "We don't want to miss the party. Lead the way, Liv."

I stepped over Mr. Gardner and pulled the curtain aside. "Wow." The front of the shop was tiny, with standing room for maybe three people on the customer side of the counter. Behind the counter had been a bit more spacious, but it was nothing compared to this.

Fennel whistled beside me. "Is this what they mean by looking behind the curtain?"

"I guess so."

He took a breath, squinting at the machinery and racks of suspended garments. Each one was covered in cellophane and tagged with an order number. "Fancy operation." A narrow walkway led past the conveyor belt of clothing and the large machines for cleaning, pressing, and folding. At the end was an office where a thin, bald man sat with his head in his hands while Sgt. Chambliss spoke gently to him.

Fennel knocked on the doorjamb, and Chambliss turned to us. "Detectives," he greeted, "this is Arthur

Lee. He owns Star Cleaners. He arrived around 5:45 this morning and found Jonathan Gardner dead. He came back here, unlocked the door, and called us. He's been here ever since. He doesn't want to go back out there until the body's been cleared away." Chambliss gave us a look. He didn't like this any more than I did.

"I'm sorry," I said, stepping into the room.

Mr. Lee looked up at the sound of my voice. "I knew today was going to be a bad day. My horoscope warned me about this. I just didn't think it'd be this bad."

Chambliss met Fennel's eyes and jerked his chin toward the door. "Excuse me for just a minute, Mr. Lee. I need to have a word with Detective Fennel. Detective DeMarco will pick up where we left off."

"Sure." Mr. Lee nodded, something he seemed to do more often than a bobblehead doll. Clearly, he was in shock. "As I was telling the sergeant, I don't know the security guard. Not really. I have a service. A night watchman was included in the deal."

"So you don't know Mr. Gardner?"

Lee shook his head.

"How long has he worked here?"

"I don't know."

I stopped writing and looked up from my notepad. "You don't know?"

"No, I don't. That's what I was saying to your boss."

My jaw set, but I didn't offer a correction to his statement. Sgt. Chambliss wasn't my boss. And explaining the command structure of the police department would be a waste of time. "Explain that to me."

"Like I said, Moonlight Security provides a guard. He comes in at night. They have the details. I don't know how long that man's been working here. They've assigned several different night watchmen. I didn't bother paying attention to who's who."

"Okay. Why don't you tell me when you hired Moonlight Security?"

His brow furrowed. "Um... three weeks ago?" He turned toward the filing cabinet behind the desk. "I have the contract here somewhere." He got up and opened the drawer. Automatically, my hand moved to the holstered weapon at my hip and rested on top of it. It never hurt to be safe instead of sorry, but he pulled out a folder and returned to the desk without incident. "Eighteen days ago." He held out the contract for me to read.

I skimmed the details. Star Cleaners bought new locks for the front and rear doors and had alarms installed. They also had new security cameras mounted out back and a remote control opener installed for the metal gate to make it easier and safer for the delivery van to get in and out.

"They offered me a package deal on the night watchman," Mr. Lee said, "if I upgraded."

"Sure, that makes sense, I guess." I handed back the folder, wondering if I should ask for a copy now or wait until later. "But I'm fuzzy on one thing."

"What's that?"

"Why does a dry cleaner need a night watchman?"

Mr. Lee's mouth dropped, and he gawked at me. "To make sure no one breaks in to steal the drugs."

TWO

"What?" I couldn't have heard him right. "Did you say drugs?"

"Yes." He gave me a bewildered look. "You passed them on your way in. The dry cleaning chemicals," he pointed out the door, "they can be huffed. Used as inhalants. They make great gateway drugs. I saw that on one of those primetime news shows. You're a cop. Don't you know that?"

"Have you ever huffed them?"

He jerked backward as if I slapped him. "God no. Do I look like a drug addict to you?"

"No, sir," I said, growing more uncertain of this fact. "But most people wouldn't think to huff dry cleaning chemicals. Has this been a problem in the past? Have you had a lot of break-ins?"

"No, but I've had problems with a number of employees. They were supposed to be working, and instead, they'd sneak off and get high."

"And you caught them huffing the chemicals?"

"Well, no. But they'd be gone for a few minutes,

come back, and y'know, it was obvious they were on something. What else could it have been?"

A number of things, but Mr. Lee could be right. "How many times did this happen?"

"More than I care to count."

I sighed, not wanting to think how bleak life must be to inhale dry cleaning chemicals for kicks. Frankly, I despised dry cleaning after my best friend Emma had forced me to read studies on the neurotoxins and cancer causing chemicals involved in the process. Sure, some places used safer and more eco-friendly substances, but I still wasn't convinced it was a good idea, specifically after I learned it didn't actually do much to penetrate the fabrics and make them any cleaner. And after hearing how frequently Mr. Lee's employees allegedly huffed them, I had another reason to despise dry cleaning. Not to mention, Jonathan Gardner probably wasn't a fan either.

"Can I get a copy of this?" I tapped the security contract with my pointer finger. "And a list of your past and current employees with the troublemakers highlighted?"

Mr. Lee opened the top drawer of his desk. "Sure. Do you think one of them broke in here and killed that man?"

"I don't know."

He grabbed a highlighter and opened another drawer. "Frankly, I wouldn't be surprised."

"Did any of them hold a grudge after you fired them or give you reason to think they might want to harm or steal from you? Have you received any threats?" To hire a night watchman, something must have happened.

"Not that I recall."

"Okay." That didn't help me any. I took in the rest of the office. From what I could tell, it hadn't been ransacked. "Did you happen to notice if anything's missing?"

Lee pursed his lips while he rummaged through the drawer. "Like I told the sergeant, the office was locked when I got here. The cash drawer had two hundred and fifty dollars in it. That's gone. But that's all I can say for certain. I haven't had time to inventory the chemicals in the storeroom, but at first glance, everything appears to be there. Unless they filled the jugs with water or something."

"DeMarco," Fennel called, "do you have a minute?"

"Hold that thought, Mr. Lee. I'll be right back."

Chambliss gave me a look as I came out the door. "The guy's a little off his rocker, but he's pretty damn shaken. CSU tested his hands for GSR, but it came back negative. Same with blood. He doesn't own a gun or have any priors. I don't think he killed the security guard."

Lee had given me the same impression, but I'd learned long ago not to be quick to pass judgment, at least at work. "Did he explain to you why he has a night watchman?"

"He got a discount or freebie. It has something to do with the new security system he installed."

"What did the security company say?"

"Moonlight didn't have anything to say. The alarm was never tripped. The disarm code was entered around four. Your partner has the details." Chambliss glanced into the office. "All right, I'll finish up with Mr. Lee and take him down to the station to fill out a report, unless you need more time to ask questions."

"I think he's given us enough for now. We can always follow up." I poked my head back into the office. "Mr. Lee, is there anything else you wanted to tell me?"

Lee thought for a moment. "No, but if you need dry

cleaning, I have a uniform discount. Twenty percent off."

"Okay." I kept my face neutral in the professional manner I had practiced in the mirror, "just get us that paperwork as soon as you can. If you need anything or remember anything else, here's my card. Don't hesitate." I placed it on his desk. "Sgt. Chambliss will finish taking your statement." I passed Chambliss in the doorway and went back into the cavernous dry cleaning area to meet Fennel.

He rubbed a hand over his mouth and stared at the endless row of hanging garments. They were attached to a conveyor belt that circled, making it easier to find a customer's order for pickup. He glanced back at the office, listening to Chambliss' voice drift into the hallway.

"The ME's here. He placed time of death between 3 and 5 a.m. I'd wager it was around 4:12," Fennel said as he led the way back to the front of the building.

"That's precise. Are you clairvoyant now?"

"Only when it comes to reading your mind." He held the curtain to the side so I could walk through. "But the security system logged an entry at 4:12."

"The alarms never went off," I said. "That's when the system was disarmed?"

"Yeah." Fennel glanced down at Gardner as we carefully maneuvered around the medical examiner and his assistant as they photographed the body. Simmons crouched beside them, gathering evidence and taking more photos as they prepared the slain guard for transport. "Someone knew the disarm code." He handed me a sheet of paper with a list of names. "Those are Star Cleaners' employees and previous employees who knew the code."

"Inside job?"

"It reads like it. I just don't understand the point.

Why break in just to kill a guard and empty a register? Did Lee say anything?"

"He might be crazy, but he's under the impression drug addicts want to steal the dry cleaning chemicals."

"That'd be a first." Fennel exited the shop and took a moment to stare up into the bright morning sky. He took a few deep breaths, the color slowly returning to his face. "Then again, anything's possible. We should check with narcotics and see if they've heard anything about this. It could be the newest craze."

"Perhaps."

"This isn't the safest neighborhood. According to dispatch, they get about a dozen calls a day for the area. Mr. Lee could be on to something. Or the killer broke in just to kill Gardner, and the money was a bonus."

I didn't like that theory, but it made the most sense. "No one reported gunfire?"

"Not according to dispatch."

That didn't sit right with me.

"It was one shot, Liv. The bastard didn't miss. He fired point blank. He couldn't have been any farther from his victim than I am from you."

"So why'd Gardner let some asshole with a gun get that close to him?" I tried to think, but it was too early in the morning for this. I hadn't even had my coffee yet. "It reads almost like a mugging gone wrong."

"Maybe it was." Fennel scanned the perimeter, following the crime scene tape that blocked off the front of the dry cleaner's from the rest of the sidewalk. "Gardner could have gone to grab lunch or take a smoke break. He stepped outside, met the killer, and promised to hand over his wallet and the register in exchange for his life. At least, that's what the sergeant thinks might have happened."

"It's a possibility." I called to the nearest uniformed

officer, "We're going to need copies of the surveillance footage. Everything Star Cleaners caught and whatever we can get from nearby shops. I was told Chambliss sent officers to perform a canvass."

"We're already on it, Detective DeMarco."

"All right, good."

Fennel quietly snickered. "You know, I took care of that while you were inside chatting with Mr. Lee."

"How would I know that?"

"Because you know me."

"Yeah, well, I also thought you were going to blow chunks all over Gardner. Maybe I really don't know you that well." I nudged his shoulder. "How about Ellie? Does she know you better than I do?"

"Are you trying to ask me something?"

"You know what I'm asking."

Fennel gave me the evil eye. "Let's check out back. That's where the disarm code had been entered. I want to see the setup. Chambliss thinks the killer might have come in from the back and left through the front. Ellie found several sets of footprints near the rear gate. It could lead to something."

"Muggers don't usually lie in wait."

"Maybe it was a slow night."

We went through the alley, which opened behind the building and crossed to the remote-controlled gate. Two security cameras stood watch over the back of the building. One was posted on the wall, perpendicular to the gate, and the other covered the two double doors that led into the back of Star Cleaners. A patrol officer monitored the back while another crime scene tech dusted for prints and collected trace evidence.

"Have you pulled security footage yet?" Fennel pushed his jacket aside to expose his badge to the unfamiliar officer.

"Yeah, but I doubt you'll get much. The cameras have been sprayed with some kind of oil," the officer said.

The CSU tech didn't even bother looking in our direction before chiming in, "My guess is the perp used cooking spray. It's cheap, easy to find, and did a hell of a number on the lens."

"What else did you find?" Fennel asked.

While they went over the rest of the details, I studied the tight walls, barely spread far enough to accommodate the delivery van. Frankly, being back here was making me claustrophobic. So instead, I focused my attention on the conversation, but something didn't make sense. "Do you think the killer came in through the back?"

"That's what the cameras would suggest," the tech said. "He probably followed the guard inside after he entered the code."

"And that's the panel where the disarm code was entered." Fennel jerked his chin toward the number pad beside the double doors. "Did you print it?"

"It's smudged too badly. We didn't get anything usable."

"But if the killer came in through the back, who broke the front door?" I asked.

"Maybe he went out that way," the uniformed officer suggested, parroting the sergeant's theory.

Fennel chewed on the inside of his lip. "Most of the glass landed on the inside. That means he broke the glass door from outside the shop. We could be dealing with more than one attacker."

"Gardner could have been in on it and got double-crossed. Or something else went down, and he got caught in the crossfire." I stared at the keypad. "We need to determine who used that panel to enter the disarm code."

Fennel reached for the folded sheet of paper. "Well, we got a list."

THREE

Five names were on the list. Four, if we excluded Arthur Lee. "This can't be everyone."

"It isn't," Brad said as he drove toward the first person's home address. "Moonlight Security installed the system. They must have the disarm codes too. And who knows how many people that might include."

"Great." I flipped down the visor and checked to make sure my ponytail was smooth.

"And it doesn't include the people these people told. We might have to spend the entire day hunting down the person who entered the code, and it could be for nothing. We don't even know if that's how the killer got inside."

I gave my partner a look. "Why are you causing trouble? Can't some things be easy?"

"Me?" He let out a snort. "You started it. I'm just doing my job. I don't want Jonathan Gardner's killer to get away with murder. So we're going to find this guy or girl or team. Whoever they may be."

"Okay." I rubbed a hand down my face and studied the list of employees, current and former. "This is a lot of turnover for a dry cleaner's. Half of these people don't work for Star Cleaners anymore."

"Red flag?" Brad asked.

"Possibly."

A yellow coupe pulled out of a space a few spots away, and Brad parked in the now empty space. "Perfect timing."

I looked at the clock on the dash. "Not really. The world's on its way to work and school." I hated early mornings.

"Can't we at least celebrate the little things? This job's hard enough. You don't have to be so cynical about everything." He winked at me and climbed out of the car.

I followed him down the sidewalk and up the steps to a fourth floor walkup. He knocked on the door and waited. Thirty seconds later, the front door opened a few inches, the chain holding it in place.

"Ms. Rivera?" Brad asked.

"Yes? May I help you?"

"We're the police, ma'am. I'm Detective Fennel, and this is Detective DeMarco. We just have a few questions. May we come inside?"

"Questions?"

"About Star Cleaners," Fennel said. "Please, it'll only take a few minutes."

"Okay." Catelyn Rivera closed the door, removed the chain, and pushed the door wide to allow us to enter. Her studio apartment didn't hide any secrets. "I don't work for Mr. Lee anymore. I quit three days ago."

"May I ask why?" I watched her cross the room and pour a cup of coffee while placing a frozen waffle in the toaster. My stomach growled, surprising me. After visiting the crime scene, I thought I had lost my appetite.

"Mr. Lee's an asshole." She opened the fridge and pulled out some jam. When the waffle popped, she flipped it over and pushed it back into the toaster. "He pays minimum wage. No benefits. No nothing. But he acts like he's doing me some huge favor by letting me work there. Like it's a privilege instead of one step above slave labor. I told him I couldn't work Tuesdays or Thursdays. I have class those days, but he didn't care. He thought my work schedule should take priority over my class schedule. So I told him what he could do with the job."

"How long did you work there?" I asked.

Fennel wandered toward the kitchen table and scanned the stack of textbooks.

"I got the job right after finals and worked through the break, so a few weeks. He knew when he hired me I was working on my bachelor's. I'm a senior."

"European history?" Fennel held up one of the textbooks.

"No, economics. But I failed history my freshman year, and I've been putting off retaking it. Now I don't have a choice."

"And you can't afford to fail again," I said.

She gave me a determined look. "I won't. Nothing's going to stop me this time."

"Where were you between the hours of three and five this morning?" Fennel asked.

"I was still at the library at three. Then I came back here to get some sleep before my eight a.m. class." She gave me a bewildered look, and I noted the dark circles beneath her eyes. "Why? What happened? Did something happen to Mr. Lee?"

"Can anyone vouch for your whereabouts?" Fennel asked.

She blinked a few times. "No, I was here by myself. I was sleeping."

"Do you know Jonathan Gardner?" I asked.

She shook her head.

"According to Mr. Lee, you know how to disarm Star Cleaners' security system," I said. "Have you ever done that? Or have you shared the disarm code with anyone else?"

Her waffle popped, and she reached for it, slathering butter and jam on it before taking a bite. "No," she said while she chewed, "I wouldn't give out the code. I only used it twice, those two days he had me open for him." She wiped her mouth on the back of her hand. "Honestly, I probably wouldn't even remember it if it didn't spell out STAR."

"What?" Fennel asked.

"You know, like on the telephone. The numbers coordinate with the letters." She looked embarrassed. "On the keypad, each number has letters above it. So I just hit the digits to make the word. It was easy enough."

"And the code spells out STAR." That didn't make the security system seem particularly secure, but I wasn't sure how many people would think to do that. Then again, after trying the street number and 1-2-3-4, that would probably be the next logical guess.

"For the record, you never told anyone that?" Fennel asked.

"Why would I? It's not like I had someone picking up my shifts at the dry cleaner's. Twelve hour days in the steamy back with those stinky chemicals and stinkier clothing." She crinkled her nose. "No one I know is desperate enough to work in a place like that for a miser like Mr. Lee." She gulped down some coffee. "I have to get ready."

"Do you own a gun?" Fennel asked.

"No." She shifted her gaze from my partner to me. "Is Mr. Lee okay? I might not have liked him as a boss, but he's still a person."

"He's fine," I said. "Do you mind if we look around?"

"Help yourself, just make it quick. I can't be late for class."

"Sure thing." Fennel and I checked the apartment, but we didn't find a gun, bloody clothing, or broken glass. Nothing indicated Ms. Rivera had been anywhere near Star Cleaners. "Thanks for your time. We may be back to follow up."

"Follow up on what?" she asked as we made our way to the door. "You still haven't told me what happened."

I glanced at my partner. He wanted to play this close to the vest. "Don't worry about it." I jerked my chin at her textbooks. "You have more important things to think about. Good luck."

She smiled, but her eyes held a question. "Uh, thanks."

Brad and I didn't speak until we were inside the cruiser. "I don't think she did it," he said. "And given the security code, anyone could have guessed it."

"Still, according to the security logs, the code was only entered once. That's a lucky first guess." But I didn't think she was responsible either. "Let's move on to the next name on the list."

"Roger that." Brad turned the key in the ignition.

Sgt. Chambliss had patrol officers checking the same things we were checking, but since patrol had to conduct a canvass and probably grab coffee, I had a feeling we'd get through the entire list before they did.

The next name on the list was Guy Kellerman. He still worked at Star Cleaners but hadn't been scheduled to work the rest of the week. When we knocked on his door, no one answered. After some quick checking and a few calls, we discovered Mr.

Kellerman had gone on vacation and flew out yesterday afternoon.

We spoke to him on the phone, but he claimed he never gave out the security code. When asked if he knew Jonathan Gardner, he told me he did not. Since he wasn't in town, had no priors, and a pregnant wife, I decided his alibi was airtight.

"Check his social media for overlap," Fennel said as he drove to the next location.

"How could Kellerman kill someone from hundreds of miles away?" I asked, but I checked anyway. Besides working for Star Cleaners, Guy Kellerman also worked as a janitor at the baseball stadium. He just picked up the gig with Mr. Lee in order to put some money away in case his wife decided to become a stay-at-home mom after their little one was born. "I don't see anything."

Brad rubbed the backs of his fingers against his freshly shaved cheek. "This is a waste."

"You said no stone, remember?"

He growled and reached for the radio. Patrol had already questioned Pamela Aiker, the other current Star Cleaners employee. She also had an airtight alibi, but since she was the delivery driver, she used the code the most. "She could have had someone fill in and told him the code. But she'd never confess to sharing it. She'd lose her job. Then again, Arthur Lee found the body. When the cops arrived, he was inside the shop. He could have done it."

"Okay, what's his motive?" I asked.

"I don't know. It's just something else to consider."

"Maybe we need to treat this like a robbery because, right now, that's what it looks like." Except I wasn't sure.

"Fine, but once we finish up with Star Cleaners' employees, we move on to Jonathan Gardner.

Someone killed him, Liv. And I'm guessing it had more to do with him than the money in the register."

FOUR

"Who is it?" the third man asked.

Carter peered through the peephole. "Shit. It's the cops. They found us. How the hell did they find us?"

"Easy, man. Just breathe." Diego put a hand on Carter's shoulder. "It might not have anything to do with us. Your roomie had a party last night. Three guys are passed out on the bathroom floor. I bet it's about that. Your neighbors probably called in a noise complaint. That's probably all it is."

"It better be." The third man grabbed the two duffel bags and peered down the hallway. They couldn't risk running. The police would catch them on the fire escape. Plus, running would make them look guilty. "Play it cool. Go see what they want. I'll hide our stash."

"What they want?" Carter gawked. "You know what they want. You–"

The third man slapped his palm over Carter's mouth. "That's right. And if you tell them that, so help me, I will put a bullet through you right now. And then they'll have to investigate two murders. You got it?"

Diego scowled. "Easy. Carter's just paranoid."

"Paranoid?" Carter put out the joint and spun in a circle, looking for a place to hide it. "This isn't paranoid." He pointed emphatically at the door.

"Don't freak out." Diego took the joint from between his fingers. "You're not thinking straight. All right? Just answer the door and see what they want. Play it cool. Tell them you were with Mike all night. No one's going to question it. You were there, weren't you?"

"Yeah, but I left after an hour to meet you guys."

"No," the third man insisted, "you were with them the entire time. If the cops ask you something, just say you don't remember because you were drunk or high. It doesn't matter what you say, just as long as you keep your mouth shut about what really happened." He narrowed his eyes. "Do not let them search the house." He opened the coat closet and tucked the bags inside. "You blow this, and I'll blow your fucking head off. And don't try anything stupid. I'll be listening to every word you say."

He opened the first door and entered the room. Two men were passed out on opposite ends of the bed, another one was asleep on the floor. A moment later, Diego joined him.

"At least we showered and changed," Diego muttered as he kicked off his shoes and found a spot on the ground to get comfortable.

"I don't trust Carter," the third man said. "He's too squirrely. You told me he could handle this. But he's ready to crack. If he does, it's on you."

"He won't crack." Diego glanced down at the joint he'd taken from Carter. "He might just need a few more puffs of courage."

*   *   *

Fennel stopped in front of apartment 602, cocked his head to the side, and glanced at me. "You smell that?"

"Someone's having a party."

"This ought to be fun." He knocked on the door again and waited. "Five bucks says no one answers."

"You're on."

From behind the door, I heard movement and whispers. The light shifted beneath the doorframe, and Fennel and I stepped to the side. The place smelled like marijuana, but that didn't mean they didn't have other narcotics inside. And if panicked, people often behaved badly. After a few more whispers, the door creaked open.

"Michael Tolliver?" I asked. The man in the doorway didn't look anything like the photo I'd seen when checking his social media account on the way here. Michael Tolliver had dark brown hair and an olive complexion. This guy was bleach blond and pale. His red, glassy eyes looked like they belonged to an albino rabbit.

"He's sleeping." The man looked down at our badges and guns. "What do you want?"

"And you are?" Fennel asked.

The man rubbed his forehead before wiping his palm on his pants leg. "Carter Moore, Mike's roommate." He stepped back, his gaze darting down the hallway. "If you want to talk to him, I can wake him up."

"Do you mind if we come inside?" Fennel asked.

"No. I mean yes. I mean...what do you want?" Carter rubbed his eyes. A fresh layer of perspiration burst from his pores, giving his skin a slight sheen.

"We just need to speak to your roommate. It'd be

best if we do that inside." Fennel stared at the man.

"So this is about Mike?" Carter asked, nearly breathing a sigh of relief. "Did he do something wrong?"

"We just need to ask him a few questions and find out where he was last night," I said.

Fennel narrowed his eyes. "Are you on something, sir?"

"Me?" Carter shook his head vehemently. "No...uh...just hungover." He turned to look behind him. After several seconds, he let go of the door. "I guess it'd be okay if you came inside."

Fennel and I exchanged a look and cautiously entered the apartment. The smell of pot grew stronger, but I didn't see a burning joint anywhere in sight. Carter led us into the living room, fidgeting uncontrollably. The man was practically shaking.

"Is something wrong?" Fennel asked. Obviously, our presence had made him uneasy, probably on account of the pot, but I couldn't be sure that's all it was.

"No, nothing. Just battling a hellacious hangover. You know how those go." Carter headed for the hallway. "Stay right here. I'll get Mike for you." Voices emanated from down the hall, but I couldn't make out what they were saying.

I kept watch while Fennel examined every inch of the living room. He found an empty ashtray and a vase that doubled as a bong but no contraband. Fennel stopped in front of the entertainment center and knelt down, examining the lower shelves. When I heard a doorknob turn, I cleared my throat. Fennel stood up and straightened his jacket.

A moment later, Carter returned. "Mike's getting dressed. He'll be right out." He leaned against the wall. The nervousness had been replaced by an unsettling mellow. Maybe they'd been smoking in the bedrooms. "Want to tell me what this is about, officers?"

"Was Mike here all night?" I asked.

Carter stared at me and licked his lips. "Not all night. We spent most of the night at a strip club." He chuckled. "Bachelor party." He eyed me again. "None of those women even came close to holding a candle to you. You're the prettiest thing I've seen in a long time."

"Thanks," Fennel said, "I exfoliate."

Carter turned to look at my partner. "What?"

"Who's getting married?" Fennel asked.

"Huh?" Carter grew even more confused.

"You said you were at a bachelor party. Who's getting married?" Fennel asked again.

"Oh, um, my buddy. Well, he's really Mike's buddy. Mike got the invite. I just tagged along. Who wouldn't?" Carter swallowed. "So yeah, that's where we were until like...." He blinked a few times. "Four. And then we called a car to drive us back."

"What strip club?" I asked.

"Dimples."

Another man stumbled down the hallway, using both hands to bounce off one wall and then the other, like a pinball. He got to the end and dropped into a recliner. Even disheveled, this guy looked like his profile pictures.

"Michael Tolliver?" I asked.

He forced his eyes open and leaned his head back to look up at me. "Yeah. What can I do for you? Carter said the police were here." He caught sight of my badge and gun beneath my jacket. "I thought he was lying. I thought you might have been a strippergram. Do they still have those?"

"I wouldn't know."

"Sorry." He held up his palms. "Is this about last night? We paid our tab. And the girl in the cake, that was supposed to have been taken care of."

"That's not why we're here." I glanced at Fennel. It'd be best if we split up. "May we speak in the kitchen, Mr. Tolliver?"

Michael hauled himself out of the chair. "Yeah. I need coffee. And water. And aspirin."

I followed him into the kitchen while Fennel continued to drill Carter about the bachelor party and details on their whereabouts.

"I'm sorry to bother you so early in the morning. But you work for Star Cleaners, right?" I asked.

"Yeah." Mr. Tolliver opened a cabinet and grabbed a box of instant coffee. Then he reached for a mug. "Would you like some?"

I would love some. But something about this place and these men left me uneasy. "No, thanks."

He nodded before filling a mug with tap water and placing it inside the microwave. "Did something happen at work?"

"There was a break-in. Mr. Lee said you had the access code." I watched Tolliver's expression carefully, but his surprise was genuine.

"I didn't do it. That's why you're here, isn't it? Shit." He took the mug out and stirred the coffee crystals into it. "Look, whatever you need, Detective...?"

"DeMarco," I said. "I'll need names of the people who can vouch for you, what time you left the strip club, all of that."

He clung to the counter as he made his way toward an abandoned smart phone. He tapped on the screen a few times, blinking in an attempt to focus what must have been blurry double-vision. "Here's the receipt from my rideshare." He held out the device. "And Gary saw me. Hell, everyone did. There were like a million of us there. If you check the photo roll, there are probably pictures. I'm not sure if there's a timestamp or whatever."

I read the receipt. Carter was right. They didn't leave until four, when the club closed. After copying down all the pertinent information, I checked Tolliver's recent photos. "I thought strip clubs didn't allow flash photography."

"Not of the girls on stage, but Gary's brother rented out the entire place. We were the only ones there. So it shouldn't have been a problem."

"What happened with the girl in the cake?" I asked.

He blushed. "Nothing. She was great. Delicious. No, Tasty." He turned a deeper shade of crimson. "That was her stage name. Apparently, she cost extra. Or the cake did. I don't know, but Bart's credit card got declined. I think Willie or Kevin picked up the tab."

He came over and pointed to the screen. "That's Willie. That's Gary. The one with the bra on his head, that's Kevin."

I thumbed back through the photographs, finding more shots of the group outside the club. Twenty-three men had gone to the bachelor party. I handed Tolliver my notepad. "I need names and whatever numbers you have, just in case. Where did you go after the club?"

"Several of us came back here for the after party." Tolliver gulped down some coffee. "Half of them are passed out on my bedroom floor, if you want to ask them any questions."

"Liv," Fennel called, stepping into the kitchen, "you almost through in here?"

"Do you know Jonathan Gardner?" I asked.

Tolliver blew on the rising steam and took a sip. "He's the night watchman. Why? Did he say I did this?"

"No, sir," Fennel said. "He's dead."

"Dead?" Tolliver sputtered, choking on coffee. "No way. I just saw him yesterday. What happened?"

"He was shot inside Star Cleaners." Fennel glanced back into the living room, but Carter appeared to be in a daze. "Do you own a gun?"

"A shotgun. I keep it at my parent's hunting cabin." He paled, looking like he might be sick. "Do I need a lawyer?"

"No, sir. We just have to figure out what happened. Do you remember any problems arising at work? Did you see or hear anything suspicious? Did Mr. Gardner mention any threats or problems with anyone?"

"No, nothing like that. I just do my job and go home. It's hi and bye. Nothing more. Mr. Lee doesn't exactly let us talk much. It's just about doing the work." Tolliver dropped into a chair. "I can't believe this. This is insane. When did it happen?"

"Last night," I said.

Tolliver appeared lost in thought. "God."

"Half the party's passed out in the back bedrooms." I looked at my partner, surprised he had said so much. We didn't mention any of this to Catelyn Rivera.

"So I heard." Fennel turned to find Carter still leaning against the wall. "The groom-to-be wandered out in search of the bathroom, and I asked him about his night. I think we're done here."

"I just have one last question, Mr. Tolliver. By chance, did you tell anyone how to disarm Star Cleaners' security system?"

"No, I wouldn't do something like that."

I nodded to him. "Get some sleep. We're sorry to have bothered you."

Carter walked us to the door. He stared at me with

those bloodshot eyes. He looked like he wanted to say something. Finally, he cleared his throat. "I'm sorry," he swallowed, "y'know, that I couldn't be more helpful."

FIVE

"Did you find anything in the MDT?" Fennel asked as he drove to the address we pulled off the victim's license.

"Jonathan Gardner doesn't have a record. I don't think he's ever even had a parking ticket." I stopped tapping on the mobile data terminal and pulled out my phone. "Let me see if I can find anything else on social media."

"We're going to have to make the notification." Fennel chewed on his bottom lip. Every cop hated this part of the job. Most were lucky enough to avoid having to do it. But we weren't so lucky. "I didn't see a ring on his finger. Do you think he's married?"

"No."

My partner let out a sigh. "Okay. What about kids?"

"Just give me a second."

"I hope he doesn't have kids."

"Me too."

"According to his license, he's twenty-eight. He could have kids. Then again, I'm a little older than he is and I don't have any kids. So I guess that doesn't mean anything."

"Are you sure about that, Brown Eyes? It's not like you'd necessarily know if you did."

"I don't."

"Are you sure?" I teased.

"Stop that, Liv. I would know. I'm not that kind of guy."

"Does Ellie have kids? Oh hey, wasn't she out on maternity leave these last few months?"

"You're not funny." Fennel intentionally hit a pothole just to rattle me.

"I'm hilarious. You just don't appreciate my wit." I tapped on my phone, scrolling through the photos on Gardner's social media page. It appeared he had lots of friends but no steady girlfriend, at least not anymore. "I don't think Gardner has kids. No wife. No girlfriend."

"Boyfriend?" Fennel asked.

"According to this, he's into women."

"Are you looking at his dating profile?" Fennel's lip quirked in the corner. "You know, you could try one of those dating sites."

"To search for our victim?"

"No, to search for someone to share your wit with."

"Is that what you shared with Ellie?"

"For the record, we never went out. We're friendly. You know me. I'm a considerate guy, who doesn't have a problem showing his appreciation for our hard-working support teams, so whenever I need a favor, she makes sure our evidence gets processed ahead of schedule. No harm, no foul."

"I always knew you were good for something. I should pimp you out more often. But I don't trust you not to break hearts left and right."

"Do I look like Jake Voletek to you?"

"You might if you didn't shave for a week." Voletek was another homicide detective we worked with. He hit on anything that moved, including me until I set him straight, but despite that, my gut said he was a good cop, dedicated and with a lot to prove, kind of like me. Thankfully, my partner rarely hit on anyone, but that didn't stop most of the women from shamelessly flirting with him. And Fennel and I had been partners long enough for me to know he wasn't exactly a choir boy either. He was just more subtle about it.

"Regardless, you can't pimp me out, Liv. We don't work vice."

"But we could. You might like it better than homicide." I tried to hide the concern from my eyes. Fennel never wanted to work homicide, but he transferred because it's what I wanted. He could have stayed in intelligence, but he wouldn't leave me. He made it clear we were in this together, even if it meant starting some days with his head in a barf bag.

He pulled into a space and cut the engine. "Let me see that." He took the phone from my hand and scanned Jonathan Gardner's page. But there was nothing damning on it. No one had posted any threats. "What are we doing?" He glanced around, but he didn't spot any patrol cars. "The sergeant said he called for a search warrant. But it doesn't look like the paper's here yet."

"We could knock."

Fennel scrolled through Gardner's details one more time and handed back my phone. "Yeah, all right. For all we know, the guy could have a secret harem upstairs. Someone could be inside who knows why Gardner was killed."

"We just left a harem of sorts. What did you make of Michael Tolliver and his roommate?"

"I'm going with potheads. Carter was so fidgety. I swear he went in the bedroom and took a hit because, when he came back, he was chill."

"Yeah." But something still bothered me about that.

"Hey," Fennel nudged me, "do you think Michael Tolliver had something to do with Gardner's murder?"

"No. He seemed genuinely shocked when he heard the news."

"That might not have been shock." Fennel let out a breath. "I spotted what was left of the after party. Half of them were passed out on the bathroom floor. I'll put a call into the rideshare guy and make sure he picked them up and dropped them off at that address, but if he did, I'd say they have a solid alibi."

"You said the killer could be working with a team."

"Not an entire bachelor party. We'd have eyewitness accounts if that were the case."

"True, but that apartment gave me a bad feeling."

"Probably because they hoped you were a strippergram." He handed back my phone. "I bet the pay's nice. You could do it on the side. You wouldn't need to buy any props, you already have a nightstick and handcuffs, and Mr. Lee would give you a discount on uniform cleanings."

"Hey, now. Stripping is an equal opportunity business. You could just as easily shake it for some rolled up dollar bills." I laughed, recalling my first encounter with Voletek.

"What? You don't think women would be into this?" He gestured at his body.

"And some men too."

He snickered. "Equal opportunities, huh?" He reached for the door handle.

We went up the steps and knocked on Gardner's door. Not surprisingly, no one answered. So we did the next best thing. We knocked on his neighbors' doors. No one remembered seeing anyone new dropping by for a visit. No suspicious vehicles had been parked outside, and no one recalled hearing arguments or fights coming from Gardner's apartment. As far as his neighbors were concerned, Jonathan Gardner was a quiet guy who threw barbeques on the weekends during the summer and picked up groceries for the two old ladies who lived upstairs.

I called to check on the status of the warrant while my partner paced just outside the building. When he worked off the nervous energy, he took to leaning against the car. "How long?" he asked.

"It's signed and on the way."

He stared up at the looming apartment building. "I doubt we'll find anything inside. I keep running over it in my head. The broken front door and the punched in security code at the rear, along with the disabled cameras, don't make a lot of sense." He checked his phone again. "According to Mr. Lee, the register was emptied but nothing else was taken."

"Aside from the contents of our victim's wallet."

"What could Gardner even have had in there? I doubt he carried more than a hundred bucks, if he even had that much." Fennel let out a sigh. "This is ridiculous. The only thing I can come up with is it was a robbery, possibly a stickup or mugging, gone wrong. Why kill a man over two hundred and fifty bucks? That's insane."

"It happens."

"No shit, Liv." He blew out a breath. "Sorry."

"It's okay. You're mad. I am too." I thought about Star Cleaners' security system. "It's a bad neighborhood, but still, the scene doesn't make much sense."

Fennel straightened and stepped away from the

car. "Okay, let's say I'm Jonathan Gardner. For some reason I went outside to check on something. I came back in at 4:12 and entered the code, but someone was casing the place and sprayed the cameras."

"Do you think that's why Gardner went outside?" I asked. "He noticed something weird on the camera feed or heard a noise out back? Maybe he spooked the shooter, so the guy went around the front and broke in."

"Except there are two obvious problems with that theory."

"What are they?"

"The killer fired from behind the counter."

"So he emptied the register, then shot Gardner."

"Except I don't see why the security guard would let him do that. He had a gun. He's trained to deal with trouble. Why didn't he pull his piece?"

"It's one thing to read a manual and go over instructions. It's another when you're in the middle of the action. You know that better than anyone."

"Except I always pull my piece," Fennel said, "and so do you."

"We're cops, not security guards."

"All right, I'll give him the benefit of the doubt. But that doesn't explain the security system logs."

"You checked them?"

"I did. And Chambliss said the log showed someone entered the disarm code at 4:12 a.m. from outside the dry cleaner's. The sergeant assumed Gardner must have stepped out for a breath of fresh air and was coming back inside, but wouldn't he have needed to disarm the system before opening the door in order to step outside?" He waited for the light bulb to flick on over my head. "There were two other men inside Star Cleaners besides Jonathan Gardner."

"Unless the front door was broken after Gardner

was already dead," I suggested. "Maybe someone entered from the rear door, killed the guard, emptied the register, and retreated out the back. With the security system disengaged, we have no idea what doors were opened or when. And then someone else wanders by, notices the body peeking out from behind the counter, busts through the front door, and..."

"And what? Empties his wallet?" Fennel asked.

"Well, he was already dead."

My partner rubbed his eyes. "We need to watch the surveillance footage." But before he could say or do anything else, a police cruiser pulled up beside us.

Officer Roberts got out. "Did someone call for a search warrant?"

Fennel took the folded document from Roberts' hand, checked the details to make sure everything was correct, and tucked it into his breast pocket. "All right. Let's see what we find."

We returned to Gardner's apartment. Officer Roberts bumped the lock for us, and we pushed open the front door. Sunlight filtered in through the partially opened blinds. The living room looked as you'd expect a bachelor pad to look. Oversized leather couch, big screen TV, a pile of old pizza boxes and empty beer cans on the coffee table, and a video game system, headset, and a pile of games beside one of the two black gaming chairs that sat on the floor in front of the coffee table.

"Damn," Fennel rubbed his mouth, "it looks like my place."

"You're neater than this," I said.

He gave me a sideways look. "I pick up before you come over."

"Bullshit. You're a neat freak. Everything on your desk is organized in some weird system I still don't understand. Living like this would make you crazy." I headed for the kitchenette. A stack of unopened mail sat on one of the stools at the counter. Water bill, electric bill, credit card application, an advertisement for a new Chinese restaurant, a coupon for a free carwash, and a letter addressed to Richard Golden.

Frowning, I checked the address to see if our victim had gotten his neighbor's mail. But the address matched. "Brad, check the bedroom. I don't think we're alone."

SIX

I cleared the rest of the apartment, checking everything, including the closets before following Fennel into the master bedroom. Crusty brownish-red streaks ran down the man's yellow t-shirt. He remained prone on the bed, his eyes closed.

"Mr. Golden?" I kicked the corner of the mattress, but he didn't stir. "Do you think that's blood?"

Fennel sidestepped around a pile of clothes, glanced into the attached bathroom to make sure the assailant wasn't hiding, and then approached the body on the bed. He reached out with a gloved hand to check for a pulse.

The man screamed, startling us. "Who the hell are you?" He scooted across the mattress and fell off the other side of the bed. Scrambling up, he grabbed a tennis racket and held it in both hands directly in front of his body. He looked like he was about to play Wimbledon.

"Whoa," Fennel held up one palm while he reached for his badge with the other, "take it easy. We thought you were dead."

"What?" Golden yelled.

"Sir, please. We're the police."

"What?" Golden cocked his head to the side, finally noticing the badge in my partner's left hand. Shifting the tennis racket to one hand, he tugged an earbud out of his left ear.

"We thought you were dead," I repeated, hearing an unrecognizable rock song coming from the displaced wireless earbud.

"Why would you think that?" he asked. "Did Johnny put you up to this? Is this some kind of prank?" He pointed the end of the tennis racket at Fennel's badge. "Is that even real?"

Fennel's hand shook for a moment before he hooked his badge to the side of his belt and made a fist. "It's real."

"Mr. Golden?" I asked.

He glanced at me, still unsure about my partner who hadn't moved from the bedside. "Who wants to know?" He edged backward toward the bathroom door, and I wondered if he planned to lock himself inside. Or maybe he needed to change his pants.

"I'm Detective Liv DeMarco. That's Brad Fennel. We knocked earlier. Didn't you hear us?" We should have knocked again before we entered.

His gaze shifted from my partner to me. "No." He gave us an odd look. "If Johnny didn't send you, what are you doing in my apartment?"

"Your apartment?" Fennel let out an exhale. "The lease is in Jonathan Gardner's name."

Golden tucked the racket back beneath the bed and rubbed his eyes. "Yeah, so? I live here too. Is that a problem?"

"No, sir," I said.

He nodded, unsure of what was happening. "So I'll

ask you one more time. What are you doing inside my apartment besides scaring the shit out of me?"

Fennel opened his mouth, but I beat him to the punch. "Mr. Golden, maybe you should sit down."

He crossed his arms over his chest. "You got five seconds, lady. Make this good."

"I'm sorry to have to tell you this, but your roommate's dead."

He snickered. "Uh-huh. Sure." He scratched his left eyebrow. "Let me guess. You two work with him at Moonlight, and he thought it'd be fun to send you over here to scare me. But I'm not an idiot. Cops can't just bust into someone's home."

"We didn't." Fennel removed the court order from his jacket. "We have a search warrant. We knocked, like Liv said, but you didn't answer."

Golden took the offered paperwork, the grin still plastered on his face. But as he read the details, the joy left his eyes. His lips drooped, and he stumbled backward, catching himself on the dresser. He held on to the paper but leaned heavily against the waist-high piece of furniture. Without it, he'd be on the floor.

"My condolences," Fennel said.

"How did it happen? When?" Golden looked up from the paperwork. "I just saw him a few hours ago."

"What time?" I asked.

Golden looked at the clock. "Shit. That was last night. I... oh god. I got home from work. And we played video games until he had to leave. That was 8:30. Somewhere around there." He rubbed a hand down his face. "God, that was just last night. It doesn't feel like it. I..."

"Where were you?" Fennel asked.

"Right here. Well, there." Golden jerked his chin toward the living room. "I got caught up in a game. I didn't go to bed until the sun came up."

"Can anyone verify your whereabouts?" Fennel asked. Until now, I hadn't thought of Golden as a suspect, but everyone was a potential person of interest at this stage, especially with possible blood spatter dripping down his t-shirt. "Was anyone else here?"

"The guys online know I was here. We just made it to level 17. We were talking the entire time."

"Over the headsets?" Fennel asked.

Golden nodded. "And I ordered some pizza around one. I don't remember who delivered it. I just grabbed it."

"Are those the boxes on the coffee table?" I asked.

"Yeah."

"Okay, we'll need your friends' names or handles in order to verify your whereabouts," Fennel said. "Liv, why don't you check with the pizza place?"

I gave Fennel an odd look. "Okay, boss."

He squinted at me. I didn't know what he was thinking, but I returned to the living room and left him alone with Richard Golden. I just hung up with the pizza joint, which verified a delivery had been made to the apartment and was paid for with Golden's credit card and his signature was on the receipt, when Fennel stepped out of the bedroom.

"What's going on?" I asked.

"I told him to get dressed since we have more questions. He's in a state of shock, but I didn't want to leave him alone until I knew for certain he couldn't escape out the window or pull a gun."

"Does he have any weapons?"

"Just the tennis racket."

"What about the stains on his shirt?"

"Ketchup. He works at the Corndog Hut." Fennel placed his palm against the game console. "It's still warm. I don't think he's lying." He peered into the other bedroom. "That must be Jonathan Gardner's room. Do you want to get started in there?"

"Let's wait and see what his roommate has to say before we do anything."

Fennel nodded and took another deep breath. "He scared the shit out of me."

"Me too." I glanced down at Fennel's hand, but it was no longer shaking. "I'm glad he's not dead. Hopefully, he'll be able to give us some answers."

Fennel looked around the apartment. "That'd be nice, but I'm not holding my breath." He went into the kitchen and opened the fridge. Then he checked the cabinets, closing each of the doors as he went.

"What are you looking for?" I knew my partner. He was always professional, but the small voice in the back of my mind that worried about him and could never quite shake the memory of that one time I found him passed out on the floor of his apartment couldn't help but wonder if he was looking for a drink.

"Motive." He came around the counter just as Golden emerged from the bedroom, dressed in a black t-shirt and sweatpants.

"Johnny's really dead?" Golden licked his lips and looked uncertainly at the mess on the coffee table. "Like dead dead? Not like Halloween dead or like in a coma but he might still come out of it but doornail dead?"

"I'm sorry for your loss." I nodded to the sofa. "Why don't you sit down? Brad, get him a glass of water."

Golden rubbed his face. "And you're not with Moonlight?"

"No, sir." I sat down beside him. My partner came around the couch and placed the glass on top of one of the pizza boxes. "What can you tell us about your roommate? Do you know anyone who would want to harm him?"

"No. Johnny was that guy. You know that guy." He looked up at my partner. "The one you can always count on. The one who lets you crash on his couch when your girlfriend kicks you out. The guy who always invites everyone over for a barbeque or a party. He's always so calm and chill. People gravitate toward him. He makes everyone feel better. He's that guy. No one would hurt him. Are you sure he's dead? Maybe I should call him." Golden stood abruptly. "I'm gonna call him."

"Mr. Golden," I began.

"Liv," Fennel shook his head, "let him be."

We watched him dial and wait. When no one answered, he hung up. "You know, Johnny should be back by now."

"What time does he usually get back?" Fennel asked, deciding it was easier to play along than to pound reality into Golden's head.

"A little after eight. He works ten to six. The dry cleaner's opens at seven, and once Mr. Lee shows up, Johnny heads back to the office and clocks out or whatever."

"Do you know why Mr. Lee hired a night watchman?" I asked.

"That was Moonlight Security's brilliant idea. Anyone who upgraded to the deluxe package was assigned a guard for the first thirty days or six weeks or something. I don't know. But that's why Johnny started working there. He spends his nights watching TV and movies on his phone." Golden glanced down at his cell phone. "Maybe his battery's dead."

I'd seen grief and denial but never to this extreme. "Does Johnny have any family or relatives close by?"

"Nah. He moved out here for college and never went back. His folks live out of state."

Fennel handed him his notepad and pen. "Can you write down their names and a phone number, if you have it?"

Golden took the paper and reached for his phone. "Sure." He scrolled through his contact information and copied the phone number and address into my partner's notebook. At least we wouldn't have to make the notification.

"When's the last time they visited?" Fennel entered the details into his phone and shot off a text to someone at the precinct to get the ball rolling. We'd have to contact the local police, and they'd make the notification in person. It was only marginally better than us calling long distance to give Jonathan Gardner's parents the bad news.

"Not since the summer. Johnny went home for the holidays to see them, but they only get together about twice a year. He's busy, and they don't like to travel. He always says he should visit them more often." He swallowed as the facts sunk in, but he was determined for this to not be real. I couldn't fault him for that, but it made our job more difficult. And watching him was heartbreaking enough, even more so than finding the body. At least then, Gardner was just another victim. Now he was a person with people who cared about him. "He wanted to go see them for his little sister's birthday. She's turning twenty-one at the end of next month."

"Tell us about Johnny," Fennel said. "When did you meet? What does he do? Where does he hang out? Who are his friends?"

"We met freshman year. We shared a dorm and have been best friends ever since. Johnny used to work as a bartender, but then the manager asked him if he could work as a bouncer instead. So that's what Johnny did. He liked it okay, but it didn't pay much.

Eventually, he found a job at Moonlight Security. I guess that was two years ago. Most of it was just stupid night watchman shit. He worked in an office building for a while. But these last six months, he's been reassigned like five times. He hates it. He's been looking for something else, but he hasn't found anything yet." Golden jerked his head to the side, as if the glitch in his brain had resulted in a physical manifestation. "Needless to say, ever since they screwed with his hours and schedule, he hasn't had much time to hang out with friends. We tend to stay around here. The last time he had a day off, he ran some errands."

"What kind of errands?" Fennel asked.

"Just basic stuff. Getting his oil changed, grocery shopping, that kind of thing."

"Does he have a girlfriend?" I asked.

Golden shook his head. "Mary did a real number on him. He's sworn off dating for the time being. One of these days, he'll come around. I keep telling him that. But in the meantime, he still makes a hell of a wingman, if I can ever convince him to grab a beer. Ever since he worked in a bar, he doesn't exactly enjoy going to them. It's probably why I hate corndogs and hotdogs and tater tots." He cringed.

"Mary?" Fennel flipped his notepad to a new page.

"Yeah, Mary Winsor. They broke up ten months ago. The heartless bitch. They'd been together for six years, since college. I don't know what her deal was, other than the fact she's psycho." He rolled his eyes.

"Has Johnny seen her since? Has she contacted him at all?" Fennel asked.

"No. He tried calling her a couple of times after she broke up with him, but she wouldn't give him the time of day. She said she had to find herself and she couldn't do that with him." He shook his head. "I heard from a friend of a friend that she went to some ashram or temple or something, but then I noticed photos online of Mary in California with some other guy. From the way she was hanging all over him, I don't think he's a monk."

"Did Johnny know about this?" Fennel asked.

"I don't know. Maybe. But she's ancient history. He just hasn't gotten over the heartbreak yet. I told him the best way is to get some. That'll put everything back in perspective. But I think he was happy with it just being us. No nagging girlfriends or wives. We got it made. This is the good life." Suddenly, his cheeks turned red and his eyes filled with tears. "God." He held his fist to his mouth and bit his knuckle. "What am I supposed to do now? He's my best friend. And now you're telling me he's dead."

While I attempted to comfort Richard Golden, my partner searched Jonathan Gardner's bedroom and the rest of the apartment. But we didn't find anything that would explain why someone shot him in the face. When Fennel finished the search, he called for an officer to keep an eye on Mr. Golden. Neither of us wanted to leave the distraught man alone.

SEVEN

"Are you going to cry?" Brad asked.

"No, that wouldn't be professional." I sniffed and looked out the window.

"Are you sure? Because if you do, I will too. And then it'll just be our little secret. No one has to know." He took one hand off the steering wheel and gave mine a squeeze. "That was brutal."

"At least he alibied out. It would have been worse if we had to drag him in as a person of interest."

"True." Brad pulled into a parking space near the Moonlight Security office building. Half a block away was a coffee shop. "I could use some caffeine. How about you?"

"Coffee, chocolate, answers. At this point, it makes no difference to me."

"Come on. It's my treat. And if you want to go crazy and splurge on something insanely unhealthy, I won't tell Emma."

I thought about my best friend. I felt the same way

about her that Richard Golden felt about Jonathan Gardner. There was a time in my life when it was just the two of us against the world. But then I became a cop. And my world got a lot bigger. And then I met Brad, and now most days, it was just him and me, fighting the good fight. Or trying to. Even if today felt like an epic loss.

"Don't you think it's weird none of the neighbors mentioned Jonathan Gardner had a roommate?" he asked.

"We didn't ask."

"He has an alibi. And I don't think anyone could fake that level of grief." Brad stared up at the menu, but his mind was elsewhere. "But it's just weird."

"Maybe it has to do with Gardner's lease agreement."

"That could be," he agreed. The woman in front of us moved out of the way, so Brad and I stepped up to the counter. "What do you want, Liv?"

"Large, organic dark roast."

"Make that two." Brad reached into his pocket for his wallet.

The barista noticed his badge and shook her head. "It's on the house."

"No, I insist." Brad paid for our coffees and picked up a bag of chocolate covered espresso beans and read the ingredients on the back. "And two bags of these." He handed her another fifteen dollars. "Keep the change."

We went to the end of the counter to wait for our order, and Brad handed me one of the bags. "You said you wanted chocolate and coffee."

"You're the best."

"I know."

"Since you're into wish fulfillment today, are you going to get answers too?" I tore open the candy and offered him some, but he shook his head and opened his own bag. He shook a few into his mouth and crunched on them.

"That's the plan."

I smiled. "I like it." I had eaten three by the time our drinks were ready. Brad shook two packets of raw sugar into his and gave it a stir. Most days, I drank mine black, but today wasn't most days. So I followed suit and added a splash of almond milk, ignoring the amused snort that came from my partner. "You said you wouldn't tell Emma."

"My lips are sealed."

We stepped back into the morning light, the weight of the last few hours crushing me beneath it. "I don't think Jonathan Gardner was killed for personal reasons, but we should look into Mary Winsor and her new boyfriend, just in case."

"We should also run down Gardner's gaming buddies. Some people can get really competitive with these online games. They spend hundreds of hours building up their characters, so they get testy when things don't go the way they want."

"Yeah, but don't you think Mr. Golden would have mentioned something like that happening?" I asked.

"Maybe. Or Gardner did something wrong and screwed one of his teammates or shot his friend's character. I've lost many online campaigns due to friendly fire."

"Now you're making this sound like some military op."

"They aren't that dissimilar, except of course for the obvious differences. Unless that's why Gardner's dead. One of his friends might have shot him as payback, in real life."

"I don't know."

Brad shrugged. "My gut says that's not what

happened either, but we leave no stone unturned."

"When we get back to the precinct, I'll ask Mac to look into it."

"Laura Mackenzie? Really?"

"Why? What's wrong with her? She's the best tech the department has and the least utilized."

"Yeah, but you let a gamer near a game, and it'll be three days before she surfaces."

"Puh-lease." I rolled my eyes and sipped my coffee, wondering if I could take it into the office building or if they strictly enforced the no food and beverage policy stenciled on the front door. "Mac's a professional." I gave him a sideways look. "But you seem to know a lot about this. I'm guessing that means I shouldn't let you anywhere near this unless I want to work the case on my own."

"Don't worry, Liv. I'm a reformed addict. I gave up the first person shooters when I got back stateside. Now it's just car racing and third person adventure games. Not that I have much time for any of that." He nudged my shoulder. "You keep me busy."

"It's not me. It's the job."

"Sure, sure." He watched a few people through the front window while he finished his coffee. Then he tossed the paper cup into the bin. I took a final sip and followed suit, amused to see a phone number scribbled on the side of his cup. "Are you sure you don't need that?" I pointed at it.

Brad glanced down. "Nah."

"She was cute."

"I'm good, thanks." He waited for me to let it go. Then he rubbed his hands together. "All right. You wanted coffee, chocolate, and answers. Let's see if I can go three for three."

We entered the lobby, checked the directory, and went up two floors to Moonlight Security. The frosted glass door and the stenciling reminded me more of a private eye's office from a noir flick than any security firm I'd ever seen. Brad opened the door, glancing up when the bell dinged above us.

The receptionist behind the pressed-wood desk popped her gum and smiled. "What can I do for you?"

"Police." My partner held out his badge.

She climbed out of the chair and leaned over the counter, her cleavage spilling out from the top three opened buttons of her blouse. "Detective," she nodded to herself, "nice." She glanced at me, but I didn't hold out my badge. I didn't need to see any more of her cleavage. She was young and perky and had probably used that trick to get out of several speeding tickets.

"We need to speak to whoever's in charge," I said.

"The big boss isn't in. But you can speak to my supervisor," she turned her attention to Brad, "or you can leave me your number. I'll have him call you. Or I could call you."

What was up with these women today? Jeez. Brad was right. He could probably go three for three.

"Where can I find your supervisor?" I asked.

She pointed to an open door that led into a back office.

"Thanks." Without waiting for an invitation, I headed for the office. Brad and I had done this enough times that we didn't have to voice our intentions. I'd start with the supervisor while he convinced the perky twenty-four year old to spill her guts, along with her boobs, about the operation and everything she knew about our vic. Damn, now my internal voice was starting to sound like a hard-boiled detective from the black and white movies. I definitely didn't need to spend any extra time in this security office.

Shaking it off, I knocked on the doorjamb and opened my jacket to reveal my badge. "Detective Liv

DeMarco, homicide. I need to speak to you about one of your employees."

Connor McFarland gestured that I enter. "Please, have a seat. I knew someone would be here. This is about Jonathan Gardner and the shooting at Star Cleaners, right?"

"Yes, sir."

"A sergeant called earlier to ask me some questions. I figured it was just a matter of time until officers came knocking." He took off his glasses and squeezed the bridge of his nose. "What can I do to help?"

"You can start by telling me why Star Cleaners hired a night watchman."

"It was part of a promotion we had running. In case you haven't noticed, this isn't some fancy operation. Originally, we sold home security systems. Eventually, Mr. Denisten decided to branch out. So we started installing security systems for small businesses, and then he came up with the bright idea to provide guards."

"Mr. Denisten?"

"The guy who owns this place." McFarland opened the drawer and removed a business card with his boss's name and contact information. "I assume you'll want that."

"Thanks." I tucked it into the back of my notepad. "I take it from your tone you didn't think it was a good idea."

"We didn't have the manpower. At the time, it was just me, Mr. Denisten, Ava, and Ralph, the other technician. So we had to hire people, and that cut down on profits. So we had to take more jobs. And hire more people. You can see where this is going."

"How many people does Moonlight Security currently employ?"

"Eleven, if you count me and the owner. It used to be fourteen, but we had to let three of the regulars go last month when none of our promotional customers wanted to sign a contract to keep a night watchman on hand. So now, we have six full-time security guards and one floater." He handed me another sheet of paper before I could ask. "That's our employee list. I took the liberty of circling the three who were let go. The sergeant said you'd want that."

"Yes, thanks." I read the names, but they didn't mean anything to me. Golden hadn't mentioned any of these people when I asked about Jonathan Gardner's friends. "Did you ever have any problems with Mr. Gardner?"

"No, Johnny was topnotch. Truthfully, he was too good for this place. He had real potential. The kid could have gotten a better job somewhere else. He had a bachelor's in psychology. If he'd just gone a bit further, he would have had tons of opportunities. Maybe then he'd still be alive." He choked up, and I gave him a moment to compose himself. "Have you spoken to his parents yet? He talked about his family all the time. I just can't imagine what they're going through. I have a son, a few years older than Johnny. I just...I can't imagine. I wanted to call them to express my condolences."

"I'm not sure if they've been notified yet, so you might want to hold off."

McFarland nodded. "I'll send flowers. Everyone around here will pitch in. We'll get a nice arrangement."

"So Mr. Gardner didn't have any problems with anyone at work?"

"No, of course not. He was a gentle soul. Everyone loved him."

That's the only thing I'd heard about our victim.

"What about personal issues? Anything you can think of?"

"Sorry."

"Did he ever talk about a girlfriend or some girl he met?"

"Nah, Johnny had been burned pretty badly. He wasn't ready to put himself out there again."

"So no jealous husbands or vengeful exes? No one threatening him? What about money issues? Did he have any?"

"We all have money issues, but Johnny never complained about it. He always showed up for his shifts. He never called in sick. He offered to cover if someone else called in, but I don't think that was about money. I just think he was a good guy. He liked helping people."

"All right," that left only one possibility, "what about Star Cleaners?"

"What about them?"

"Any idea why Mr. Lee wanted to hire a night watchman? Did Mr. Gardner or any of your other security guards ever report any problems?"

Something flickered across McFarland's face. "Star Cleaners hired us to install a new security system less than a month ago. Mr. Lee wanted the best system we had to offer. Top of the line. He went for all the bells and whistles, and when we offered him a night watchman for a thirty day trial, he jumped at the opportunity. Our clients are never that eager. I thought it was weird, but given that neighborhood, I figured maybe he'd had more than his share of break-ins and hold-ups. That's why I insisted Johnny be armed. He's licensed. All of our security guards are. But he didn't like carrying the gun. I told him it was better to be safe than sorry, but I guess it didn't make much of a difference."

"So you think Gardner intervened in the midst of a break-in?"

"Isn't that what happened?" McFarland cocked his head to the side, mentally replaying the questions I had asked him. "You think Johnny was killed for some other reason?"

"I don't know, sir. That's why we're investigating."

"It seems simple to me. Some asshole breaks in, Johnny tries to stop him, and for his trouble, he gets himself killed." He inhaled, shaking his head. "And it's my fault because I sent him over there." He deflated, sinking deeper into the chair.

"Sir, it's not your fault." At least, nothing indicated he was responsible. "We noticed some discrepancies with Star Cleaners' security logs. Would you mind taking a look?"

McFarland put his glasses back on and sat up straighter in his chair. "I'll do anything to help you find the person who hurt Johnny. Where are they?"

I glanced out the doorway. Ava held Brad's left wrist against the counter while she wrote something in black ink on his palm. "Detective Fennel," I called, and she released the grip on his wrist and tucked the pen into her cleavage, "are you almost finished out there? Mr. McFarland would like to see the security logs."

My partner straightened his jacket and strode toward us. From the look on his face, I wasn't sure if he had made progress on identifying the killer or on getting some buxom blonde to tour his bedroom. Either way, his mood had improved.

EIGHT

After Mr. McFarland reviewed the security logs and the data Moonlight Security's servers received during the night, we still weren't any closer to figuring out what happened. If the perimeter had been breached, the disarm code would have to be entered, but the code was entered before the perimeter was breached. And it had been entered from outside the shop.

"At least we know Jonathan Gardner didn't disarm the system," Fennel said. "Mr. Lee told Sgt. Chambliss that Gardner arrived for his shift at his normal time, took up his post inside the dry cleaner's, and then Mr. Lee activated the system once he let himself out. That's their routine. They did the same thing every night."

"So someone waited until 4:12 a.m. to enter the disarm code. Do we know if the person who entered the code had a key to gain entry?"

"We'll check with CSU and find out if the rear doors were tampered with." My partner jotted down a note, so we wouldn't forget.

"Or the killer and his accomplice entered the

disarm code, then went around the front, and broke the glass, so it wouldn't trigger the alarm."

"That means the killer could be working solo," Fennel said. "The system beeps when it's accessed. So Jonathan Gardner heard the beep, went into the back room to check the panel, and the killer broke through the front door. Gardner heard the noise, ran back out front, and got himself killed."

"Damn. That makes sense. It also makes this a random act of violence." It'd be a lot harder to find the killer if he had no connection to the victim or Star Cleaners. "Where do we go from here?"

"Dammit." He tried to think, but his stomach let out an audible growl. "Are you hungry?"

"I'm not sure. Is it possible to have no appetite and be starving at the same time?"

"I think so." He checked the time. "Let's pick up lunch and take it back to the precinct. We need to review the security feed from outside the shop and find out if the canvass turned up anything useful."

"Sounds like a plan."

By the time we got back to the station, Sgt. Chambliss had sent officers with Mr. Lee to take inventory. The sergeant left copies of Lee's statement and the reports with us, but we'd already been over all of it.

I speared a carrot and popped it into my mouth. "I thought we agreed this was a random act of violence. Why are you still scouring the internet for sordid details on Jonathan Gardner?"

"Because it's all I can do." Fennel leaned back, holding the bowl beneath his mouth so he wouldn't spill while he ate his salad. "Did Chambliss say anything to you about Mr. Lee?"

"He's leaving it up to us since we're the detectives."

"That means he doesn't think Lee's the killer."

Fennel swallowed another bite and rocked forward, putting his lunch down on his desk. "According to patrol, Mr. Lee's wife said he didn't leave their house until 5:25. But since it's his wife, she could be lying."

"Or that's the truth. CSU checked him for GSR and blood spatter. He didn't shoot Gardner. At least that's what the evidence indicates." I recalled our early morning interview. Perhaps, if I'd been more awake and alert, I would have paid more attention. "Arthur Lee's an odd one. He thinks drug addicts want his dry cleaning chemicals. And he wanted top of the line security for his dry cleaning business."

"Do you think it's a front for something?"

I shrugged and focused on the few remaining bits of hardboiled egg and avocado slices hidden beneath the spring mix. When I finished eating, I wiped my hands and entered a few searches into the database. No other department had Mr. Lee or Star Cleaners under surveillance. And I couldn't find any reports of previous break-ins or crimes happening at that location.

"Hey," Fennel swiveled his monitor around, "a month and a half ago, someone broke into Mr. Lee's apartment."

"Who filed the report?" I asked.

"His wife. Mr. Lee was attending a dry cleaning convention when the break-in occurred." He scanned the report for additional details. "The stolen property was recovered three weeks later, along with property from half a dozen other break-ins in that neighborhood. That would explain why he insisted on topnotch security."

"Did Moonlight install a system at his home too?"

It was Fennel's turn to shrug. "Want to call and find out?"

I picked up the receiver and dialed the number on

McFarland's business card. Three rings later, he answered and I asked him the same question I just asked Fennel. After getting affirmation, I hung up, only to find Fennel on the phone asking Mr. Lee the same question.

He snickered and put down the phone. "Well, that explains it."

"Let me guess, Mr. Lee got a discount on Star Cleaners' security system after having had his home security system installed."

"Something like that." Fennel sifted through the documents again. "Is it just me or does Mr. Lee enjoy a discount a bit too much? I'm going to run his financials and check with his insurance company to see if that might be motive for the break-in and murder. He didn't pull the trigger, but he might have had someone else do it for him."

"Do contract killers have coupons?" I asked.

"I don't know, Liv. The next time we arrest one, you should ask."

I stuck my tongue out at him and picked up my notepad. A lump formed in my stomach, and I regretted eating. Reaching for the phone, I dialed an unfamiliar number and waited for verification that Jonathan Gardner's next of kin had received notification. At the moment, they were making arrangements to fly in and claim the body. We'd have to question them once they arrived, but for now, I could let them grieve in peace.

Fennel quirked an eyebrow. "Are you okay?"

"Uh-huh." I blew out a steady breath. "Gardner's parents should be arriving on Monday."

"Okay." He reached for the baseball on his desk, palming it as he thought. "You know...I wonder..."

I stopped what I was doing and stared at my partner. "Go on. The suspense might kill me."

He scowled. "Bad choice of words, Liv." Opening his notepad, he double-checked some facts. "Michael Tolliver had the same gaming system and game as Jonathan Gardner."

"So? Didn't you say you played the same game?"

"It's probably nothing, but we said we'd have Mac run down their online teammates and verify Richard Golden's alibi. We might as well have her check to see if they ever played together."

"They worked together, so it's possible. Maybe Mr. Bachelor Party downplayed their relationship." I reached for the phone and dialed Mac's extension. After updating her on the situation, I handed the handset to Fennel so he could give her the pertinent details.

While he did that, I dug through our records for anything on Moonlight Security, but the company was too new. They had filed the proper forms and were adequately licensed. Their employees passed the required background checks and had no previous criminal records. Another dead end, I thought, snorting when my internal voice, which sounded suspiciously like Brad, chastised me for the play on words.

"I'm cracking up," I mumbled.

"What?" Fennel raised an eyebrow. "They sell crack?"

"No. Maybe. I'm going to check with narcotics and see if they know anything."

"All right. I'll drop by gangs. It's possible someone's been charging shop owners a protection fee, and Mr. Lee doesn't strike me as the type who'd pay. It could be something." He got up from his desk and went up the stairs.

After giving my computer a dirty look, I went to see if the detectives in narcotics knew anything I didn't.

But aside from the usual drug traffic in that part of town, they hadn't heard anything. And no one had been selling dry cleaning chemicals or huffable materials on the streets.

Reassured that I wasn't crazy and Mr. Lee was paranoid, I decided to give the dry cleaner a call to check on the progress he made taking inventory and to ask about the employees who allegedly got high at work. Our conversation was brief. None of the chemicals had been stolen.

"Are you sure nothing else is missing?"

"Everything's here. Oh no. Wait a minute," Mr. Lee put the phone down, and I waited for him to get back on the line, "the thief took something else."

"What?" I asked.

"My ticket pad. It has carbon copies of everyone's order."

"What else? Names? Addresses?"

"Yes."

"Credit card numbers?" I asked.

"No."

"What about checks?"

For a moment, he sounded offended. "I don't accept checks."

"Okay." Could this be about identity theft? "Are you sure no one's account numbers were listed?"

"No. Those are run through the machine. It only lists the last four digits. Nothing else."

"What information do you record on your ticket pad?" I thought about dry cleaning tickets I'd had in the past. But they never contained private information.

"Name, address, items to be cleaned, and phone numbers. Nothing else." He cleared his throat. "Why would someone want that?"

"I have no idea. Are you sure it's gone?"

"Yes, it was right here, on the counter beside the register." Mr. Lee sounded almost frantic.

"Thank you for your help, if you remember anything else, please give me a call."

I disconnected and went to speak to the crime scene unit to find out if the ticket pad had been bagged for evidence collection. But they hadn't seen it. I found Ellie hunched over a table, running a lighted wand over Gardner's bloody shirt.

"Hey," I hoped since I worked with Brown Eyes she'd offer me the same perks, "do you mind if I look through the photos you took of Star Cleaners?"

She pointed to a camera on the table behind her. "Knock yourself out."

I scrolled through the snapshots, but I didn't see any order pads or dry cleaning tickets. So the killer took something else besides the money in the register. I just didn't know why.

"Hey, Ellie, did anyone check the exterior camera feed from Star Cleaners?"

She stopped what she was doing and spun around to face me. "I'm not sure. I know Mr. Lee didn't have any cameras posted out front, and the ones in the back were too badly damaged to give us anything. But the sarge said he was going to pull nearby traffic cams. You might want to check with him."

"Thanks."

On my way back upstairs, I stopped to speak to the watch commander. Nearby CCTVs saw a silver sedan drive away from Star Cleaners at 4:37 a.m. The plates had been removed and every window had an illegal tint, making it impossible to see who was inside the vehicle.

"Did you get any visuals on the suspect?" I asked.

Chambliss shook his head. "We backtracked. The car appeared in the vicinity around 3:30 a.m., but the driver parked in one of the few blind spots. And since none of the shops to the west of Star Cleaners have exterior cameras on that block, we didn't see anyone get in or out of the vehicle. A BOLO's been issued, and patrol knows to keep their eyes peeled. I'll let you know if it turns up."

"I appreciate it." But something told me even if we found it, it wouldn't lead to anything.

NINE

"I finally figured it out," I said triumphantly. "Actually, it makes a lot of sense now that I think about it."

Brad glanced at me. "What does?"

"The reason you weren't into the barista. You only date blondes."

"What?"

"Ellie has black hair, and you said there was no chemistry. But you and Carrie have lasted a while, and she's blonde. You have a thing for blondes."

"I do not have a thing for blondes." He glanced around to make sure no one was eavesdropping. "And you know Carrie and I aren't a thing. We're just having fun."

"It's okay. We all have a type."

"Oh yeah?" Brad cocked an eyebrow at me. "What's yours?"

"I know it when I see it."

He snickered. "Fine, Liv. Don't tell me." He rubbed his eyes and leaned back in his chair, tossing the baseball up in the air and catching it. "Narcotics, gangs, vice, and intelligence all came up blank. Jonathan Gardner's the most beloved guy in the entire world. His ex and her boyfriend are too far away to have done anything to him, not that they would. I'm sure when she broke his heart, she must have told him it was all her fault since he was perfect." He glanced at me. "I bet he would have been your type. The all-American, straight white teeth, crooked smile, heart of gold type. Damn. A guy like that shouldn't go out like this."

"At least it was quick." I couldn't bring myself to look at the horrific crime scene photos of what little was left of Gardner's face. "Based on what his boss at the security firm said, I think the reason Gardner didn't draw on the killer was because he didn't like guns."

"It could be why he was killed. The thief might have asked for his wallet, thought Gardner was going for the gun, and shot him preemptively."

"I don't know, but based on what we've learned, I don't think Gardner was involved in the break-in. I think he was just a victim."

"Not the target?" Brad asked, playing devil's advocate, as usual.

"Okay, smart guy, I'll go along with that if you can tell me who wants him dead or what motive they have for killing him. It's not like he had a life insurance policy for a few million. Or any life insurance at all. Unless you think this has something to do with a video game."

"Nope," Laura 'Mac' Mackenzie said, startling me. "I checked, but Gardner's gaming buddies have their characters intact. If anything, they were quite the kick ass team." She dragged a straight-back chair beside my desk and plopped down. "Damn, Fennel, you're looking fine today."

"Thank you. I'm glad somebody noticed." He looked pointedly at me.

"Who are you kidding? Everybody noticed. I thought I was going to have to call for riot gear or an emergency evac. First, Ellie, then the barista, and don't even get me started on Ava."

"The receptionist from Moonlight Security?" he asked.

"You know damn well what her name is. She tattooed it on your wrist." I grabbed Brad's hand and held it up.

Mac laughed. "Sorry, I didn't mean to start anything."

"Too late." Brad took the list of video game handles from her outstretched hand. "You got their real names and contact info. That's great. You're a goddess."

"I can probably tell you where they're logging in to play, if they're online," Mac offered.

"Even better." Brad winked at her. "So, do you think I should stick with the dark dress shirt with my jacket? Or go back to the white shirt and tie?"

"Definitely dark dress shirt and no tie. At the risk of having to report for sensitivity training, I'd say you should lose another button." She nudged me. "What do you think, Liv? He could drop a button, right? Show off those pecs. You work out enough. You ought to flaunt it."

"Don't get him started," I warned.

"You're no fun," she said.

My partner beamed. "I'm glad someone notices all the hard work that goes into this." He waved his hand down his body.

"All right, I have to get back to work. I'll call you if any of those guys log-in and get you their locations. Do you think one of them is your killer?" Mac asked.

"It's tough to say. We don't have any real leads. Every avenue leads to nowhere. But it doesn't hurt to gather as much information as possible," Brad said.

"That sucks. If there's anything you guys need, let me know."

"Hey, Mac," I said before she could walk away, "any idea why someone would steal the ticket pad from a dry cleaner's?"

She chewed on her lip while she thought. "I got nothing." That made three of us.

Brad continued to stare at me, even after Mac walked away. "What?" I asked, wondering if I had salad dressing on my shirt or spinach in my teeth.

"Did you ever consider maybe I dress nicely so you have something pretty to look at all day?"

I stifled a laugh, nearly choking in the process. "Who are you kidding?"

He shrugged and turned back to the report Mac had handed him. "She's on the ball." He held out the file for me to read.

"I'm guessing that means our vic spoke to these people regularly. That these are his friends."

"Not necessarily, but there's a good possibility. Gardner's roommate would know his gaming habits the best. But Golden said Gardner only played with friends. Whether that means he knew them in the real world, I don't know."

I scanned the list of names. "Turns out our vic and Michael Tolliver had more than just the passing interaction at work." I handed the list back to Brad. "Do you want to run down the names, or do you want to delve deeper into Michael Tolliver's alibi?"

"I'll take one for the team and contact the strip club. I might even have to go down there and flash his photograph around to make sure the management remembers him." Brad shuffled the papers on his desk. "We already verified the information with the rideshare guy, but it's possible Michael booked the car and instead of riding home with his buddies, he detoured to Star Cleaners to rob the place. As far as we know, Michael Tolliver had no reason to want to kill Gardner, but that would explain why Gardner allowed his killer to get so close and why he didn't try to shoot the guy."

"It might even explain why Gardner was killed. After all, he could definitely ID the thief."

Brad pushed away from the desk. "All right. I'll check it out and ask around. Maybe someone at the club remembers Michael Tolliver becoming angry or belligerent."

"Check with the girl who popped out of the cake. I'm sure she'd remember."

"Why? Don't you think all drunk, horny men look the same?"

"Yeah, they kind of do. But if he was angry or possibly dangerous, she would have caught on. From the photos I saw on Michael's phone, the men were all over her. She would have known who to avoid."

"All right. I'll call you if I find something."

"Be careful. With the way you're dressed, the ladies may eat you alive."

He licked his lips, the comeback obvious from the smirk on his face. But my partner was too classy to say it out loud.

After he left, I ran each of the names Mac had pulled. Aside from two counts of public intoxication and one for public urination, these guys had no records. I turned my search back to Jonathan Gardner's social media profile. I found most of the names on his friends list. They were mainly his college buddies. They'd all been in the same fraternity house. That also explained the public intoxication and urination.

I checked every person's social media page, including Michael Tolliver's, but they were the basic this is what I ate for dinner, this is my hot girlfriend, and here's a funny video of a cat. Why couldn't this be simple?

Banging my head against the desk seemed like a wonderful idea, but I didn't want the other members in my unit to think I was crazy. They didn't know me that well, and they might get the wrong idea. Instead, I pushed my chair back and rested my forehead on the edge of the desk, waiting for brilliance to strike.

"Hey, princess," Detective Jake Voletek dropped into Brad's empty chair, "where's your other half?"

"Strip club. And I told you not to call me that."

Voletek laughed, thinking it was a joke. "You guys always catch the best cases."

"No, we don't." I sat up and pushed the case file toward him. "We got a dead security guard and an empty cash register."

"You're serious?"

"Yeah."

"The guard worked at the strip club?"

"No, Jake, he worked at a dry cleaner's."

"Okay, now I know you're yanking my chain." Voletek read the jacket. "Sorry, I thought you were joking."

"No, and we're having a lousy time accepting the obvious motive. The perp also stole the ticket pad and the cash from our victim's wallet." I thought for a moment and reached for the phone. Gardner's wallet had been emptied except for his gym membership. I needed to know if his debit or credit cards had been used since the murder.

The voice on the other end didn't seem surprised to hear from me. "I was just about to notify you,

Detective DeMarco. We ran Jonathan Gardner's financial report. There haven't been any charges since we found the body and started monitoring his financial activity, but the last charge came in at 5:17 a.m."

"Where?"

"A twenty-four hour liquor store, 24/7 Spirits." He gave me the address.

"Thanks." I tore off the sheet and slipped into my jacket.

Voletek quirked an eyebrow. "Where are you going?"

"On a tequila run."

"Your partner's at a strip club, and you're going out for tequila. Are you looking to get into trouble?"

"Not me, but someone is."

TEN

"I don't know." The clerk remained behind the counter with his arms folded across his chest. "It was some guy."

"Was he alone?" I asked.

The clerk shrugged.

"It's a simple question, sir."

"One guy came to the counter to pay for his purchase. He might have had someone else with him. I didn't pay much attention."

"But you were here at five o'clock this morning?"

"Yeah."

"And you're still here?" That didn't make much sense.

"So?"

I looked around for obvious violations. "Do you card?"

"Yeah, minors or people who might pass for minors. This guy, he was no minor."

"Okay, so what did he look like?"

"He was just some guy. Some old guy."

"Old, great. How old?"

The clerk picked at something stuck between his back teeth. "Dunno. Forty?"

"So not that old. And you still didn't card him."

"He's over the legal age."

"What about your security camera?" The red light in the corner remained on. It could have gotten a look at our killer.

"You want to see what's on it?"

"Yes, sir."

He pulled a step stool from beneath the counter and climbed up to the camera. A moment later, he pulled it down. It didn't connect to anything. "Good luck."

I checked, but the internal storage only saved a few minutes of data. It re-recorded on a continuous loop. Unless someone manually stopped the recording, it was useless. "You're joking. What good is this?"

"The red light on the front is a great theft deterrent. I haven't had a problem since I installed it."

"You didn't happen to get it from Moonlight Security, did you?"

The clerk scoffed. "I ordered it on the internet."

Blowing out a breath, I wondered if I could arrest him for obstruction, but I couldn't prove he remembered anything. And it wasn't a crime to be unhelpful. "Okay, let's go over this one more time. A man came in here at five o'clock this morning to purchase what?"

"Whiskey."

"What did he look like?"

The clerk glared at me. "Like a guy, probably in his forties. He paid with a credit card."

"Why didn't you ask for ID when he used his card?"

"Because he swiped it through the reader. I didn't even touch it." He held up his palms. "Not my business. Not my property."

"So he touched the card reader?"

"Yep."

All right, now I was getting somewhere. CSU might have luck pulling his prints. I stared down at the faded buttons and hanging pen.

"Don't waste your time. I wiped it down at end of shift, along with the counter. I'm sure Shelly did the same thing when her shift ended."

"What time was that?"

"Four."

"Your shift ended at four a.m.?"

"No, Shelly went home at four this afternoon. My shift ended at seven a.m. I'm part owner, so I work the overnight and stock. Aside from a couple of regulars, no one usually stops by in the middle of the night. But business picks up at shift change, and we stay busy until almost eight." He looked down at my badge. "A lot of first responders drop by after working graveyard. They probably need a little something to help them sleep."

"Was anyone else in the store at 5:17 this morning?"

He sighed. "I dunno. It's work. I do my job, ring up customers, card the ones I have to, and that's that."

I stared at the register. "Don't you have to enter a birthdate in order for the transaction to complete?"

"Uh-huh."

"Okay, great. So what was this guy's birthdate?"

"You gonna buy him a card?"

I hated unhelpful civilians. "Yep, so I need to know his birthday. And before you say you don't remember, I'm sure it must get recorded somewhere."

He stared at the counter. "Unless you have a warrant or something, I'm done cooperating. You have no reason to harass me, and I have work to do."

"You just enter the same date for everyone, don't

you?" I asked, but he didn't answer. I took a step back, suddenly developing a terrible headache. "Look, the guy who bought a bottle of Jack from you this morning killed someone for no reason. He broke into a place, emptied the register, and killed a guy. I don't want that to happen again. You don't want to be his next victim, do you?"

"Nice try, but I don't know anything. I don't remember him, and you can't prove that I do. I mind my business. I don't get involved. I don't look for trouble. Don't bring trouble to me."

Once I got back to the car, I called Fennel to update him on the situation. While we spoke, I watched the clerk mount the camera back on the wall. So much for high-tech security measures. No wonder Moonlight Security had branched out.

"Dammit," Fennel cursed. "The strip club was also a bust. The girls remembered Michael Tolliver. He left with his friends. The bouncer even saw him get into the car with his buddies once it pulled up. He didn't kill Jonathan Gardner."

"At least that's one name off our list."

"We have a list?" Fennel asked.

"No, but we could make one and then cross Michael Tolliver's name off of it." I looked around. 24/7 Spirits was twenty blocks away from Star Cleaners. It was too far to walk, so how did the killer get here? "Why did he use Gardner's credit card?" I mused out loud.

"He probably did it right after he killed him. He must have figured it was safe since we hadn't found the body yet. Or maybe he wanted to screw with our TOD by making us think Gardner made the purchase."

"Perhaps. But for him to choose this liquor store, he must have known there were no security cameras. He's been here before. You have the address, right?"

Papers ruffled in the background. "Yep."

"Okay, see if there are any traffic cams nearby and pull the footage. And contact dispatch and find out what officers walk this beat. They'll know which shops in the area have security cameras, and they'll know who to talk to for intel."

"All right, I'll get the ball rolling. Are you heading back to the precinct?"

I didn't want to go back to the station since I knew Lt. Winston didn't like it when we worked beyond end of shift without permission and was liable to tell us to go home. The killer had a plan. Breaking into Star Cleaners and killing Gardner was part of it, so was stopping by 24/7 Spirits to buy a bottle of Jack, and I wouldn't be able to figure out what that plan was from inside my apartment.

"Liv?" Fennel asked.

"Yeah," I turned the key in the ignition, "I'm on my way."

ELEVEN

"The cops came here." Carter ran both hands through his hair, his entire body trembling. "They know. They know what you did."

The third man peered down the hall, but Michael Tolliver's bedroom door remained closed. "Lower your fucking voice. You don't want to wake up your roommate, or I'll have to permanently silence him. You get that, right?"

Carter gulped and rubbed his mouth. He had to get out of here.

"You need to stop smoking that shit, man. It's making you paranoid." Diego sat at the kitchen table, sipping whiskey from a juice glass. "At least the rest of the bachelor party finally cleared out. The last thing we need is more people in our business." When he signed on to this, Diego knew people might end up dead. He just didn't realize it'd happen so soon. The police investigation meant they had to be careful. "We should probably clear out too. What do you think?"

The third man took a deep breath. Unlike the other

two, he was stone-cold sober and cool as a cucumber. This is what he planned. He just didn't think the cops would get their act together this quickly. But they didn't know anything. They were just covering their bases. Still, he would have preferred them flapping their gums at some donut shop instead of following up with the other Star Cleaners employees. On the bright side, Michael Tolliver had an airtight alibi. That was one of the reasons why he chose last night to strike. Innocent men shouldn't go to prison.

"What are you thinking?" Carter asked, cringing when the third man met his eyes. "You know I didn't tell them anything. You listened to everything they asked and everything I said."

"Then why are you so nervous?" The third man took a step closer, watching Carter shrink in on himself. "You said we were cool. Now you're about to piss yourself. If this is too much for you, tell me. We have sixteen hours until go-time. If I have to replace you, I will."

"No."

"So you're in?"

"I'm...uh...I'm in." Carter bit his lip.

"Diego?" the third man asked.

Diego downed the rest of the whiskey in one gulp. "You know I am. One hundred million dollars here we come."

Carter glanced at his friend. That's why they were doing this. One hundred million split three ways was a hell of a lot of money. He could disappear to someplace where his violent partner couldn't find him. The money might even make him forget seeing that man's face explode out of the back of his skull. Or he'd buy enough booze, drugs, and tail to make him forget. Or so he hoped.

The third man eyed Carter, his unease growing

with every jitter. "Until the job's done, we stick together. I don't want anyone getting antsy or doing something stupid and getting picked up by the cops."

"Yeah, no. That'd be bad," Carter said, though it was clear his mind was elsewhere.

Coming back to Carter's apartment had been stupid enough, but if Michael hadn't seen his roommate home safe and sound, he would have started calling and texting, which would have led to questions. This was easier. This went along with Carter's bogus alibi about attending the bachelor party, and since Carter was their connection to Star Cleaners, the third man needed to keep him alive and out of trouble for now. He couldn't afford for Carter to go blabbing their plan to the first person who asked. But once the job was done, that would no longer be the case.

He looked at Diego and grinned. By this time tomorrow, everything would be different.

*   *   *

"Sgt. Chambliss said a vehicle was seen driving away from Star Cleaners around the time of the murder. And since we know Jonathan Gardner's credit card was used at 24/7 Spirits, which is twenty blocks from Star Cleaners, I'm going out on a limb and saying the killer drove there. We'll need to pull traffic cam footage from outside the liquor store and see if we spot it."

"Already done," Fennel said. "As soon as we got off the phone, I ran with it. No silver sedan with illegal tinting went anywhere near the liquor store during that timeframe. And before you ask, nothing's turned up yet on the BOLO, but it's probably just a matter of time. A car like that is gonna stick out."

"Dammit." How could we already be scraping the

bottom of the barrel? "What about ballistics?"

Fennel rubbed his eyes. "Nothing yet. Are you surprised?"

"Not even a little bit." I let out a sigh. "Okay, so we don't know if the gun used to kill Gardner's been used in any other crimes. That's not helpful. Did the ME have anything to add?"

"Like what?"

"I don't know."

Fennel reached for the phone. "Let me see what I can find out."

I read the intel again, but it was just a jumble. Maybe it was me. I was tired, frustrated, and had the mother of all headaches. Emma would probably tell me it was from eating the entire bag of chocolate covered espresso beans. The caffeine and sugar apparently weren't good for me. There was a chance she wasn't wrong, but this felt more like a stress headache. The kind I got when I was missing something.

"Detective," a familiar voice called from behind.

I spun in my chair to find ADA Logan Winters standing behind me. "Dammit."

He quirked an eyebrow. "You forgot?"

"Yeah, sorry. We caught a case." I gestured at the mess of papers on my desk.

"Do you need to reschedule?" He pulled out his phone and tapped on the screen. "I'm free Monday night and for a few hours on Wednesday." He nodded to my partner, who whispered a few things on the phone. From his posture, it appeared Fennel was in the midst of a social call instead of a work call. "But the court date's set for Thursday, so Wednesday's pushing it."

Fennel hung up the phone. "Carrie said the prelim suggests cause of death is a fatal gunshot wound to the head. They found some week-old bruises on the guy's shins and one on his shoulder. That could be something. But he might have been kickboxing or playing soccer. Didn't he have some photos like that on social media?"

"Lacrosse," I said. "Or it could have been field hockey."

"Right." Fennel rocked back in his chair and tossed the baseball in the air. "That would explain it."

"Add his teammates to the list."

"They're already on there. He does everything with the same group of guys. If he's not hanging out with them, he's hanging out with his neighbors. Guess you can never take the frat out of the guy." My partner looked pointedly at Winters. "Am I right, counselor?"

Winters snickered. "What makes you think I was a frat guy?"

"Your ties."

I put a hand over my mouth to stifle my laugh. Fennel glanced at me and winked.

"Well, I did live in a frat house, but we weren't the crazy, fun ones. We studied and conducted moot court trials and organized student government."

"I didn't realize that's how one becomes an expert at beer pong," Fennel mused.

Winters smiled. "Anytime you want a rematch, just let me know." He checked his watch. "Are you about ready, Liv? Or should I set up in the conference room?"

"At this point, it feels like I may never leave." But Lt. Winston had told us to go home. Until more evidence was collected and analyzed, there wasn't much we could do. The rest would have to wait until tomorrow.

"She's ready," Fennel said, earning my patented glare. "You heard the LT. Unless we're ready to make an arrest, whatever we're working on has to wait until tomorrow." Fennel turned off his computer and organized the top of his desk. "So what are you two doing tonight? Hot date? Secret rendezvous?"

"Actually, I was hoping your lovely partner would agree to dinner," Winters said, "but you're welcome to join us."

"I don't want to be a third wheel. Liv could use some TLC."

My cheeks turned red from both anger and embarrassment. "It's not a date," I hissed. "It's trial prep. Correct me if I'm wrong, but aren't you on the roster to testify too?"

"That's right," Winters said. "It'd probably be easier if the three of us went over everything together. We need to go over the facts and your testimonies and make sure the defense can't hit us with any surprises. C'mon, Brad, dinner's on me. And if we finish early enough, I'll let you take me at beer pong."

"I can't tonight," Fennel said. "I have plans."

"With the barista?" I asked.

He shook his head. "Carrie."

"Oh. Just now?" I jerked my chin toward his desk phone.

"No." Something flitted across his eyes. Normally, he and Carrie didn't make plans ahead of time. It had always been spur of the moment booty calls. Maybe she wanted to take their "just having fun" to the next level.

"That explains why you're dressed like that."

"I'm telling you, Liv, this is for you." Fennel slipped on his jacket and grabbed his keys. "Don't keep her out too late, Winters. Unlike some people, homicide detectives have to work on Saturdays. And this case is a bitch."

"I wouldn't dream of it. Well, I would, but Liv

would probably shoot me."

"Liv might still shoot you," I said. I watched my partner push his chair beneath his desk. Something wasn't right. "Logan, I'll meet you downstairs in a few minutes. I just need to finish some things up first with Brad."

"Yeah, sure, no problem." Logan looked down at his phone again. "You and me need to get something on the books before you make your court appearance. How does Monday sound, Brad?"

"Works for me," Fennel said.

After Winters left us alone, I turned off my computer and watched my partner anxiously smooth his hair back, not that his short hair even had enough length to get unruly, but that was beside the point. "Are you okay?"

"Not really. The only thing I can figure is the robber killed Jonathan Gardner just because he was there. So unless we find evidence, video footage, or an eyewitness account that leads straight to the killer, I'm not sure we'll get this guy."

"Or guys. It could be a team."

"$250 bucks is a lousy payoff for one person, let alone two or more." He sighed. "I guess we'll figure it out tomorrow. You don't want to keep Logan waiting."

"What about Carrie?" I asked. "Normally, you'd already be out the door and halfway to her place by now."

"Don't worry about it."

"I'm worried."

He held the door for me. "I promise this won't affect any of our cases. The ME's office isn't going to shun us or toss us to the back of the list. It'll be fine."

"Are you breaking up with her?"

"Liv, don't."

I held up my palms. "Sorry."

He softened and nudged me. "I'll see you tomorrow at noon. I might be a few minutes late. Can you cover for me? Or are you planning on showing up a few minutes late too? I mean Winters is the entire package. He's the kind of guy every mom hopes their daughter will marry."

"Oh god, tell me you didn't have this conversation with my mom."

"Not yet. But I hear wedding bells."

An officer walked past us, going up the steps, and I elbowed Fennel in the ribs. "Don't start shit like that here. I don't want rumors floating around."

"Fine." He leaned in close. "Just don't do anything I wouldn't do." And then we went out the double doors, past the front desk, and out of the precinct. By the time I turned to tell him good night, he was already gone.

"Liv," Winters waved me over to his fancy car, "you want a ride?"

"No, I'll follow you. Where are we going?"

"My place, if that's okay. All of my notes are there, and I have tuna steaks marinating in the fridge. I thought I'd make us dinner."

I was too tired to fight. "That sounds perfect."

TWELVE

"Liv?"

"Huh?" I blinked my eyes open, only to squeeze them shut a moment later. "Too bright."

The assistant district attorney laughed. "I take it you don't rise with the sun."

"Not if I don't have to." Why did I stay the night? For the life of me, I couldn't remember what possessed me to think this was a good idea. And now I had to deal with the fallout.

"I didn't want to wake you, but you left your phone in the living room. And it's been buzzing for the last twenty minutes."

Rolling onto my side, I caught sight of the clock. "Shit."

"What's wrong?" Logan held out the device, and I dragged myself off his bed and grabbed it from his hand.

The alarm notification pinged on the main screen. I was supposed to be across town in thirty minutes. This was a nightmare. I wouldn't get there in time if I went home to change. And I needed to change. "I'm late."

"For work?"

"Not exactly."

"Okay." He gave me an odd look. "Do you want to share with the class, Detective?"

I grabbed my gun and badge off his nightstand, clipping them onto my belt. "This was such a bad idea. Why did you let me stay? What's wrong with you? Professional boundaries, remember?"

"Oh, sure. Blame me. You're the one who came down with a killer migraine last night. Most women use that as an excuse not to crawl into my bed."

"I don't follow convention. And the champagne you opened only made it worse."

"Then let me make it up to you." He jerked his chin at my phone. "What's so important it can't wait until after breakfast?"

I blinked again, feeling a buzzing headache behind my eyes. "You made breakfast?"

"Made might be too strong of a word. I'd say I'm offering you breakfast. But I did make coffee. Does that impress you?"

"Did it come from a pod or k-cup?"

Logan looked at the floor. "Maybe."

"Not impressed."

"Are you always this difficult?"

"Ask Brad." I looked around the unfamiliar room. "Mind if I use your bathroom?"

"Not at all." He pointed to a closed door. "I put out fresh towels. And if you look in the middle drawer, you should find some travel items I took from a hotel."

"Stealing's a crime. Didn't they teach you anything in law school?" I went into the bathroom and shut the door.

By the time I came out, Logan was seated on the

couch, typing up the details we'd gone over last night concerning a pending trial. "Are you sure you don't want breakfast? At least take a cup of coffee for the road."

"No, thanks." My partner would spot an unfamiliar coffee cup a mile away. And the last thing I wanted to tell him was I spent the night in Logan Winters' apartment after I gave him such a hard time yesterday. I glanced at the screen. "Are we done with the trial prep? Or is there something else we need to go over?"

"No, I think we're good." He clicked another tab. "But I will need to review Fennel's statement with him before Thursday." Logan looked up at me. "So when you see your partner, tell him don't forget."

"On one condition." I grabbed my purse and jacket from one of the stools and headed for the door. "You don't mention this to him."

"Mention what?"

"Good." I turned back around to make sure I had everything.

"Forget something?" Logan held out my notebook.

"Right. Thanks." I tried to take it from him, but he didn't let go.

"Did you forget something else?" His blue eyes sparkled. He was enjoying this.

"Like what?"

"C'mon, Liv, you're really going to make me beg? Don't I at least get a good night kiss?"

That stopped me dead in my tracks. "What?"

"That's how dates usually conclude."

"This wasn't a date."

He rubbed the stubble on his cheek. "May I present to you exhibit A." He pointed to the kitchen sink filled with dirty dishes. "Dinner." Then he tapped his pen against the side of an empty champagne bottle.

"Exhibit B, drinks." He grinned, looking back into his bedroom. "And exhibit C, you spent the night in my bed. That's how my better dates end."

"That's sad." I patted him sympathetically on the shoulder and eyed the blanket on the couch. "If you date a lot, you should probably invest in a pull-out. After all, I spent the night alone in your bed. And you were out here. That's how it usually goes, huh?"

He laughed. "Don't focus so much on the details."

"Sorry, hazard of the job." I opened the door. "I'll see you around, counselor."

"Not if I see you first."

Logan liked to flirt and tease. It was harmless. He was harmless, but I didn't want word getting out or rumors spreading. The last thing I needed were other people in the department thinking I was having a fling with an ADA. It was bad enough most cops questioned my abilities since my father had been a legend at the precinct, and they figured that meant I hadn't earned my position. So being a DeMarco was already one strike against me. Being a woman was strike two. And any type of relationship with a coworker would be strike three. I couldn't risk that, so why didn't I call a cab and go home last night? Oh right, I thought my head would explode. Plus, I was too tired and inebriated to think clearly. That was why.

Grumbling to myself, I walked out of the building and cursed the bright sunlight. On top of it, I was hungover. "Stop it, Liv. There's nothing you can do about it now." I unlocked my car. The digital clock on the dash reminded me I was already behind schedule, so I sent a text to Emma, drove home, brushed my teeth, washed my face, changed clothes, and tied back my hair. I didn't have time to shower, but it didn't matter. I was going to spend the next few hours at the softball field. However, since the game might last until it was time to start my shift, I grabbed my gear, just in case.

When I arrived, I was surprised to find most of the parking spots occupied. Brad had downplayed these games as nothing more than a few guys from the precinct tossing a ball around. From the looks of it, this was a big deal. Or maybe that was just because it was the big police versus fire department game. The two departments worked well together, but no one could deny we had a friendly rivalry dating back to the dawn of time, or whenever the city first formed a police and fire department.

"Hey," Emma called, waving at me from her spot on the bleachers, "where've you been?" I bounded up the two steps and took a seat beside her. My best friend handed me a travel cup. "I thought we might have gotten our signals crossed."

"No, I'm just running late." I took a sip, pleased Emma had brought me a green smoothie for breakfast. "Have you seen Brad yet?"

"No, but I've been distracted." She jerked her chin toward the dirty blond firefighter currently taking practice swings near the dugout. From the quirk of her lips, I knew devious thoughts were running through her mind. Obviously, her recent hiccup in the dating world hadn't been traumatic enough to cause her to swear off men. I probably should have been relieved. Instead, I was concerned. She tore her eyes away from him and focused on me. "Doesn't he look familiar?"

"I don't know him. Could he be an EMT?"

Emma turned back to the field and tilted her head from side to side. "No, I don't recognize him from the hospital. We would have crossed paths in the ER. I would have made sure of that."

I snorted and gulped down more smoothie. Even

though I was queasy, I knew the smoothie would help. Water would be good too.

Emma bumped her knee against mine. "Where were you? I thought we were meeting at your parents' house since they left us in charge of housesitting and dogsitting while they're on their Mediterranean cruise."

"I'm sorry about that. Did Gunnie give you any problems?"

"Nah, he's such a cutie. But he's so big. He practically walks me. It's a good thing your dad has him trained."

"He's a Bernese mountain dog. They grow fast. You remember the movie Beethoven?"

"Wasn't that a Saint Bernard?"

"Close enough."

"At least he doesn't slobber that much." She eyed me. "Did you oversleep?"

"Yeah."

She nodded a few times before saying, "You smell like men's cologne. Who's the lucky fella? Did he oversleep too?"

"Em," I scoped out our surroundings, but we weren't that close to anyone else, "be quiet."

She looked at me with disapproval, which she had mastered by observing my mother. "The answer is obviously no, or you'd be in a better mood."

"I have a headache. Leave me alone."

"I bet you told him the same thing. Who is he, Liv? You know I'm going to annoy you until you tell me. Is this why you wanted to move out of my apartment? I told you I didn't mind if you had sleepovers."

"I was with Logan. We were doing trial prep."

Emma made a face. "Never mind."

"Told ya."

"No wonder you have a headache. I'll get you a

bottle of water from the concession stand. Do you want anything else?"

"No, thanks."

"I'll see if they have a banana. You could use something solid in your stomach."

While Emma was gone, I searched for our team's dugout. As predicted, our uniforms were blue. At the far end, I spotted my partner loosening up his shoulder. Oh, that's right. He pitches, I thought. He rotated his shoulder a few times and made some exaggerated throwing gestures.

"Good morning, Liv." Detective Jake Voletek sauntered over to the fence which separated the stands from the field. He rested his forearm against the chain-link and took off his cap. He used the same hand to rub his forehead and then put the cap back on. "Are you here to cheer me on?"

"I doubt you need any more cheering. You have an entire section dedicated just to you." I caught sight of several women on the other end who giggled and pointed at my fellow homicide detective.

He crooked his finger for me to come closer, so I climbed down the two rows and stood in front of him. "You understand how badge bunnies work, right? They'll jump on anyone with a badge. They aren't here for me. Well, not specifically." He turned to face them. "Morning, ladies." A few giggled, and one even did that coquettish wave, waggling each of her fingers separately. He turned back to me. "How come you never do that when I wish you a good morning?"

"Because I have more than one brain cell. But I could always just wave to you with one finger."

"Ouch." He took a step back from the fence. "I should warm up. Does Brad know you're here?"

"Not yet."

"Oh, this should be fun."

"Thanks for the heads up about my partner's secret double life and the invite to the game."

"Anytime." Someone called his name. "I'll catch you later." Voletek turned and jogged across the field.

As I headed back to my seat, I spotted Emma coming up the steps with some fruit cups and a bottle of water. "Who was that?" she asked, handing me the water.

"Voletek."

She unfolded a napkin and placed it on my thigh before popping the lid on a fruit cup and handing it to me with a spoon. "What's wrong with him?"

"Nothing." I looked down at the fruit cup. "Stop mothering me. I can take care of myself."

"I'm sorry, but you know Maria gave me specific instructions on what to do while she and your dad are on their month-long cruise. That included watching the house, feeding and walking the dog, and taking care of you."

"She didn't tell you to feed me too, did she?"

"No, but," Emma glanced down at the smoothie and fruit cup, "someone has to, and obviously, Bradley isn't doing a very good job. After all, he let you go home with a strange man." She squinted in the direction of the dugout. "So that was Jack?"

"Jake."

"Right. He's kinda cute. I bet he cleans up nicely."

"No."

"Not for you." She gave me a look. "Well, you get first dibs. Did you call dibs?"

My headache had gone from an annoying buzzing behind my eyes to a constant throbbing and an annoying buzzing in my ears. Or maybe that was just Emma. "The last thing I need is for you to date someone in homicide. I just transferred. Lt. Winston doesn't like me. My coworkers don't know what to make of me."

She let out a huff. "Fine."

We silently drank our green smoothies. I picked the orange and banana slices out of the fruit cup and ate them. But I couldn't stomach the pineapple or kiwi, so I gave those to Emma. By the time I finished breakfast and most of my water, my headache had dropped to a tolerable level and the guys had finished their warm-up.

After some sort of ceremonial sports thing I didn't understand, the players jogged out to take their places.

"Go Brad," a pretty blonde called from the other side of the stands. Brad smiled at Carrie and gave a little wave without waggling each of his fingers separately. Or maybe he did, but I couldn't tell since he had a glove on.

"Yeah, go Bradley," Emma cheered.

Brad turned at the unexpected sound of Emma's voice. His eyes zeroed in on me. I held up my palms and shrugged. He tucked the ball into his glove and pointed at his eyes and then at me. Perhaps, I should have waggled my fingers at him coquettishly, but I knew my partner. He wasn't mad. He just wanted me to think he was.

Emma nudged me in the ribs. "Who's that?" She jerked her chin in Carrie's direction, and I turned to look at the medical examiner's assistant with a smile and friendly nod.

"That's Carrie."

"Carrie? When did Brad get a girlfriend?" Emma asked.

"She's not his girlfriend. They're friends." Except that might have changed in the last twelve hours. After all, she was here. That had to mean something. Maybe after the game, they'd go shopping for rings.

"Right," Emma exaggerated the word. "How long has she been sleeping with him?"

"I don't know."

"You don't know?" Emma cocked an eyebrow. "I don't believe that. You and Brad don't have any secrets. Though, that does explain it."

"Explains what?"

"Never mind." She linked her arm through mine. "So how long has Brad been playing softball?"

I watched him throw out another pitch. The ball whizzed past the batter, and Brad took a step back to reposition for his next pitch with the same cocky swagger he had whenever he noticed something or found a piece of evidence at a crime scene that everyone else had missed. "According to Jake, he's been on the team for years. He just never told me. See, we have secrets." But I couldn't figure out why.

Three innings in, my phone rang.

THIRTEEN

"Fennel," I shouted, holding up my phone, "we have to go."

Someone called a timeout or whatever the equivalent was in softball, and Brad jogged over to me from where he'd been waiting on the bench for his turn at bat. "What's going on?"

"We caught a case."

"So much for a morning off."

"It's not a morning off. We're on call. You know that."

"Up until now, it felt like a break. You don't mind giving me a ride, do you?" He took off his cap. "I don't have my car."

"See, it's a good thing I showed up today to watch you play." I gave him a teasing smile, though my insides were currently doing the mambo. I'd been on the force long enough not to have jitters. It must have been the hangover or fear of what this call meant. I hadn't gotten many details, just that more security guards were dead. I didn't know if it was connected to our current case, but I had a bad feeling. I just hoped this scene wasn't gruesome. I didn't think I could stomach gruesome at the present.

"Okay. Give me a minute. I'll meet you in the parking lot." His gaze darted to Carrie.

I took a step back. "Sure, no problem." I tried to wave goodbye to Emma, but she had lost interest in me the moment I answered the phone. She knew what it meant. Instead, she continued to eyeball the fire department's third baseman. My mind made several inappropriate hose jokes, which made me snort. At least I amused myself.

I'd just unlocked the car doors when Brad sprinted toward me with his bag thrown over his shoulder. He hadn't bothered to change, but at least he'd taken off his cleats. He climbed into the passenger seat.

"Two dead. Responding officer said it looks like an armored truck heist gone wrong." He unzipped his bag and pulled out his holster. "At least that's what Lt. Winston left on my voicemail. For some reason, he thinks this is related to yesterday's robbery."

"I guess he called you too." I checked the rearview mirror before backing out of the space.

"What did he say when he spoke to you?"

"The same thing. You know the LT. He doesn't give anything away." I glanced at my partner from the corner of my eye. "I'm still not sure if that means he doesn't know, doesn't care, or just doesn't want to cloud our judgment."

"Who knows?" Brad dug through his bag, pulling out his cuffs and badge. He clipped them to his belt and unbuttoned the softball jersey and slipped into a long-sleeved t-shirt and police windbreaker. "Do you think anyone's going to notice I'm not wearing regulation attire?"

"You mean that isn't the police department's

official softball uniform?" I gasped in mock horror.

He squinted in my direction. "Has anyone mentioned you're not that funny?"

"Really? The voices in my head think I'm hilarious."

He chuckled, a deep velvety sound that eased the unsettled feeling in the pit of my stomach. "I hate to break it to you, but they're wrong."

"Pfft." I slowed as the traffic light turned yellow. "You're just jealous you don't have a built-in audience to give you unfettered adulation. But I guess you don't need it. You had your own cheering section at the game this morning."

"I can't believe you invited Emma. See, this is why I didn't tell you about softball."

"Seriously?"

He chuckled. "Sure." Except he knew I didn't believe him. "You hate watching sports. And you saw what it was like. Aside from the families, everyone else enjoying the game has ulterior motives. You already break my balls enough over my dating life."

For the first time, the complaint actually sounded sincere. "I'm sorry."

He shook it off. "How'd last night go with Logan?"

"We're all set for court. He wanted me to remind you that you have to meet up with him."

Brad tapped his temple. "Like a steel trap." He turned sideways to face me. "You didn't wash your hair."

"How do you know that?" I felt the top of my head. "Does it look greasy?"

"No, you look fine. But you only wear your hair like that when you don't have time to shower."

I cocked an eyebrow at him. "I wear my hair up all the time."

"I know, but you rarely do the twisty thing." He leaned closer. "And you smell like cologne. So unless you bought some very manly scented soap, I think you have some explaining to do."

I couldn't believe he just said that. Apparently, I'd also underestimated his detecting skills. He might be the greatest sleuth since Sherlock Holmes. At this rate, Emma could be his Watson. "Oh, like you inviting Carrie to watch you pitch? We've been partners for nearly two years. You're the one who has some explaining to do."

"The light's green." He shook his head and pointed at the windshield, just as the driver behind me honked his horn. "And we've been partners for over two years. You don't like sports. And I knew if you knew, you'd feel obligated to go. Honestly, Liv, I was saving you from countless hours on the bleachers, lumped in with all the wives, girlfriends, and families."

"And you were afraid I'd hurt your game."

"You're not that much of a distraction."

"I wasn't talking about your pitching, Romeo."

Brad's cheeks reddened, and he turned his head to stare out the window. "Did you and Emma enjoy yourselves?"

"Emma definitely did. What do you know about the other team's third baseman?"

"He's a firefighter. He might have been in the calendar. I heard some guys teasing him about it."

I realized that's why he looked familiar. "Mr. August." That spelled trouble with a capital T, but it was just the kind of trouble Emma would want to get into. At least this guy was a legitimate firefighter and not a killer in disguise.

Brad cocked an eyebrow at me, but I shook off the question. He didn't need me to connect the dots. He knew my best friend almost as well as I did. "So you didn't have a good time busting my balls?"

"I didn't show up to bust your balls. You should

know me better than that. For what it's worth, you looked pretty damn impressive out there. You have a good arm."

"Thanks."

At the sight of the parked police cars, I turned and pulled in at the end of the row. Our conversation had been a distraction to ease our nerves, but now we were here. And it was bad. Worse than I thought it would be, and I hadn't even stepped out of the car yet.

The crime scene techs were already hard at work. Two officers guarded the perimeter of the police tape, so I identified myself and flashed my badge.

"What do we know so far?" Brad asked while I ducked under the tape.

The officer consulted his notepad. "The call came in around 8:30 this morning. Shots fired. When we arrived on scene, we found them." He gestured to two tarps. One on the sidewalk, the other near the rear of an opened armored truck. "The store's alarm had been triggered. The door was open, but we didn't notice any obvious signs of a break-in. No signs of forced entry. Nothing to indicate the killer took anything from inside. We don't even know if he went inside."

"He didn't have to," I said. "He waited for the guards to wheel it out. The cash they collected and whatever was inside the back of the truck is what he wanted."

"Has the armored truck company been notified?" Brad asked.

"The sergeant's handling it."

"Where's the shop owner?" I asked.

The officer shook his head. "The EMTs don't think he'll make it." He pointed to a marker on the sidewalk near the front entrance. The stain on the concrete could only be one thing.

"Did anyone see anything?" Brad asked.

"Customers? Employees? People on the street?"

"Shop was closed. It doesn't open until ten. When we arrived, the looky-loos scattered. We have yet to speak to any witnesses."

"What about the shop owner?" I asked. "Did he say anything before they took him to the hospital?"

The officer shook his head. "He was too busy choking on his own blood." He sucked in a breath and stared into the distance. "I'm guessing if anyone was around to see what happened, they took off the moment the thief opened fire."

"Still, someone made the 9-1-1 call. Did dispatch trace the number? We need to ID the caller." Brad ducked beneath the tape to stand beside me. From here, he turned to look into the rear of the armored truck. It wasn't supposed to be that easy to get inside one of those. "Two guards. That means there must have been another one or two inside the truck. Did they make the 9-1-1 call?"

The officer shrugged. "Ask the sarge."

Brad nodded and led the way past the bodies to Sergeant Chambliss, who stood just outside the police tape. He sipped coffee from a paper cup and rubbed his eyes. When he saw us approach, he drained his cup and handed the empty to a nearby rookie.

"Are you sure you're first responders?" Chambliss glanced at his watch. "You're a couple hours too late." He looked down at my partner's softball pants. "At least tell me we kicked some firefighter ass."

"I don't know. We only made it three innings."

"Damn. Nothing good's gonna come from today." Chambliss blew out a breath. "All right. So here's the kicker. The dispensary," he pointed to the building surrounded by crime scene tape, "is protected by Moonlight Security. The night guard got off duty at eight a.m. The armored truck pickup came a little late today, after the night watchman had already gone home. We don't know anything yet, but that's one hell of a coinkydink. It's a good thing you detectives are here to figure that out, huh?"

I narrowed my eyes at the sarcasm, but Brad let it roll off his back. "What about the armored truck company and the guards inside?" he asked.

"They're all dead."

"That doesn't make sense," Brad said. "If two of the armored truck guys went in to collect the money, what happened to the guards who remained inside the truck?"

Chambliss swallowed. "Your guess is as good as mine."

FOURTEEN

I checked the inside of the shop, but nothing looked like it had been taken or disturbed. The sign on the desk insisted cash-only, and given the nature of the shop, I wasn't surprised. According to LockBox, the truck company, cash was picked up by armored truck every Saturday before the start of business. They had several other dispensaries on their route, along with other cash-only businesses. By the time they made it here, they should have had close to an entire pallet in the back of the truck, roughly one hundred million dollars, except the original truck had broken down. So LockBox sent an empty truck to make this pickup while they emptied out the other truck and had it towed for repair.

"Our killer has the worst luck ever," Fennel said, stepping into the main room. "Did you find anything?"

"Nope. Nothing's been disturbed. Do you think this could be another inside job? I contacted Moonlight Security, and Mr. McFarland told me Jonathan

Gardner used to work as a night watchman here before he got transferred to Star Cleaners. That gives us a solid connection."

Fennel bit his lip and stared into the room he just came from. "The dispensary has a ton of security cameras. They're all working. Two LockBox guards came in, the owner opened the safe, they unloaded it onto two separate, locked carts, and they wheeled it out of the shop."

"Okay, so the shooter didn't enter the store. He's not an idiot."

"No, I guess not." But a question itched at Fennel's mind.

"You want to know how the alarm got triggered if everything appeared to be on the up and up."

He pointed at me. "Bingo."

"What about the owner? Could he have hit the alarm when he saw the shooter?"

"I haven't found any big red button that says press in case of an emergency, but there might be one." He got onto his hands and knees and peered underneath the counter. "Anything on the walls?"

"No." And now I wondered how the alarm had gotten tripped. "Let's have someone bring Mr. McFarland in for questioning, along with the night watchman. Two businesses protected by Moonlight Security were hit in the last two days. That has to mean something."

"Besides the fact they have lousy security?" Fennel stood up and wiped his palms on his pants. "Have you checked out the truck yet?"

"Just a brief glance. CSU's checking for GSR and blood." I marched out of the fragrant shop and knelt down beside one of the tarps. The medical examiner wasn't in any hurry to move the bodies. I didn't know if that was because he slept in on Saturday mornings or if it was because he was short-staffed on account of one of his assistant's watching the softball game.

Beneath the tarp, blood had congealed around the man's head and chest. Just like Jonathan Gardner, he'd been shot in the face at close range. But unlike Gardner, this guard had made a move for his gun. The strap was open, and his weapon was missing. According to the crime techs, they'd found it a few inches from his body. It had recently been fired, with two bullets missing from the clip.

"The vest would have saved his life if the asshole hadn't shot him in the head," Fennel said from behind me. He pointed to two bullet holes in the guy's shirt with the silver slugs poking out from beneath the torn material.

"At least he tried to shoot back."

Fennel studied the ground, careful to maneuver around the markers, but he didn't find any blood drops. At least none that had been marked. "Looks like he missed."

He went to the second tarp, this one much closer to the rear of the truck. "Same thing here. Two shots to the chest. One to the head."

"Nice grouping."

"You're thinking our killer's been trained?"

"Maybe." I didn't know what to think, except this had to stop before more people died. I rubbed my mouth, replaced the tarp, and said a silent prayer. Were these two robbery-homicides connected?

While my partner spoke to the officers and crime techs, I walked around the area. The responding officers had done a good job containing the scene. Too bad they hadn't arrived sooner to stop the killer. But why hadn't LockBox sent more than two guards to make the pickup? Armored trucks had three, sometimes four, men inside when it came to large pickups and deliveries like this. One always stayed inside the truck to call for help.

I peered into a nearby dumpster, unsure what I expected to find, but all I saw was trash. So I moved on, farther from the dispensary and the crime scene. How far could the killer have gotten? Even though he didn't score hundreds of millions or even millions, he probably picked up several thousand dollars, maybe more. That would be heavy, especially in those sealed cash boxes the guards had wheeled out.

The killer must have had a getaway vehicle waiting. He must have parked close to the dispensary. Dialing LockBox, I waited for someone to answer. Before the call was transferred to someone in charge, an armored SUV pulled up beside my car. The LockBox insignia had been stenciled on the doors, and two men who looked like they should have been extras in a spy thriller stepped out of the vehicle.

Two officers stopped them at the police tape, and I came up behind them. "I'm Detective DeMarco. Who are you, gentlemen?"

"Leslie Tatem and Nicholas Pandori," one of the men said. He didn't offer his hand. Instead, he stared at the tarp over my shoulder. "Have you IDed them yet?"

I nodded. "Case Jeffers and Alan Croft."

"Damn."

Pandori swallowed and removed his sunglasses. Tears were in his eyes. "Do you know what happened?"

"We're working on it. Why did LockBox send a truck with only two guards?"

"Two?" Tatem shook his head. "No way." He held up his fingers. "Three."

Pandori studied the scene but made no attempt to cross the tape. "You didn't find Lindsey?"

"Lindsey?" I asked.

"Lindsey Rook." Pandori bit his upper lip. "That means he might still be alive, right?"

"Who's Lindsey Rook?" I repeated, not wanting to give him false hope.

"He works with us," Tatem said. "He liked to drive. Used to be a school bus driver but said this was better. He always joked if he'd had the gun back then, the brats on the bus might have behaved themselves."

"Does Lindsey have any outstanding debts? Personal issues?" I asked.

Pandori scowled at me. "You think someone from LockBox is involved?"

"I'm just trying to find out what happened. Right now, my priority is locating your friend. He could be hurt or worse. Anything you say can only help the situation."

Pandori didn't look convinced, and he eyed Tatem. Tatem blew out a breath. "Of course, Detective DeMarco. We'd be happy to answer any questions you have, but Lindsey's an upstanding guy. One of the best guys I know. He's the guy you'd want watching your back if you were pinned down in a firefight."

"So you think he got out of the truck to help Jeffers and Croft?"

"You bet your ass," Tatem said. "LockBox received a garbled radio transmission hours ago, but we couldn't make heads or tails out of it. Less than an hour later, the police contacted us with the news. I'm guessing Lindsey called it in, but it didn't go through."

"They probably used jammers," Fennel said, stepping up beside me. He introduced himself to the two men. "Excuse us, gentlemen." Fennel grabbed my elbow and steered me away from them. "9-1-1 just received a call about a body fifteen blocks from here. According to the caller, two security guards stripped the man down to his skivvies, shot him in the chest, and headed down to the train station. Dispatch has already advised the metro cops to be aware of active shooters in the area. We need to move. Now."

FIFTEEN

"Shit." Carter sucked down a few breaths. The world had dimmed around him.

"Stop being such a pussy." Diego tossed the man's shirt to him. "Put that on."

Carter shoved one arm through the sleeve and then the other. With trembling hands, he tucked the too large shirt into the too short pants and went to work on the buttons.

"Hurry it up," the third man hissed. He had already opened the first lockbox and emptied the cash into a duffel bag. Now, he filled the second bag with the cash from the second lockbox. "It's taking you longer to dress than it took me to get the boxes open."

"So what?" Carter asked, shaking his head from side to side in the hopes of getting the world to right itself. "You stole this guy's keys. How hard is it to stick a key in the hole?"

"How hard is it to dress yourself?" the third man retorted.

"I don't understand why I have to wear this." Carter

finished with the buttons but felt the wet bloodstain at the tip of the collar. Hopefully, no one would notice that. That's why Diego had waited to shoot the guard, instead of killing him the moment he stepped foot outside the armored truck.

"I don't understand a lot of things." The third man tossed the second duffel over his shoulder and got out of the car. They already wiped the vehicle as best they could. It wouldn't link back to them, but the dead guard's head wound had left a stain on the floormat. Instead of worrying about it, the third man hoped it would lead the police on another wild goose chase to track the car's origin and give him and his team more time to escape. "Namely, why the armored truck was empty." He slammed the door. "Care to explain that to me, Carter?"

Carter gulped. "Huh-how should I know?"

"You're the one who said it'd be filled to the brim. You said it'd be there forty-five minutes before it showed up. Let me see your phone. Did you call someone? Did you tip someone off?"

"No fucking way. I just told you what I heard. It's not my fault if something went wrong."

But the third man yanked Carter's phone out of his pocket, checked his call log and messages, threw the device to the ground, and stomped on it. "You better be telling me the truth."

"Why would I lie?"

The third man grabbed him and slammed him against the dumpster, causing a booming rattle. "Are you trying to double cross me? Do you want all the money for yourself? Or did you grow a conscience and lose your balls?"

"Uh, guys," Diego whispered urgently, "we need to go."

The third man kept Carter pinned to the dumpster.

"Give me one reason why I shouldn't kill you right here and now."

Diego grabbed his arm. "I'm serious. I thought I saw someone over there." He pointed to one of the windows in the building across the street. A few slats in the blinds remained askew. "Someone's watching us. We can't stay here."

The third man shoved Carter one final time and stepped back. "I'm not walking away without my payday. You better find a way to make this up to me."

*   *   *

"Out of the way." I raced down the steps. Fennel and I had arrived at the crime scene, immediately identified the naked man as Lindsey Rook, and headed for the nearest train station. The vast subway system would make our killer's escape inevitable if we didn't stop him in time.

Fennel headed for the information center while I went straight for the station agent. Nowadays, most of the subway system was automated, but a few people still got their metro cards from the station agent. But before I could maneuver around the throng of people, a blood-curdling scream echoed through the interior, causing the constant droning to suddenly quiet. And then the droning came back with a renewed roar, and additional surprised screams joined the first.

"Police." I pushed my way toward the commotion. The report of gunfire boomed in the cavernous tunnels. "Everyone get down."

I couldn't see through the mass of people, but just like animals in the wild running from fire, people raced toward me, away from the deadly sound.

"He has a gun," someone said, not slowing.

"He shot the ticket lady." At least, I thought that's

what someone else said as they darted past me.

Grabbing my weapon, I held it at an odd angle at hip-height. I didn't want to aim and panic the frenzied mob. They were already primed to stampede. Instead, I held up my badge and pushed my way toward the booth, telling people to get back as I went.

"Oh god." A woman crouched at the open door to the station agent's booth. "Help. Someone, help me. She needs help."

I rushed forward, kneeling down beside her. "Are you hurt?"

She shook her head, eyeing my badge as I clipped it back on my belt. "No, but she is."

She held the woman's head in her lap. I nearly missed the gunshot wound amid the station agent's tight red braids. The shot had gone to the side, entering just beyond her temple and coming out the other side behind her ear. Regardless, I checked for a pulse, but she was gone. Her body just hadn't gotten the message yet, and her pointer and middle fingers twitched.

I scanned the area for danger. The shooter was here. Close. He could have escaped in the fracas. "Did you see who did this?"

She swallowed, clutching the dead station agent's hand. "Two security guards. They had those khaki shirts with the black. Lock Stock or something?"

"LockBox?" I asked.

"Yeah, that's it."

"Did you see where they went?" I hadn't heard any other shots. The area had cleared, except for a few people who probably lived down here and the folks who were too wrapped up in their own lives or busy listening to their earbuds to notice the world around them.

She pointed with a shaky hand toward the nearest

platform. "There."

I reached for my phone and hit the speed dial for dispatch. "Shots fired." I gave the pertinent details. The cops stationed inside the subway station had to prioritize their actions. The majority were busy making sure everyone evacuated safely. But a few made it through to pursue the shooter. By the time I hung up, three uniformed officers had clustered around me.

I left the woman and the dead station agent in their care and headed for the platform. After jumping the turnstile, I aimed ahead of me, silently clearing out the few remaining civilians as I made my way across the platform. At the far end, I glimpsed a khaki-colored uniform.

"Freeze," I yelled.

The man hesitated for a split second. He faced the track, staring into the tunnel. Even if he jumped onto the tracks, he'd have thirty feet to clear before he could disappear into the darkness, and that was assuming he didn't get splattered by a train or hit the third rail.

"Don't even think about it."

He cocked his head to the side. From here, I couldn't make out much about his profile. He had short, dark hair. He held up one hand, bending his elbow at a right angle, as if he was announcing a touchdown, and then he turned sideways and fired. He kept his gun pressed against his stomach, practically out of my line of sight.

The first shot impacted against the metal bench directly in front of me, and I returned fire. He ducked behind one of the large, concrete support pillars and continued to fire blindly, keeping himself out of sight.

Diving behind a metal trashcan, I edged closer until I could take cover behind another one of the support pillars in that row. I pressed my back against it, spotting my partner making his way along the platform directly across from me.

After taking another breath, I poked my head out and returned fire, hoping if I couldn't hit the offender, I'd at least be able to distract him long enough for Fennel to get to him. He fired again. His shots getting closer and closer to my head. I ducked back into cover, my heart pounding in my chest. If I couldn't see him clearly, how could he see me?

Quickly, I searched for any mirrors or monitors, but I didn't see anything that would give away my position. Did he have a sixth sense or a spotter? The woman who attempted to provide aid to the dead station agent said there had been two of them. Where was the second shooter?

The ground beneath my feet vibrated, followed by the telltale rumble of an arriving train. Disregarding my own well-being, I broke from cover just as the subway came to a stop, blocking my view of the other side. The doors opened, and dozens of unsuspecting passengers exited the row of cars.

For the briefest moment, I caught sight of a khaki-colored shirt moving with the throng. And then it was gone. I shoved people aside, announcing myself, but it was already too late.

Fennel appeared in the open doorway of the emptying subway car. "Where the hell is he?"

I squinted into the distance. I didn't see him head for the stairs. "Did he get on the train? Or go in the tunnel?" I couldn't see into the tunnel since the stopped train blocked it from view.

"I'll check the train." My partner disappeared back inside, moving from the middle car toward the far end, closest to where the shooter had been positioned.

I shouted to the officers who had arrived to assist to

have the train stopped and to be on the lookout for anyone wearing a security guard uniform. Thankfully, they had already radioed the description to all officers in the area after speaking to the woman.

By the time I made it to the end of the platform, the shooter had vanished. Spent casings littered the ground, and I picked one up and tucked it into my pocket. At this rate, I didn't need anything else to disappear.

"He's not here." Fennel emerged from the first car. He kept his back to mine, covering me while I checked around the pillar and the alcoves near the end where the homeless liked to sleep and people could lock their bikes. "Did you get a look at him?"

"No, but he killed the station agent. A woman saw what happened. She said there's two of them."

"That goes along with what the 9-1-1 caller said." He took a step back. I could feel his reassuring presence behind me. "What about the men's room?"

"I don't know." I stared into the darkness. "I think he went into the tunnel."

He pulled out a radio, asking for an ETA on our backup. With so many people, most officers had been diverted to crowd control and evacs. "On our way," came a clipped response.

Fennel kept his eyes on the door to the public restrooms. "I say we check there first. If they went into the tunnels, who knows where they might pop up?"

Several anti-crime officers approached our position, their badges out and exposed, but they identified themselves just to be on the safe side. They kept an eye on the tunnel entrance while Fennel and I cleared the restrooms.

By the time we were finished hauling the few occupants out, more cops had arrived on the scene.

The trains had been shut down, and several went into the tunnels in search of our suspects. Fennel and I questioned the few people we dragged out of the bathrooms, but they hadn't seen anything. And since they tested negative for GSR and didn't fit the description of our offenders, we let them go.

We swept the area again, questioning anyone and everyone we could find, but the descriptions varied drastically. Most people I spoke to didn't see anything. They heard the shot or the screaming and followed the crowd to safety.

"Do you think the offenders blended in and escaped?" Fennel asked as we made our way back to the traumatized woman. She sat on top of a gurney with a blanket around her while EMTs checked her pulse.

"We already had their descriptions even before the station agent was killed. No cop would let a security guard slip away."

"They could have changed clothes."

"We would have found the discarded uniforms in the trash or on the ground. I didn't find anything. Did you?"

"No." Fennel sighed, glancing back at the stopped train. Officers were questioning the remaining passengers and checking IDs. Aside from pissing off the commuters and getting several complaints lodged against the department for the holdup, I didn't think this would achieve anything. "How did they get past us?"

Security camera footage was already being pulled and compiled, so we'd know soon enough. In the meantime, we had a few eyewitnesses to question.

SIXTEEN

From what we gathered, two men shot and killed the LockBox security guards, left the scene of that crime, found someplace to hang out for a couple of hours, and then dumped Lindsey Rook's body several blocks away from the dispensary, dressed in his clothes, and abandoned their getaway vehicle. They went down into the subway tunnels and tried to rob the station agent. She must have unlocked the door, possibly in an attempt to go for help or to appease their demands, but either way, they shot her and fled.

The woman who had been behind them in line hadn't seen what happened until they knocked her over on their way out. By then, everyone else who'd been clustered around the booth had literally run for their lives. She had crawled to the open door, found the station agent, whom she spoke to every week when she renewed her metro card, and tried to save her. She didn't know the station agent was already dead, and as far as I could tell, no one had told her yet.

"Gloria," she said. "Her name's Gloria. I don't know her last name, but she has a son. A teenager. Someone needs to call him. She'd want him to know what happened."

"We'll make sure that's taken care of," Fennel promised. "Try not to focus on that. Think back, before that happened. You were waiting in line, like you always do. Was there anything different about today? Did you notice anything weird? Did you happen to overhear anyone's conversation? Possibly you heard what the men in front of you might have been saying?"

She shook her head. "I wasn't paying attention. I tune everything out. It's the usual. Well, it was. Now," she blinked and looked around, "nothing seems normal."

"It's okay," I said. "Just try to remember."

"There were two of them in the same khaki shirts and dark work pants. They had belts like that." She pointed to a nearby officer. "Thick with the holes and the gadgets."

"Did they have guns?" I asked.

She nodded. "I didn't think anything of it. They had uniforms. That made it okay. At least, I thought it did."

"Did you see a name tag?" Fennel asked.

She bit her lip and stared at the turnstiles.

"What about their height or hair color?" I asked.

"Dark hair. Both of them. One was darker than the other, skin too."

"Could you guess their race?" Fennel asked.

"I don't know. Probably white, maybe Latino, Asian, or Middle Eastern. Hell, one of them could have been a light skinned black man for all I know."

Fennel glanced at me. That didn't help us any. "Okay, but they were both men?"

"Yeah. I'm sure of that." She sized him up. "About your size." She gave his pants an odd look. "Are you a baseball player?"

"No, I'm a homicide detective."

She arched an eyebrow. "Undercover?"

"No, ma'am."

A thought dawned on her. "Their clothes didn't fit right."

"What do you mean?" Fennel and I asked simultaneously.

She shifted her gaze from me to my partner. "It looked like they grabbed the wrong uniforms. One guy's shirt was snug, and his sleeves didn't come down all the way. And the other guy, his pants were baggy, like they might have fallen off if he loosened his belt. I don't know. It was just weird. But I kinda thought maybe they just had a one size fits all kind of thing going on. I mean, it's a uniform, right?"

"But they both had the same uniforms?" Fennel asked.

"Yeah."

"Not just similar clothes, but uniforms?"

"That's what I said," she insisted. "Why? Does that mean something?"

The EMTs stepped closer. "We should take her to get checked out, just to make sure she's okay. She took quite the fall." He nodded at a few of the bandages they'd placed on her scraped knees and forearm. "It'd be best to make sure she didn't hit her head or lose consciousness."

"Okay." I copied down her information, told her we'd follow up if we had more questions, and watched the paramedics wheel her away.

"They both had uniforms," Fennel said. "But they only stripped one of the LockBox guards. That would mean the second offender is part of LockBox."

"You saw Pandori and whatshisface. They looked sharp. Even the two slain guards were dressed nicely."

"You paid attention to that?" Fennel asked. "You didn't notice what I was wearing yesterday."

I rolled my eyes. "We would have noticed if their clothes didn't fit right." A theory wormed its way through my brain. "Assuming these are the same assholes who knocked over Star Cleaners, I'd say they stole more than the ticket pad and the cash in the register. I think they took someone's dry cleaning too."

"You think they stole a security guard uniform. That would make sense. That's why Gardner's killer needed the ticket pad." Fennel let out a low whistle. "Didn't you say Mr. Lee runs a uniform special? We should find out if he cleans any of LockBox's uniforms."

"Or if Star Cleaners is one of LockBox's clients," I said.

After getting a progress report on the officers in the tunnel and an update on the passengers who had been questioned, Fennel and I made our way up the steps. The morning had turned to afternoon. But even the midday sun couldn't improve my mood. Four more dead and at least one woman injured, and the bastards responsible had gotten away again.

We backtracked to the alley where we'd left Lindsey Rook's body with a few uniformed officers. The scene had been roped off. The coroner's van had parked at the mouth. Two police cars and one unmarked cruiser had boxed in our vehicle, but it didn't matter. Right now, this was where we needed to be.

"What do we know?" Fennel asked the medical examiner.

The ME pointed to the vehicle. "Blunt force trauma to the head. It probably knocked him out. He did quite a bit of bleeding in the back of the car. But you can see here," he turned the guy's head to the side, "it didn't trickle down. Most of it is in his hair. They probably had him upside down."

"They didn't want to get blood on the uniform," I said.

"Any idea what hit him?" Fennel asked.

"The impact is focused here." He pointed to an ugly, uneven gash at the side of the man's head. "But I don't recognize it. Once we get the area cleaned and take a mold, I should have an answer for you. I just told your two pals from homicide the same thing." He jerked his chin toward the nearby dumpster where they'd fished out Rook's body.

"Thanks, Doc." Fennel took a slow, deep breath and peered into the dumpster, jumping back when Jake Voletek stood up. "Jesus."

Voletek laughed. "And I didn't even get a chance to yell 'surprise'."

"Now's not the time, Jake." I glared at him.

"Tell me about it," Detective Lisco said. She stepped into the alley. "I just finished up with the 9-1-1 caller. But he didn't get a look at the shooter. When he heard car doors slam, he looked out his window. He saw a security guard drag this guy," she jerked her head down at the body, "out of the back of the car, pull off his pants and shirt, and then carry him to the dumpster. A few minutes later, he heard a loud bang. He thought the car backfired, and they were leaving, but the car hadn't moved. That's when he realized it had been a gunshot and called us."

"What else did he see?" I asked.

"Nothing. He gave us a vague description of the two men he saw near the dumpster. Both had dark hair, were fairly tall, and athletic looking." She gazed at Fennel's pants. "Hey, Jake, do you have a pair of those on under your slacks?"

Voletek snickered. "I didn't know you were interested in what's under my slacks." He grabbed the edge of the dumpster and swung one leg out and then the other.

"How'd the game end?" Fennel asked, though I could tell he was focused on the case.

"We called it a tie. Too many calls coming in for us to figure it out." Voletek looked at me. "It's not every day two top detectives abandon not one, but two crime scenes. Tell me you had a good reason. I'm sure Lt. Winston's dying to hear it."

"The 9-1-1 caller said the men headed into the subway station. We thought we might have had a chance to stop them. But we didn't."

"Shit," Voletek swore. "Any idea who they are?"

"I think we're tracking the same men from yesterday," I said. "First they broke into Star Cleaners to steal a LockBox uniform. I verified that with Mr. Lee on our way back here. And then they hit the truck."

"Okay, so why'd they take this guy hostage, strip him, and dump him if they already finished their armored truck heist?" Voletek asked. Fennel looked at me. Neither of us had figured that out yet. "Do you think Rook could have been an inside man and this was a double cross?"

"Could be," Fennel said.

Voletek nodded, but a thought gnawed at him. "What do you think, princess?"

"I think if you call me that again, I'll toss you back inside that dumpster and shut the lid."

Lisco stifled a laugh.

"Seriously," Voletek stared at me, all joking aside, "is that what you think happened?" He held out his phone. "I ran our DB through the database. No outstanding debts. No record. The guys who work for LockBox are squeaky and not in a wheel's falling off kind of way. They get good benefits, a pension plan, retirement, vacation. It's one of the better companies. Apparently, they realized it'd be wise to keep their employees happy so they don't get robbed blind."

I scanned the details. Lindsey Rook appeared to be just as clean and wholesome as Jonathan Gardner. "The killings aren't personal. These were good men who were just doing their jobs." I handed Voletek back his phone and crouched down beside the dumpster, hoping a different position would give me a new perspective.

"Who do they have in common?" Fennel asked.

But no one had an answer. The name Lindsey Rook hadn't come up yesterday. And from what I recalled from Moonlight Security's records, he had never been one of theirs. As far as I knew, Gardner and Rook never crossed paths. But that didn't mean anything. They might have traveled in the same circles or concentric circles. Something like that.

"I guess we better find out." But something told me that wasn't our connection. I just didn't know what was.

SEVENTEEN

As soon as we returned to the precinct, I tore through everything we had. But I didn't find a connection. I had Mac and every available tech and uniformed officer reviewing the data, searching social media, and analyzing the surveillance footage we had gathered. But we still hadn't come up with anything solid.

"Ballistics said the same gun that killed Jonathan Gardner also killed Case Jeffers and Alan Croft." Fennel rubbed a hand over his mouth.

"What about Lindsey Rook?"

"Different gun."

"And the slugs they found in the subway station?"

"Those were too badly damaged, but they matched the caliber used to shoot Rook." He rocked back in his chair and rubbed his palms on his pants, probably glad to be out of the softball uniform and back in business attire. "We're dealing with two shooters."

"We knew that already."

"But now we have proof." He leaned forward, his fingers flying over the keyboard. "I'm guessing they're working together." He squinted at the screen. "Have you found any overlap with LockBox and Moonlight?"

"Aside from Gardner working as night watchman at the pot shop, I haven't found anything else. They never shared any employees. No one we investigated from Gardner's past has anything to do with the armored truck company or vice versa."

"DeMarco, you need to see this." Lt. Winston stood in the doorway to the conference room where most of the geek squad had set up. "You too, Fennel."

We exchanged a glance and crossed the bullpen. "What is it, sir?" I asked.

He pointed to the screen. "It turns out LockBox didn't make their pickup today."

"You mean the truck that broke down?" Fennel asked.

Winston didn't even bother answering my partner. He pointed to one of the techs. "Johnson, play the traffic cam footage."

A moment later, the large monitor flipped to a shot of the LockBox truck arriving and parking at the end of the block. Jeffers opened the passenger door and climbed out. He went around to the back of the truck and opened the rear door. After that, we couldn't see what was happening. The camera angle didn't allow us to see inside the truck, but they must have been prepping the interior for the pickup. That was the only thing that would explain the delay.

"Johnson, switch to the store's exterior feed. Same timestamp," Winston said. While the LockBox crew was occupied, two similarly dressed men entered the pot shop. "Freeze it there."

I narrowed my eyes at the grainy feed. "Son of a bitch."

"We're attempting to run them through facial rec, but that'll probably be a bust."

"Those guys don't work for LockBox," I said.

Winston rolled his eyes. "You think?"

"What about the interior footage?" Fennel asked. "That shop had cameras coming out the wazoo. Did any of them catch anything?"

Winston crossed his arms over his chest and leaned back against the table while the tech cycled through the various feeds. "Nothing but the bills of their caps and some chin."

"Their uniforms don't fit." Just like our eyewitness had told us. I thought about the shop owner, but I'd been notified ten minutes ago that he didn't make it. "What about after they left the shop?"

The tech switched the feed again. "They're on their way out, but the shop owner stops them."

"He probably realized something was off about them," Fennel said.

"Yeah, so they killed him." Winston turned away while the one on the right struck the owner in the throat with a baton. Blood splashed against the bottom of the door, just like you'd see in a Tarantino film, except this violence was real. I grimaced.

"That's probably the weapon used to knock Rook unconscious." Fennel tightened his jaw but kept his eyes glued to the screen. "Do we have footage of the firefight?"

"Nope." Winston spun to face the conference table. A sketch had been made to scale of the area with points of interest marked. "Forensics determined this is where the bulk of the action happened. It's in a blind spot. It's out of range of the shop and the traffic cams. No other cameras in the vicinity caught it. We aren't sure how Lindsey Rook managed to get himself taken or how he became another victim, but LockBox has turned over their recordings from inside their truck. Unfortunately, right before this massacre happened, the footage turns to static."

"Jammer," Fennel said.

"Or inside job." Winston shrugged. "Guess that's up to you two to decide. But I want this mess put to bed quickly and quietly. Shutting down a subway station at lunchtime on a Saturday isn't something my detectives should be doing. Understood?"

"But, sir, the shooters were right there," I protested. And they'd basically used the same play they had at the cleaner's, except this time four men were killed.

"Then why didn't you arrest them?" Winston asked.

"They got away," Fennel said.

Winston kept his gaze on me. "How? You stopped the trains. Where did they go?"

"I don't know. I only saw one. He might have escaped into the tunnel when the train stopped," I said.

"And the other?" Winston asked. He pointed at the image still on the screen. "I count two, and so did the 9-1-1 caller and the eyewitness you questioned."

"We only encountered one shooter," Fennel said. "They split up before we arrived."

"I don't give a shit what they did. You just have to find them and arrest them." He jerked his chin at the door. "Get to it."

"Yes, sir," Fennel said before I could open my mouth. I glared at the lieutenant, but he was right. This was our case, and if we'd handled it better yesterday, five people might still be alive today. The thought sickened me as we returned to our desks.

You can't think like that, Olive, my dad's voice said. All you can do is your job. The rest is up to them. Shitheads will always find a way, no matter what you do. Leave that behind. It won't help you.

"Liv," Fennel nudged me, "you okay? You don't

look so good."

"I'm just thinking about something my dad used to say." I slammed my palm on the desk. "I wish I'd realized it sooner. The uniforms. The dry cleaner's. They must have had this planned all along. If only I'd figured it out, connected the dots."

"Go easy on yourself. We didn't have anything to go on." He straightened the papers on his desk and reached across to organize the stack at the edge of mine. "But now we do."

"We do?"

He offered a wan smile. "Yeah." He grabbed the legal pad he'd been using and flipped to a clean page. "The target couldn't have been the couple dozen grand they got from the dispensary. The target was the hundred million that should have been in the back of the truck. They wouldn't have gone to that kind of trouble to steal uniforms and time everything so perfectly if they just wanted to rob one place."

"Yeah, but how would that have worked?"

"It's elementary, my dear. They probably didn't count on the delay or the shop owner stopping them. I'm guessing they would have left the shop, found someplace to take cover, waited for LockBox's actual guards to go inside, and then they would have approached the truck. The driver would have seen the uniforms and carts and opened the doors, and once inside, they would have convinced him to take them to a predetermined location or killed him and driven the truck themselves."

"Wow, that's a lot of speculating."

"It's what I'd do. Wouldn't you do the same?"

I bit my lip. "It's a good plan, except none of it worked out, including the timing. And we still don't know where they went after they abducted Rook and before we caught up to them in the train station."

Fennel grabbed a map and marked the two locations, and then he grabbed a different colored pen and marked Star Cleaners and 24/7 Spirits. "Looks like they could have gone anywhere."

"That doesn't help us."

"No, so we need to find something that can."

The original truck's guards had come to the station to answer our questions about the breakdown and delay, but after running their names and cross-referencing them to the limited amount of intel we had, nothing pinged. Fennel and I interviewed everyone from Star Cleaners, Moonlight Security, and LockBox, but as far as we could tell, none of them had been involved.

"God, I'm so sick of dead ends." I sat up straight, my neck cracking in the process. "We're looking at this wrong. We have to be. This isn't a disgruntled employee, an inside job, or a double cross. I don't know how the killers knew to disarm Star Cleaners' security system, but at this point, I'm willing to say it was a lucky guess."

"It's a professional crew," Fennel said. "I spoke to a few of the other units, but they haven't heard much. I put a call in to the Feds, but so far, no dice. But you said it, Liv. The grouping on the shots was done by a pro. They avoid the cameras. At every location they've hit, it's been the same thing. They didn't get lucky. They know where the blind spots are. They must plan meticulously, including contingencies. This isn't their first rodeo. They probably did some research or staked out the dry cleaner's until they spotted someone entering the code. That's how they disarmed it. They couldn't afford for us to respond to a triggered alarm. They needed the extra time to search for the LockBox uniforms."

"Then why kill Gardner?" I asked. "Couldn't they

have just slipped in the back and slipped out?"

"I don't know. But killing him probably made it easier. No witnesses."

"Except the woman who tried to save the station agent," I said. "Any idea what happened to her?"

"Hospital released her. We have no reason to believe the shooters know her name or where she lives. And quite frankly, she never got a good look at them. I don't think they'll waste their time worrying about her."

"You're probably right." But that did little to assuage my fears. "I'm going to check with the watch commander and see if anything turned up on the canvass or the search of the subway tunnels." Remaining behind my desk and staring at a limited number of facts wouldn't solve this. I just didn't know what would.

"Yeah, okay. In the meantime, I'll work on coming up with their next possible targets."

"Next targets?" I practically choked.

"Yeah." Fennel gave me a worried look, like I'd missed a key point that should have been obvious. "Our two unsubs got up this morning thinking they'd be one hundred million dollars richer. I doubt a few grand is enough for them to walk away, especially when we have no leads."

"They don't know that."

"Don't they?" Fennel pointed to the TV in the corner of the room. "If we knew something, we wouldn't be asking anyone who had been at the train station to call the tip line. As far as these bastards know, they're still in the clear." He sighed. "Which, unfortunately, they are."

I went in search of the watch commander. Sgt. Chambliss had reported to both scenes. That's what happened when patrol called for a supervisor.

Frankly, this was as much his show as it was mine. Except, I was expected to piece together the intel.

Knocking on his office door, I took a breath and waited. He looked up and gestured that I enter. "I take it you heard."

My stomach dropped, as if I'd just plummeted from a cliff. "Heard what?"

"Guess not." He scratched the back of his head and got up from behind his desk. "I just got word back from the search of the subway system and stations. One of ours got the living daylights knocked out of him."

"Who?"

"Officer Cruz. Do you know him?"

"His name doesn't ring any bells."

"He works out of a different precinct. He and several other officers had been rerouted to connecting stations. When the 11:15 train arrived, he spotted a man in a LockBox uniform exit the train. Cruz followed him from the platform into the public restrooms. The suspect had a crowbar and attacked Cruz the moment he entered. The asshole knocked the gun from his hand, broke his leg, and several of his ribs. Before backup arrived, he stole Cruz's badge and escaped. We didn't spot him on any of the camera feeds."

"They split up before we could intervene." I thought about the train schedule. Between the woman screaming, the single gunshot, and tracking down the shooter, I hadn't noticed any other trains departing from that platform, but since there were so many different ones in the vicinity, he could have been on the other side and left before I even noticed. "I should have gotten there faster."

"We all should have. But we can't change what's already happened."

"No, sir. But I'd like to."

"Me too."

We stood in silence for a moment. "Cruz should be okay. The doctors want to keep him overnight as a precaution, but he doesn't need surgery."

"Did he get a look at his attacker?"

"LockBox uniform, blond hair, tall, athletic, his pants were too short. Other than that, the restroom was too dimly lit, and the guy had the LockBox cap on. He didn't get a look at his face. Just the back of him."

"But he noticed that the offender was blond? Are you sure?"

"That's what Cruz said."

"Any identifying marks?"

"Nothing. The guy even wore gloves. He left the crowbar behind, but we didn't find anything on it except Cruz's DNA. But I will tell you one thing, DeMarco. These bastards are attacking cops now. That means they just declared war."

"You said Cruz works patrol. Was he in uniform?"

"Yep, so this bastard knew for sure he was a cop."

At least they didn't try to steal a police uniform. That was a plus. A thought struck me, and I headed for the door. "Make sure everything gets forwarded upstairs. We need every bit of intel if we're going to stop these bastards before they kill again."

"You got it," Chambliss said. "But patrol's on the lookout. If you don't find these assholes, one of my guys will. I can almost guarantee it."

EIGHTEEN

Could it be about the uniforms? I drummed my fingers against the conference table. My desk had gotten too cluttered for me to work, so I went into the room where the techs continued to search the footage and internet for clues. Fennel followed, dragging a rolling whiteboard behind him. Then we set up our murder board.

"The 9-1-1 caller and the witness from the train station said the two men in LockBox uniforms had dark hair. But Officer Cruz said one of them was blond." Fennel chewed on his bottom lip. "The guy who shot at you looked like he had dark hair, but I wasn't that close. Most of what I could see was his cap."

"He had dark hair. Cruz was attacked by the other one. That's the only thing that would explain the timing, but the witness said both guards had similar features. I don't get it."

"Me neither. But since the restroom was out of order, it only had emergency lighting. Maybe Cruz got it wrong," Fennel suggested.

"Cops don't usually get it wrong."

"It could have been a wig. These guys like to play dress-up. Do you think they stole anything else from Star Cleaners? They could be construction workers or pirates by now."

I snorted. "Mr. Lee didn't keep any other records, just the physical carbon copies. He doesn't know what clothes were in back before the break-in, let alone after. Unless a customer tries to pick up his dry cleaning order and Lee can't find it, we won't know anything for sure."

"That could take a week or more. People don't always get around to running errands. We don't have time to wait."

"No, we don't." I rocked back in the chair. "We've compiled a list of Star Cleaners' regular customers, but none of that looks promising."

"And the employees, past and present, are in the clear. We checked alibis for today's shooting." Fennel reached for the notepad and a sharpie, marking Lee's name off the list. "Even the owner alibied out."

"The same with Moonlight Security's personnel. I want to get something on the books with the CEO, Mr. Denisten, but he's out of the office this week. McFarland said he had business meetings scheduled for every day. I left a message on his voicemail. Hopefully, he'll get back to us by tomorrow. If anyone would know anything about weaknesses in their security systems or what other lucrative targets Moonlight Security protects, it would be him."

"All right." Fennel made a note at the top and more black lines across the paper. "I got in touch with the guys who played video games with Jonathan Gardner. I just have one more to verify, but that'll probably pan out, and then we can cross off their names."

"Dammit."

"I know."

I stared up at the photo array. At this point, we didn't have any suspects left. "Six people were killed in the last thirty-six hours. And these chuckleheads still haven't gotten their big score."

"No, but they might be getting cocky. After all, one of them ended up in a shootout with us before vanishing, and the other beat the shit out of a uniformed cop in the middle of a public restroom. They aren't afraid to go toe-to-toe with the police or armed guards. At this point, it looks like they'd rather kill than run. Nothing's going to stop them from continuing to escalate."

"You're wrong. They won't take unnecessary risks. Not yet. They still have a plan."

"What makes you say that?" Fennel asked.

"According to Cruz, the maintenance sign had been on the bathroom door for a couple of days and no one else was inside. I think the bastard lured Cruz into isolation to take care of him and fled before help arrived. That's not the behavior of someone who thinks of himself as invincible."

"That's not the point, Liv. The point is these bastards don't care about killing people in uniform. Honestly, I think they revel in it. The dispensary owner is the only person they attacked who wasn't wearing some sort of uniform." Fennel swiveled around to study the board.

"That doesn't help us any."

"Maybe not," he agreed, "but it might lend itself to some kind of psychological profile. The killer hates authority, represented by people in uniform."

"Even if it's a station agent?"

"It's still authority. Perhaps, that's why they left the woman behind them in line alive. They only knocked her down. They just as easily could have shot her."

"Wow, you're so insightful."

Fennel chuckled. "I did ace psychology class."

"Apparently so did Jonathan Gardner, but that didn't help him any."

Fennel let out an unhappy grunt and reached for a map. Every point of interest had been marked and color coded. "Where do you think they went after they robbed the dispensary but before they dumped Lindsey Rook's body in the alleyway and headed for the subway station? That's two and a half hours unaccounted for."

I narrowed my eyes, seeing the crime scene unfold inside my mind. "Rook drove the LockBox truck. When he exited the vehicle to help his colleagues, the assailants knocked him out and abducted him. And they made sure to keep his uniform pristine and free of blood. That's why they shot him after they stripped him." I didn't like what I was thinking. "The killers wanted the pallet of money in the back of the truck, but the truck was empty. They must have needed the driver for something."

"Intel." Fennel let out a low whistle. "He'd know the routes, protocols, pickup times, and other stops." He dug through the stack of files and pulled out the background info we'd obtained on Lindsey Rook. Nothing indicated Rook was working with them, but Detectives Voletek and Lisco were following up to make sure. "They're going to hit another truck."

"Shit."

"Maybe that's why they wanted to take Rook's uniform. Perhaps it fits better than the two ill-fitting ones they snagged from Star Cleaners, or..."

"They got blood on theirs and needed another costume change." I stared at the mess of data covering the table and the techs who remained hard at work tracking the intel we had. For the most part, they ignored us. "What do we know for sure? At this point, the killers might be wearing wigs beneath their caps. Blond, brown, redhead? And why did they rob the dispensary if the truck was their goal?"

"They didn't think it was coming," Fennel said. "Or they got greedy."

"Twenty grand is just a drop in the bucket when we're talking about a hundred mill."

"Unless they knew the truck was empty," Fennel said.

"How?" Again, we were back to thinking this was an inside job, except we didn't have any proof.

My partner rubbed his cheek, indicating he was deep in thought. "I bet they had a radio scanner to go along with their signal jammer." He found a copy of LockBox's radio transcripts. "According to LockBox protocols, the trucks radio in when they arrive at their location and again when they depart. LockBox received the first call when Rook pulled up to the location. See this." Fennel pointed, and I read the message. Truck 304 is preparing for its first pickup of the day.

"That's how they knew. So instead of walking away, they came up with a plan B on the fly. But instead of getting away scot-free, the dispensary owner stopped them. And things got ugly." I reached for my phone. "We have to warn LockBox that another of their trucks may be hit later today."

"Or sometime this week. It'd have to be whatever routes and locations Lindsey Rook knew about."

"That's assuming he talked. Do you think they tortured him?"

"I'll get in touch with the ME's office and find out while you phone LockBox."

While I was relaying the information and getting

updates on their routes and possible targets, one of the techs waved me over and pointed to the screen. Patrol had found the silver sedan from the first scene. It had been abandoned in an alleyway and torched.

I marked the location on the map. Every location appeared random. We might not know who these assholes were, so we had to focus on the where. After setting up police escorts for all LockBox pickups, I turned to Fennel. "We should check out the car, but if another attack is imminent, it'd be a better use of our time to determine their next target. You said you were working on that earlier. Any ideas?"

"No, but this could be something. If we figure out why they dumped the car there or where they went afterward, we might find them."

"You're right." But this felt like a waste of valuable time. The clock was running out on innocent lives while these killers roamed free. I doubted this would lead to anything. They were too careful. Too meticulous. They left the car there for a reason, but my gut said it was to distract us.

NINETEEN

The once silver paint was now a peeling, scorched charcoal. The heat inside the vehicle had made the windows explode, and little bits of glass had been blown throughout the alleyway. One of the techs held up a shard with a pair of tweezers before tucking it into an evidence bag.

"We ran the VIN. The car was stolen five days ago." The patrol officer shrugged. "We never would have noticed it if we hadn't tracked it on the city's traffic cam grid. The tech guys got us close, but good old-fashioned legwork is how we found it."

"What about nearby security feeds?" I asked.

"What security feeds?" the officer asked. "There's nothing around here. It's mostly residential, and the few places," he pointed across the street, "have their cameras facing the other way."

"And as usual, no one saw anything." Fennel opened the door and peered inside the car. "What did they use? Gasoline?"

"It looks that way," the officer said.

Fennel used his pen to sift through the ashes. A moment later, he removed a latex glove from his jacket pocket and picked something up. "I found a lighter. Look's expensive. Metal. Possibly some sort of engraving."

I grabbed an evidence bag and held it open for him. "Maybe the lab can clean it up."

He reached in, searching for the trunk release, but of course whatever was left crumbled in his hand. After we pried open the trunk, we searched the inside, finding nothing but more charred ashes. At least we didn't find any skeletal remains.

"Get the rest of this bagged and tagged, and put a rush on it." I followed my partner, who wandered out of the alley and down the street. "Brad, wait up."

He halted, lost in his thoughts while his eyes took in every inch of our surroundings. "It was still dark out when they abandoned the car. No one was around. No one saw anything. The alley's narrow. They barely had enough clearance to open their doors and get out. The buildings would have blocked the blaze from view, unless you looked straight at it. They didn't just find this location. They planned it."

"What else is new?"

He quirked an eyebrow. "Okay, so where did they go from here?"

"Liquor store?" I suggested.

"Could be, except that's thirty-five blocks in that direction. How'd they get there? They sure as hell didn't walk."

I looked around. "They boosted another vehicle."

"No reports from this neighborhood."

"Okay, so they could have stolen a car from somewhere else and had it waiting for them." But that didn't feel right. I spun around to get my bearings. "They could have taken the train."

"At that time of night, the express trains run local. There's a lot more pickup and drop-off points."

"So they killed Gardner, stopped at the liquor store, and then dumped the car here."

"Or they killed Gardner, dumped the car, took the train, rode it three stops to 24/7 Spirits, and walked home."

I turned to look at the burned car. "We need to pin down the timeline. It might give us their location."

Fennel agreed, and we headed into the subway station to check the schedule before going back to the precinct. Since the traffic cam footage led us to the car, we already knew roughly what time the killers abandoned it in the alley. Now we needed to figure out how long it'd take to get from that stop to the one closest to the liquor store. Since Gardner's credit card had been used at 5:17 a.m. and the disarm code had been entered at 4:12 a.m. at Star Cleaners, that only gave us a fifty-five minute window. Could the duo have driven from the dry cleaner's to the alley, hopped a train, walked to the liquor store, and made a purchase in such a short amount of time?

After updating Lt. Winston and having our team of techs shift their focus to studying the camera feeds inside the subway stations from yesterday morning and compare them to the images we pulled of the men from this morning, Fennel and I performed some basic calculations.

"They dumped the car first," I declared. "It's the only way. Traffic cam footage puts the silver sedan in the vicinity of that alleyway at 4:42. That's the last hit we have before they entered one of the blind spots in our grid. According to the subway schedule, the train arrived at 4:50. That gave them eight minutes to torch the car and get to the train."

"It only took us three minutes to get to the train

from that alley. Five minutes is plenty of time to douse it with gasoline and light it up." He checked the schedule. "They could have gotten off at either the third or fourth stop since the liquor store is practically in the middle."

"Do you think they stuck together?"

"Probably not. It'd increase their chances of getting caught. But then again, we don't know the dynamics of their partnership. They might not trust one another. Not everyone's as lucky as we are."

"Why are you buttering me up?" I asked.

"I'm not. It's just an observation."

"Uh-huh." But I wasn't convinced. "Regardless, how long do you think it takes to walk four blocks from the train to the liquor store?"

"At that time of night, probably not long. That's a fifth of a mile, and it's not like the sidewalks are congested. Five minutes, maybe."

"Okay, so two minutes per stop, that's four minutes of waiting, plus travel time. Plus the five minutes walking."

Fennel smiled. "That's nine minutes. And figure another fifteen on the train."

"That gave the killer three minutes to buy his bottle of Jack."

"Does 24/7 Spirits have a display near the register?"

"No, the clerk said it was all along the back wall, middle shelf, near the coolers."

Fennel thought. "It doesn't take me three minutes to buy booze, unless there's a line or I have to hunt for what I want. If I go to my usual place by my apartment, it's not an issue."

"Are you sure you don't have a problem?"

"Loads." He grinned. "But you see my point."

"The killer's been there before."

"Yep."

"You think he lives around there?" I let out a sigh. "That's a ballsy move, using his victim's credit card at his favorite liquor store."

Fennel uncapped the marker, jotted down our timeline on the whiteboard, and leaned back against the table. "Yeah, you're right. They must know using Gardner's credit card at any location would attract our attention, which would explain why they haven't used it again. Maybe he thought he was in the clear."

"They had the cash from Star Cleaners. They didn't need to use plastic to pay. They wanted to lure us there for a specific reason."

"Another misdirect?" Fennel asked. "Or are we just overthinking things? Maybe we're giving these shitheads too much credit."

"I don't think they're stupid. But they are lucky."

"Speaking of lucky," Voletek said, entering the conference room, "here I am." He grinned. "We just got back from speaking to Rook's next of kin."

"We also followed up with Jeffers' and Croft's widows too," Lisco added, entering behind him. She studied the board. "We'll show you ours and then you can show us yours."

"Deal," Fennel said.

As predicted, nothing Lisco and Voletek learned contradicted what we'd already determined about the LockBox employees – they were clean. However, we didn't know they'd been forced to sign NDAs concerning their clients and job details. Given the circumstances, the company had shared details on their routes and clients with us, but we hadn't exactly asked for dollars and cents, just a list of lucrative targets and of which of those Lindsey Rook possessed intimate knowledge.

"The company even provides life insurance policies

and death benefits," Voletek concluded. "I'm thinking a change of career is in order."

Lisco rolled her eyes. "Unfortunately, Rook's near and dear didn't even know the details of his job. None of these guys talk. I'm guessing they talk to each other, and that's about it. The LockBox crew is tight."

"But it wouldn't be hard for the killers to get wind of this. All armored trucks haul roughly the same amount. The killer could have followed one of the trucks on its route, estimated the score, and made plans to rob it," I said.

"Did you check into previous employees?" Fennel asked.

"No viable leads," Lisco said.

While Fennel shared our insights with the other two homicide detectives, I hoped the pieces would connect. But no matter how hard I stared at the data, I couldn't figure out who would do this. The why was easy – one hundred million dollars. But we didn't know where the killers would strike next, but I was certain they would.

I rubbed my palms together. "So if you just missed out on making bank, what would you do now?"

"Get angry and probably drunk," Voletek said. "Then I lick my wounds and figure out how to proceed."

"But you don't give up?" I asked.

"If I had a winning lottery ticket, tore it up, and threw it in the trash, I wouldn't just say, 'tough tits'. I'd go through the trash, even if it meant scouring the entire landfill for each tiny piece that I had to tape back together."

"Are we sure Jake isn't helping these guys out?" Fennel teased. "It sounds like he's pretty damn desperate for cash."

"I was speaking metaphorically from the killers'

mindset."

Lisco stared at the board. "If you want the money so badly, and you can't grab it from the original source, you find another source."

"Why go through the trouble?" Voletek asked. "The original source is dangling in front of me. I just need a better plan to get it."

Fennel and I exchanged a glance. "Patrols are escorting the LockBox trucks on their routes. Police will be nearby to intervene," he said.

"But not forever," Voletek said. "Those are just temporary until we find these bastards or decide the threat has passed." He met my eyes, the cynicism bleeding through. "Or whenever those on high decide this is a waste of money and resources and pull the plug."

"Then we have to figure out who they are and how to stop them before that happens," Fennel said.

TWENTY

"Are you fucking insane?" Carter paced back and forth. "You're going to get us all arrested or killed."

The third man finished divvying up the cash they'd taken from the dispensary and zipped the last of the three duffel bags. "Fine. Take your cut and walk." He shoved the bag across the dusty floor. "But you're the one who knocked out that cop. That was all on you, man."

"So what?"

"So you should have killed him," the third man said.

"He was a cop. That'd be suicide." Carter took off the cap, holding the bill in one hand while he tapped it against his open palm. "I don't want to die. The entire point of this was to get enough money to disappear and start over somewhere new. To have opportunities to be someone. To be somewhere that doesn't suck balls."

"Did he see you?" Diego asked. He'd been quiet since their escape in the subway station.

"Who?" Carter asked.

"The cop, numbnuts," the third man hissed. "Can he ID you?"

Carter shook his head. "No. He didn't get a look at me. I spotted him the moment I got off the train. I knew he'd follow me, so I led him into the out of order restroom and clocked him the moment he stepped inside. Then I changed hats and jackets and walked out. He didn't see anything."

The third man resisted the urge to argue. "No witnesses. That's what we agreed."

"Yeah, we also said we were going to wait for the truck to empty out, surprise the driver, and take the cash. Why didn't we stick with that plan?" Diego asked.

The third man whipped his gaze to his other accomplice. Until now, Diego hadn't spoken out against any of their actions. But shooting the LockBox driver must have gotten to him. "Are you questioning my plan?"

"Damn right I am," Diego said. "Look, today was FUBAR. We should have walked when the truck didn't show on time. We shouldn't have stayed. We shouldn't have tried to salvage it by stealing from the dispensary. If we hadn't gone in there..."

"What?" The third man stood, one hand prepared to grab the gun holstered at the small of his back. People ought to know better than to turn on him. He wouldn't tolerate their insolence. He could carry this out himself or find others who would help.

"They wouldn't be dead," Carter muttered.

"They didn't give us a choice. They would have killed us. You know that, don't you? That's what they do. People in uniforms have no respect for us. You've seen how they act. I've told you stories. What I've seen. What I've experienced. The things they've done to me. I didn't deserve that. But that's how they all are." The third man's cheek twitched, the anger boiling up inside of him.

"I'm not saying it wasn't tough on the inside. I've heard horror stories about that place," Carter said.

"It was bad," Diego said. "But that's what it's like on the inside. Some of the guards are just as brutal as the inmates." He shifted his gaze to the third man. "I had your back on the inside. And I still have your back, but these aren't COs. The men we killed today were probably nothing more than rent-a-cops. But they saw our faces. And I can't go back to prison. I get that we didn't have a choice, but if we walked, none of that would have happened." He turned to Carter. "You wouldn't survive, man. I barely did." He glanced back at the third man. "We barely did."

"So now what do we do?" Carter asked. "The cops are on to us. They almost caught up to you guys at the train station."

"But they didn't. And I'll die before they take me," the third man vowed. "We just need to get our money and get out of here. That's been the plan all along. Nothing's gonna change it. The more heat they apply, the more driven we are to make this happen. So it's time you pick a side, Carter." He was the only one who hadn't killed, which made him a liability and the weak link.

Something in Carter's frightened blue eyes and his trembling hands gave away his true thoughts, even as he said, "I said I'm in, so I'm in."

"Then I'm going to need you to prove it," the third man replied.

Carter swallowed, perspiration lining his upper lip. "How?"

*   *   *

Brad pushed his chair under the table. "Come on."

"Where are we going? We're not finished in here."

"We need a break."

"No," I shook my head vehemently, "they're not finished yet. You said you were working on a list of possible targets. Let's go over those again. Since we have no idea who they are, we have to figure out what their next move is. It's our only shot at stopping them. We can't exactly triangulate their locations with this mess." I pointed at the map with its random smattering of points of interest. There was no pattern or rhyme or reason to their movements.

"And we will, but you're aggravated and bitchy. We need to take a moment to regroup." He cocked his head to the side. "Let's get something to eat. I could use some food for thought, and I'm sure you could too. After that, we'll swing by Star Cleaners. Maybe we'll notice something we missed before. We need fresh eyes. Everything about yesterday's break-in has changed. That means we need to reassess."

Reluctantly, I pushed my chair in. "How do you do it?"

"Do what?"

"Know exactly what to say when I know this is tearing you up as much as it is me."

He snorted. "We take turns getting frustrated and obnoxious about it. This asshole shot at you. That means you get to be the emotionally unstable one today." Something sinister passed behind Brad's eyes. "But he better not try that again." He slipped into his coat and handed me my jacket off the back of my chair. "However, I have not forgotten you crashed my softball game or that I did not get to enjoy my championship breakfast afterward. So I want brunch."

"Brunch?" I pointed at my watch. "It's dinnertime."

"Fine, breakfast for dinner. Do you have a problem with it?"

"No, but you better not pick one of those places that puts pancake batter in their omelets or I'll be very unhappy."

"You could pretend you're undercover and just eat it."

"No way, buddy. I already had one man offer me grains for breakfast. We're not doing that again."

Brad palmed a set of keys to one of the unmarked cruisers, silently asking if he could drive. Truthfully, I doubted I could concentrate on the road with all the wayward thoughts about the case floating through my mind. "What if it's almond flour pancake batter? You good with that?"

I nodded.

"So who tried to feed you breakfast?"

"No one."

"C'mon, Liv, you just said—"

"I know. It was just some guy I spoke to this morning. He tried to be charming by offering me breakfast. It didn't go over the way he thought."

"Jake?"

"Hell no. He knows better."

"He should." From Brad's tone, I wasn't entirely sure what he meant by that, but I let it go. Neither of us had the energy to continue the conversation we had started hours ago before the shit hit the fan.

Ten minutes later, Brad found a place and parked the car. "Is Nana's okay?" He pointed to the diner.

"It's great. They know us." Which meant they didn't mind our picky ordering. Regardless of what anyone said, my partner was just as difficult to please as I was. Maybe more, since he had quite a few food aversions, thanks to a bad batch of MREs and too many tours in the Middle East. Of course, partnering with me and spending lots of time with Emma had only exacerbated the situation.

We entered the diner to find a few senior citizens enjoying the early bird special. But most of the tables were empty, so we took up our preferred spot in the back corner. Since there were no windows directly beside the table, I sat with my back against one wall, and Brad sat beside me with his back against the other.

"Hey, there are my two favorite customers. I haven't seen you in a while." Beatrice handed us the laminated menus and leaned in. "I saw the news today. Is it just me, or is it getting crazy out there?"

"Crazy," I mumbled.

"Do you know what you want, or do you need a minute?" She put two water glasses down in front of us.

"Liv?" Brad asked.

"I'll have the southwest omelet with the free-range grilled chicken. No cheese. No sour cream. And the almond flour strawberry banana pancakes."

Beatrice scribbled it down on her pad. "And for you?"

"Ooh, that sounds good. Same pancakes, but I want the grass-fed steak with three eggs. Scrambled."

"Do you want the hash browns that come with it?"

"Yes, with onions." Brad handed her the menus.

"Okay. Coming right up." She put two mugs down on the table and poured us coffee without asking since she knew that's what we'd want.

After breakfast or dinner, whatever it was, which consisted of my omelet and eating the strawberries and bananas off a stack of pancakes while watching Brad clean his plate and the remaining pancakes I left on mine, we headed to Star Cleaners.

Despite the official police tape and the cardboard

covering the broken door, there were no obvious signs of what occurred yesterday morning. Mr. Lee planned to open up tomorrow afternoon, after the glass repairman fixed the door.

"What are we looking for?" An uneasiness crept into my gut.

Fennel checked the door. The crime scene guys had marked it, so he sliced through the tape and pushed the door open. Inside, remnants of their investigative tools remained, but most of the mess had been cleaned. The ficus had been removed, and the blood and tissue had been washed off the floor.

"Police," I announced. "Is anyone here?"

"Just a second," a male voice called from the back.

"Mr. Lee?" I asked, noticing my hand had traveled to my gun.

"Yes, I'm in the back office. I'll be with you in a moment."

While we waited, I surveyed the room. Evidence collection had been completed, and the scene had been turned over to professional cleaners. The security footage had been assessed, along with the security logs, but none of that yielded any results.

"Did CSU find any fingerprints on the shards of broken glass?" I asked Brad.

"Nothing. And nothing on the cameras either. The sarge had patrol check dumpsters and trashcans for discarded oil containers and cooking sprays, but we didn't find any of those either. These assholes make sure they clean up after themselves."

Mr. Lee emerged from behind the curtain with both hands visible, as if he knew we were jumpy and didn't want to risk startling us. "I was told I could come back here to clean up and check my records. I did another inventory after we spoke, but I can't be sure if any other items were taken from the clothes rack or if they'd just been picked up."

"What about uniforms? You said you run a special. You must have regulars. What kinds of uniforms do you usually get?" Brad asked.

"I have a couple of city bus drivers, some mechanics, and the LockBox truck guys. That's all I can remember. I clean police and military dress uniforms fairly regularly, but I wouldn't say my regulars drop them off." He eyed us, his inner salesman surfacing. "I could clean your uniforms regularly and give you a good price. How about a two for one discount since you're investigating the break-in?"

"No, thanks. Liv has a problem with chemical cleaning agents."

"Speaking of," I said, annoyed my partner had used me as an excuse, "you seemed positive the crime had to do with your dry cleaning chemicals being used as inhalants. Did you find any missing?"

"No. The containers in back are sealed, and the ones we've been using appear to contain the same amount and consistency as before. I even checked my records, since they are used and discarded at nearly the same rate every week, but we're right on schedule."

"Okay, good." I peered through the now open curtain, but no one else was in the shop. "We have a few more questions for you."

"Certainly. How can I help?"

"For starters, we're wondering who would know you had access to LockBox uniforms?"

Lee thought about it for a moment. "Anyone. Everyone. It's no secret. Have you seen our webpage? I post all the companies we've cleaned or have cleaned."

Brad reached for his phone and waited for Arthur

Lee to give him the url before typing it in. "Yeah, it's on here." He scanned the rest of the page but didn't find any comments or obvious tracking links.

"I also mention it on my flyers. Police, military, security guard, dress uniforms, repairmen's coveralls, any uniform, one low price, which I'll admit came back to bite me in the ass. Do you have any idea how many grease stains these mechanics wanted me to get out of their shirts? I thought they'd just buy new ones or wear them dirty. And that's just my regular customers. Of course, everyone who ever worked here or works here knows the kind of items we clean."

So much for my brilliant question.

"What about the disarm code?" Brad asked. "We spoke to the people you said knew the code. Have any other names come to mind? Have you shared that code with anyone else? Maybe you accidentally mentioned it spells out STAR to someone."

Lee blanched. "Who told you that?"

"It doesn't matter," I said. "We just need to know if this is something other people might have realized and caught on to."

"I didn't even realize that," he said. "Those bastards at Moonlight picked the code. They said it was just some random numbers. It would be completely secure. Do you believe that shit? And I fell for it. I'm wondering just how secure any of this is. The night watchman, god rest his soul, didn't even try to fight back, according to what I overhead your people saying. And the system was disarmed, but even if it wasn't, you can see for yourself just how easy it was to break-in and rob the place. I'm surprised the rear gate isn't made out of plastic instead of reinforced steel." Lee continued to rant about his displeasure with Moonlight Security, vowing to call and give them a piece of his mind.

"While you do that, do you mind if we take another look around back?" Brad asked.

"Help yourself. That's how I got inside." Lee headed toward the office in the rear. "The system won't engage since the front door's broken, so you don't have to worry about triggering the alarm." He let out another huff. "I'll probably have to sleep here tonight just to make sure none of those druggies try to break in."

I opened my mouth to ask more questions about his dogged suspicions, but Brad shook his head. "Don't waste your breath," he said. "I checked with everyone. There isn't any dry cleaning chemical ring running amok. He's just paranoid."

TWENTY-ONE

We didn't find anything out back, but Fennel wasn't willing to give up so easily. He stared at the gate which led to the double doors. "I bet this is where his precious chemicals are delivered."

"Yeah, so?"

"So maybe he has it wrong. The deliveries must come in this way, so that could explain how someone not directly connected to Star Cleaners happened to get the alarm code."

"Chambliss already asked about that, but nothing popped."

"Okay." Fennel rubbed his palms together and blew out a breath. The lock on the rear door was old and scratched. It could have been picked, or it could have just been worn. "I got nothing."

That made two of us. "I knew this was a waste. Let's split up and do a quick walk around. I'll meet you at the front door."

Fennel followed the alley around the back of the building while I went around the corner and circled around the side. Two other shops separated the dry cleaner's from the corner with large picture windows. But they didn't have any outdoor security cameras, and the shops had been closed at the time of the break-in.

"Useless," I muttered.

While I stood in front of Star Cleaners, waiting for my partner, I noticed my reflection in the windows. The glass had a dark tint which didn't allow outsiders to easily see in. Instead, it reflected a mirror image of the surrounding street. At night, it might have been a little easier to see inside the store, but the best view would still require cupping your hands around your face and pressing against the window.

"Brad," I called the moment he turned the corner, "did CSU check the windows for prints?"

"Why would they?" Mr. Lee asked, carefully opening the boarded-up door. "They weren't broken and weren't used to get inside."

"I don't know, Liv." Fennel's brow furrowed, and he tilted his head to the side to study the nearest window. "I'm not seeing any powder residue." He glanced at the dry cleaner. "Did you wipe the windows yet?"

"No, I didn't. The crew I hired spent the afternoon inside. They said they'd come back later tonight and have everything spic and span by morning."

I reached for my phone to find out if our team missed something while Fennel scrutinized the front windows. He crouched down. "I see smudges."

"Hey, this is DeMarco." I placed my request for a team to come down for some quick evidence collection.

When I got off the phone, Fennel stared up at me. "You realize we already released the scene. Anything we find now won't hold up in court."

"Does it matter?"

He pressed his lips together. We had to find these killers, but we'd need something solid to keep them off the streets. "Let's see what they find. Then we'll run it by the lieutenant and possibly the DA's office and figure out how to proceed."

"Wait, you mean you screwed up?" Mr. Lee asked.

"No, sir." But we might have overlooked some key evidence. "We just want to be extra thorough."

"That's not what Detective Fennel just said."

I glanced at my partner, hoping he'd chime in with something encouraging. But he held his hands up in front of his face, trying to judge the size of the smudge marks. Then he moved over to the next window pane to check for more smudges. "We like to cover all our bases. I'm sure you're the same way, with the way you tackle stains and all."

"Right," Mr. Lee said, though he seemed even less convinced than he did before. "But is this going to delay my reopening?"

"No, sir," Fennel said.

"Okay, then do whatever you like." Mr. Lee nodded to us and went back inside.

"If our killers were smart, they might have tried to get a peek inside to see what they were facing once they broke in. The goal had to be the uniforms in back." Fennel stood up straight. "We didn't know that before, but I'm guessing the rear door was disarmed and one killer used it to gain entry to the LockBox uniforms. The second guy remained here, keeping an eye on Jonathan Gardner."

"And as soon as the night watchman heard noise in the back, the second killer broke through the window, killed him, and emptied the register. Damn, that's brilliant."

"I just hope they didn't bother to wipe the glass afterward." Fennel smiled. "And you thought this was a waste of time."

Twenty minutes later, the mobile crime scene unit pulled to a stop in front of the dry cleaner's. Ellie climbed out of the driver's seat and opened the rear doors. "Hey, Brown Eyes and Brown Eyes' partner."

"Twice in two days," Fennel said. "I'd say it's my lucky day, but these are terrible circumstances."

She grabbed her kit and came toward us. "You think I missed something?"

"I think it's possible," Fennel said. "You had a lot of ground to cover."

She chuckled, turning to me. "Be careful. This one's a smooth talker."

"I know. I thought about putting a warning label on him but figured no one would take it seriously."

She took out what looked like a large brush for blush and opened a glass jar. "This one's a keeper. You better be nice to her, Brad."

My partner glanced at me and winked. "So I've been told."

"Well, now you've heard it a second time." After knocking the excess off the brush, Ellie gently ran it along the glass. "I'm not getting anything."

"What about here?" Fennel pointed to the smudge he'd noticed.

"Considering the amount of foot traffic, it could have come from anywhere." But when she couldn't pull a print, she swabbed the area. "It's some sort of grease. But since we didn't find prints anywhere inside, I'm guessing the killer wore gloves." She stuck the swab into a tube and sealed it. "I'll compare this to the grease we found on the rear security cameras. I'm guessing it'll match. When he sprayed or wiped the lens with it, he probably got some transfer on his gloves." She pointed to the smudges. "It looks like he ducked down low, so as not to be seen, and cupped his hands here." She held her hands up to her eyes. "Like he was looking inside."

"That's what we figured," I said.

"Gold star." Ellie checked the rest of the windows and gave the back door another check. "Unfortunately, I don't think this will give us much."

"It was worth a shot," Fennel said. "Thanks for trying. Give me a call the second you finish running the analysis."

"Absolutely." She tucked her kit into the rear of the van, gave Brad a friendly hug, waved to me, and headed back to the precinct.

"You know, I'm starting to enjoy the level of service you get. Once again, we might need to revisit the concept of pimping you out."

"Hardy har." He led the way back to the car, but our outing hadn't led to any leads. We still weren't any closer to identifying the killers or their next attempt at a large payday. "What if we do a few surprise checks?"

"On what?"

"Not what. Who. Or whom." His brow furrowed. "I don't know. We're not the grammar police." He pulled away from the shop. "The murders weren't planned. The planning comes down to the break-ins and possibly the getaways. Killing's just a side effect."

"I'd agree with that."

"So our killers didn't make a big score. Unless they did it for the thrill and got that out of their system, they'll want to go someplace safe, divide up their ill-gotten gains, and research their next target, just like Jake said."

"Sure." I didn't know where he was going with this.

"Okay, so let's follow up with everyone we spoke to yesterday and see if anyone's acting particularly squirrely. I'd say we'd check with LockBox, but I'm guessing Voletek and Lisco already gave them the third degree."

"Yeah, but we did the same with our suspects. They're clean."

"It just doesn't make sense. At least one of the killers had to possess key facts about Star Cleaners. The security code. The uniforms. The killer has to be connected somehow. We have a list. I even got Mr. Lee to name his suppliers. It's late. No one will expect us now. If we catch them off guard, we might stand a chance of getting to the bottom of this before someone else dies. C'mon, Liv, I don't know what else we can do, unless you have a better idea."

I checked the time. Once we returned to the precinct, Lt. Winston would probably send us home. Unlike Capt. Grayson, the lieutenant was a stickler about keeping to our assigned shifts. Briefly, I wondered if he had his sights set on a position at 1PP. That would explain why he had two legacy detectives working in his unit. Bureaucratic brownnoser. "Yeah, all right. But don't get your hopes up."

"I never do."

TWENTY-TWO

Michael Tolliver stared at us for a good twenty seconds before recognition kicked in. "Detectives, please, come in."

We'd already checked on Catelyn Rivera, who we found camped out in the campus library. Then we drove by Guy Kellerman's place to make sure it remained empty while he was on vacation, and then we swung by to speak to Pamela Aiker. No one acted oddly, but by now, word had spread about the murdered night watchman. Aside from being upset about losing someone who worked in the same building as they did, they didn't exhibit any signs they were responsible or display any awkward behavior which would indicate they were in the midst of planning a multi-million dollar heist.

"Is there something I can help you with?" he asked.

The smell of marijuana was nothing but a lingering memory. For the most part, the place looked about the same. "We just wanted to check on you."

He smiled at me. "Thanks."

Brad looked down the hall. "Is the party still going on?"

Tolliver laughed. "No, thank goodness. Everyone's gone home, and Carter's at work. Don't get me wrong, we had a hell of a night, but I couldn't do it every day. I'm getting too old for that."

"When's the wedding?" I asked.

"Friday." He pointed to a suit hanging from the frame of the open closet. "I'm a groomsman." He made a noise halfway between a sigh and a snort. "I got that pressed at work. Y'know, I can't believe something like that happened there. We hear about a lot of break-ins and armed robberies happening around us. That grocery store on the corner's been hit like three times this month. But I never thought it'd happen to us. We don't have anything worth taking, but we were prepared. Mr. Lee made us watch these training videos he got from the security place."

"Moonlight Security?" Fennel asked.

"Yeah. Johnny made fun of me for watching them. He said they were a joke." Tolliver's voice cracked. "I guess he should have paid more attention to them."

"So you were friends?" Fennel asked, baiting his hook.

"Friendly. We didn't talk at work much. Usually, by the time he came in, I was halfway out the door. But one time, Mr. Lee asked if I'd sweep up, so I stayed late. I guess we got to talking that day. But that was about it. I didn't really know him."

"Didn't you play online games together?" I jerked my chin at the console beneath the TV.

Tolliver smiled sadly. "Yeah, we did, sometimes. He had a whole crew. They're pretty cool guys."

"Why didn't you mention this to us yesterday?" Fennel asked.

"I didn't think about it. Honestly, I wasn't doing

much thinking when we spoke last time. But if there's anything I can do to help, please let me know. Johnny seemed like a good person."

"What did you talk about online?" Fennel asked.

"Not much, aside from killing things." Tolliver pressed his lips together. "I mean, y'know, fake things."

"I got it," Fennel said. "Did he ever mention anything about his job at Moonlight Security or being a night watchman?"

"Maybe. I don't think he liked it very much. He got bored. Moonlight isn't one of the premier companies, but it was a paycheck. I teased him about guarding people's dirty clothes and having to protect other company's security uniforms. But he knew I was just joking."

"So anybody you played with or against online could have heard you?" Fennel asked.

"I guess." Tolliver picked up one of the games and read the back of the box. "We mostly talked smack to one another and the other side, but I didn't think any of us ever took it seriously. It was just fun. Y'know, the usual ribbing."

"All right, thanks for your time." Fennel nodded at the box in Tolliver's hand. "Is that the game you usually played? Did you ever play any others?"

"Nope, just this one."

Fennel nodded. "When do you go back to work?"

"Mr. Lee wants me there on Monday, but I don't know. I had to beg for this coming Friday and the weekend off, so I don't think he'd like it if I ask for more time, especially since he's already short-staffed since Catelyn quit and Guy's on vacation." Tolliver internally debated with himself for a few more seconds before shaking it off and acknowledging us. "Lately, it just seems Star Cleaners is pretty toxic."

I asked a few quick questions about the chemicals and Mr. Lee's fears, but Michael Tolliver didn't have anything to add. Fennel and I let ourselves out. "You figured something out," I said.

My partner tried not to look smug. "I can't be sure, but if the guys online gave Gardner a good ribbing, anyone playing with them or against them heard it. That's how the communications work on that game. You can talk to your teammates on a private channel or you can talk openly to mess with the other side or make friends or whatever."

"That broadens the possibilities."

"It sure does."

We'd just gotten back into the car when Fennel's phone rang. He checked the number and hit answer, identifying himself. "That was quick. Are you sure?"

I waited, wondering what was going on.

"And it matches?" He nodded a few times, even though the caller couldn't see him. "Thanks for letting me know. I'm not sure it helps, but it's something." He hung up, frowning.

"What?" I asked.

"It's not cooking oil. It's," he made a face, "I don't know what it is. Ellie said it was a mix of commercial synthetic grease spray, CBD oil, and menthol."

"Synthetic grease?"

"The stuff that comes in a spray bottle. It can be used for just about anything with high torque and high temperatures."

"Like?"

"Carrying heavy loads."

"Like armored trucks?"

"Possibly."

"That's what was sprayed on the camera lens?"

"Yep, but Ellie said only the CBD and menthol mixture was found on the window, not the camera."

"Okay, but we're assuming it's the same source. What does synthetic grease have to do with CBD oil and menthol?"

"I'm not sure. The dispensary probably sells CBD oil," Fennel suggested.

"But it was on the killer's hands or, rather, his gloves. That's how it got transferred to the window, right? So he pressed his hands against the window to see in, and those substances were on the outside of his gloves. Menthol and CBD would be in muscle creams or rubs."

"Go on," Fennel said, fascinated by my thought process.

"So the guy could have an injury or arthritis. He used the rub, then put on his gloves, but some of the cream transferred from his skin to his gloves. Then he sprayed the cameras with the grease."

"But those sprays go everywhere. Okay. That's something. Should we swing by the dispensary again?"

"Why? CBD oil is everywhere. It doesn't mean the killer got it from the dispensary, and honestly, I don't think a customer would risk walking in disguised as a guard."

"But that could be why the owner stopped the thieves. He recognized one of them."

"Except we'll never know, unless we find something in their records." Today had turned me into a defeatist. "We need a look at the dispensary's computer and receipts. And we'll have to go through their customer database. To make a purchase, the store had to collect the customer's information. If you're right that the killer shopped at the same dispensary, then we just need to find a person who bought CBD oil and works with high torque and temperatures."

"Easy peasy," Fennel said sarcastically, heading back to the precinct.

Except it wasn't. Since Voletek and Lisco had been assigned to assist on our case, I hoped they'd already taken a look at the customer list, but they hadn't.

"I don't know, Brad." I leaned back in the chair and looked around the empty conference table. Voletek and Lisco left twenty minutes ago, and the techs had abandoned us at shift change. "It doesn't feel right." I picked up the chemical breakdown of the compound Ellie swabbed off the front window at Star Cleaners. "This looks like a prescription cream or even something over the counter, but I don't see anything like that for sale at the dispensary. This probably came from a pharmacy."

"All right, we'll hold off until the morning and contact a pharmacist to see if we can ID the product. Even if it's a generic, we might be able to pull something."

"Doubtful." With privacy laws, I didn't think we'd be able to reverse engineer a suspect list based on a prescription cream, but we could probably use that to pin down a suspect once we had one, if we ever had one. I rubbed my temples.

"We need a fresh set of eyes to look at these facts. Maybe a good night's sleep will help."

"Yeah, maybe you're right." My eye twitched, and I shoved the crime scene photos into a folder and out of sight. "I just don't want to start tomorrow the same way I started these last two days."

"Me neither."

TWENTY-THREE

Instead of going home, I headed to my parents' house. When I opened the door, I found Emma on all fours, bumping her nose against Gunnie's side. The dog looked up at me, his mouth dropping open in what appeared to be a big smile before he skittered across the floor. His back paws slid against the wood in all directions while he tried to gain enough traction to race toward me.

"Oh sure, you walk in and he immediately wants to play, but for me, he just sits there chewing on his toy and eyeing me like I might steal it."

"See, he already has you pegged." I knelt down, and the puppy jumped up, putting his paws on my chest while he tried to lap at my face. I held my head back and fluffed his ears until he calmed down enough so I could kiss him on the top of his head.

"You aren't supposed to let him do that. Vince said he needs to learn to stay down. When he's eighty pounds, he'll knock you right over."

"Dad might have said that, but he's not here right

now. I am. And I needed puppy hugs and kisses." I cuddled the dog and pulled his head into my lap.

"Are you okay, Liv?"

I stroked the white spot on the pup's nose. "I'm fine."

"Bullshit."

I covered the dog's ears. "Em, watch your language. He's just a baby." She rolled her eyes at my ridiculousness. "So how was the rest of the game?"

"It got called on account of crimes, fires, and the apocalypse, apparently. Where did you and Brad run off to?"

"Where do you think?"

She got off the floor and brushed dog fur from her pants. "You want a drink? I found a bottle of tequila your mom had hidden in the back of the freezer from her last margarita night with the ladies."

"I'm not in the mood, but whatever you do, don't tell Dad."

"What about dinner? Did you eat?" She watched as Gunnie rolled over for a tummy rub. "Did Bradley feed you?"

"Yes, and for the record, he hates it when you call him that."

"That's why I do it." With a grin on her face, she went into the kitchen and opened the fridge. "What did you eat? I can't decide if I want to defrost one of the dinner's your mom left for us or just make something quick."

"An omelet and pancakes. Well, the toppings from my pancakes. Brad ate most of the pancakes."

"That doesn't sound like dinner." She searched the freezer and pulled out a container. "How about joining me for a bowl of stew?"

"Fine." I gave the dog a final pat and stood up. He looked disappointed until he heard the sound of the cabinet opening. His ears perked up, and he happily followed me into the kitchen and waited for a treat. I gave him one, left my gun, cuffs, and badge on the counter, washed my hands, and set the table. "Oh, the firefighter you were eye-fucking, I asked Brad about him. He was in the calendar."

"I wasn't eye-fucking him," Emma said dramatically. "But you don't want to know the things he was doing to me in my mind. He definitely earned his place as third baseman."

"Eww, Emma." I cringed. "You're right. I don't want to know about your dirty daydreams."

"Speak for yourself." She grinned evilly. "But yeah, I figured that out after you left. He was July, right?"

"Wasn't it August?"

She nodded a few times. "Any idea which station he's assigned?"

"No, but it was our precinct, so all the firefighters there had to have been from the same house. It should have been on the scoreboard or something."

"Oh yeah." Emma smacked herself on the forehead. "Blonde moment."

"You'd think ER nurses wouldn't be allowed to have those, especially when you're not blonde."

"Neither should cops, but you've had plenty yourself." She flicked a strand of hair over my shoulder. "It's the highlights. You were smarter when you were a full-fledged brunette."

"Gee, thanks." I put my forearms on the counter and stretched back. "If that's the problem, we should dye my hair back to its natural color tonight so I can solve this case."

"What's it about?" Emma grabbed a bag of baby carrots from the fridge and popped one into her mouth. Gunnie looked up at her and whined, so she gave him one. He trotted into the other room, rolled it across the floor, and tossed it in the air.

"Armored truck heist, maybe. Yesterday, a dry cleaner's was knocked over, and a security guard was killed. Then today, we found out uniforms were stolen from the dry cleaner's and worn in today's crime spree."

"Didn't I see something about that on the news?"

"Probably."

"No wonder you look like that." She took the glass dish out of the microwave, stirred the stew, and put it back in to finish reheating. "Shouldn't you be out at a bar somewhere?"

"Brad has that covered." Or so I imagined. He declined when I asked if he wanted to come over and help me housesit. "We might have found a potential lead." I told her about the CBD oil and menthol mixed with the grease.

"If you send me the complete workup, I can have someone in the hospital pharmacy look at it. They might recognize it. Then again, do we know which parts are the muscle rub and which are industrial grease?"

"I hoped that would be obvious."

She snorted. "Yeah, you'd think so."

We sat down to eat, but I couldn't get the deaths I'd seen today out of my head. There had to be more I could do to stop these bastards from striking again. "If you wanted to steal millions of dollars, where would you go?"

"The bank."

"No. They don't have that much, and even if they did, it'd be too hard to get in and out. It wouldn't matter what security uniform you stole."

"What about robbing another armored truck?"

"That's what I figured. We beefed up patrols and assigned each truck an escort." I pushed my plate away. "Where else?"

"Considering the number of ODs that come into the ER, I'd say a pharmacy, but that would require a few extra steps."

"No, I don't think so. It has to be somewhere LockBox goes. One of the locations Lindsey Rook knew about." But we had the list. We had units keeping watch on every possible target. We'd catch them in the act and stop them. No one else would have to die. Officers were sent in undercover to secure the most likely locations. But what if we were wrong?

"You're worried," Emma said.

"Yeah."

She stared at her plate. We'd had this argument before. She, like my mom, thought being a cop was too dangerous. However, it was my decision. And she couldn't fault me for wanting to make a difference. After all, that's why she became a nurse.

"Why don't you take off?" Emma suggested. "I planned on sleeping over anyway. So I'll take Gunnie out for his final walk of the night and crash in my old bedroom. Unless you want to stay too. We can dye your hair, paint our nails, and talk about boys. Have you heard? I have a crush on a firefighter."

I snickered. "I heard, but I don't want to hear any more about it. I just want to go home and shower. Are you sure you got this? At least let me help with the dishes."

"You worked all day, and you spent last night with a lawyer. But tomorrow, after I get off work, I'm going to be tired and bitchy, so you can do all this fun stuff instead. Deal?"

"That's only fair."

"Be careful," Emma said.

"Yep." I grabbed my gear off the counter, gave Emma a hug, and slipped Gunnie another treat before leaving my parents' house.

On the way home, I tried calling my dad, but it went straight to voicemail. I hadn't spoken to my parents since they left the country and figured they must not have updated their phone plans for use outside the US, or Mom forgot to pack the wall adapters, or they were just having too much fun. I couldn't remember the last time my parents went on vacation.

But a part of me wanted to hear my dad's voice. Decorated police captain Vince DeMarco would know what to do with a case like this. Too bad I hadn't inherited his experience, along with his drive and instincts.

After arriving at home, I ran a couple of miles on the treadmill, did an evening yoga practice, and showered. But even the moving meditation hadn't brought me inner tranquility. I crawled into bed, unsatisfied with myself and the recent turn of events.

The ghosts of the dead haunted me. I couldn't shake Richard Golden breaking down into tears at the news of his best friend's death. And the men and woman who died today would be equally missed. The station agent had a teenaged son. What would happen to him?

I couldn't just lay here. I had to do something. No one else could lose a parent or child because of these bastards. So I reached for my laptop and brought up a city map.

"Where are you hiding?" I had memorized all of the relevant locations. But they were scattered over the map.

When this didn't get me anywhere, I called Brad. "Pick up," I mumbled, but after five rings, it went to voicemail. "Hey, it's me. I thought you might be up, but I guess not. Don't worry, it's nothing pressing. I couldn't sleep and figured we could brainstorm. Anyway, get some rest. One of us has to. I'll see you tomorrow."

Restless and determined, I decided to take a drive. As I meandered through the city, sticking to the neighborhoods and areas where the killers had been, I wondered how they knew so much about the traffic cameras to park in the blind spots.

At the next red light, I dialed dispatch. "This is Detective DeMarco." I rattled off my credentials. "I'm curious about something. Who has access to the city's traffic cam grid besides the police?" I listened to the answer, but the options were limited. "Any chance it was hacked?"

"No, Detective. We have safeties in place that would identify a breach."

"So, this isn't the Italian Job."

The dispatcher laughed. "No, ma'am."

I fell silent, hoping to come up with something that would lead to the killers. "Do you know who the city contracted to install the cameras?"

"I'm not sure."

"All right."

"Anything else I can help you with, DeMarco?"

"No, I guess not." I disconnected, again wondering about Moonlight Security's connection. Gardner had been assigned as night watchman at the dispensary and Star Cleaners. According to both Gardner's roommate and boss, he'd worked several different gigs in the last month. What other locations did he protect?

I called the precinct, but units had been assigned to sit on those places too. I should have been relieved. We were doing everything in our power to save lives, but it didn't feel like enough.

Something Brad had said came to mind. The killers

knew that liquor store. Or at least one of them did. The owner hadn't exactly been forthcoming during our previous chat, but maybe he'd be more willing to talk to me now. After all, it was the middle of the night. I wasn't on shift, and with the rising body count, he had more incentive to share what he knew. Perhaps, I could use my charms to persuade him to give up a name or description. So I turned the car around and drove to 24/7 Spirits.

TWENTY-FOUR

Aside from the neon sign out front, the liquor store looked dark, just like most other businesses in the area. Was it possible they weren't open twenty-four hours a day? I got out of the car and surveyed my surroundings. Something didn't feel right.

A dark SUV idled near the end of the block. I eyed it, watching a puff of exhaust bloom from the tailpipe. I slid my jacket to the side and rested my hand on the butt of my gun as I made my way down the sidewalk. It could be anything. But it wasn't normal for someone to be sitting around at this time of night.

I cleared two car lengths before the SUV turned on its lights and slowly pulled away from the spot. It drove a few feet to the stop sign, waited five seconds, and then proceeded on its path. I watched it disappear into the darkness, mentally repeating the license plate number a few times.

Just to be on the safe side, I ran the plates. When nothing came back on them, I asked if a patrol unit could drive by when they got a chance. Then I locked my car and walked across the street to the liquor store.

The bell above the door chimed, and the owner looked up at me from where he'd been setting up a display of Kahlua bottles. "You again?" His tone didn't sound friendly.

"So you remember me?"

"How could I forget?" He reached for another bottle and glanced around the side of the aisle. Two women in their mid-twenties whispered and giggled as they perused the racks of pre-mixed drinks. A couple were arguing next to the refrigerators about the difference between beer and lager. And a man at the back corner of the store carefully examined the various bottles of scotch. "I don't have what you want. You should try back another day." He met my eyes and flicked his gaze pointedly toward the door. "As you can see, I'm pretty busy. Maybe you should come back when you have your friends with you."

"What?" I gave him an odd look. "Are you sure you don't have me confused with someone else, I'm—"

He cut me off. "I know who you are." The girls went to the counter with their arms full of margarita, mudslide, and pina colada mixes. "You should go. I'll give you a call when I have time to look for what you wanted. I might have it in the back." He placed the final bottle of Kahlua on the top of the display and slipped behind the counter to work the register. He handed them the bags, made a point to card them, and wished them a good night. He scribbled something on the receipt and tried to hand it to the woman, but she said she didn't need it.

The owner stuffed the receipt into his pocket and went back to the display, ripping open another box. "Are you hard of hearing? I said you should come back another day."

"Sir, I think you must have me confused with someone else."

He picked up the empty cardboard box. "Fine. Follow me. I'll show you what we have in the back."

"Sir," I tried again, but he didn't wait for my protest. Instead, he grabbed the empty box and went down the aisle.

"You guys almost ready to check out?" he asked the couple.

"Yeah," the guy said.

"Oh, what about a shandy?" the woman asked her boyfriend.

The clerk didn't even slow. "Just take it to the register. I'll be right there." He paused briefly in the opposite corner of the store and called to the man examining the scotch, "I'll be out in one sec. I just gotta help this lady find something first."

"Make it quick," the guy grunted, his back to us.

The owner entered the storage room and waited for me in the doorway. I eyed the gruff customer, but he didn't appear to have any interest in anything other than the scotch bottles in front of him. Cautiously, I stepped into the dimly lit storeroom, unsure why the owner was acting so strangely.

"Sir," I said, watching as he broke down the box and added it to a large stack of cardboard, "I'm Detective DeMarco."

"Shh." He held a finger to his lips and edged toward the open door. "That's the guy. The one who came in here the other morning and bought the bottle of Jack."

"You're positive?"

The owner nodded. "He has a gun. I saw it beneath his jacket."

"How long has he been here?"

"For almost an hour. He came in when the store

was empty. He told me he was waiting for something and if I cooperated, there wouldn't be any trouble. He also said his friend is out front, and if I make a run for it, he'd kill me."

"Do you know what he wants?"

"I figured he wanted to rob the place, but that's not it. He's waiting for something. Every time the door chimes, he looks up at the mirror along the back, and he keeps checking his watch."

"Okay."

"He told me to carry on like nothing was wrong, and if I didn't..." The store owner swallowed and drew a finger horizontally across his neck. "So that's what I've been trying to do. I thought you'd get the point. Are you seriously that dense?"

"How many other people have stopped by since he's been here?" I took half a step back and peered in his direction, but I couldn't see him.

"Fifteen or twenty. They came in, got what they wanted, and left. I keep trying to get word out." He showed me the receipt where he'd written, 'Call 9-1-1, I'm being robbed.' But no one would take his note. "I don't know what he's waiting for. I thought he wanted money, but..."

"Okay, calm down."

"Calm down?" he hissed. "You told me this guy killed somebody."

"Why didn't you call the police?" I spotted the man, but he wouldn't turn away from the shelves. He didn't want anyone to see him or recognize him. Perhaps he was waiting for a lull so he could kill the owner. After all, the liquor store owner might be the only person alive who could ID him.

"How? You think I should make the call right in front of him?"

"Do you have a cell phone?"

He fished it out of his pocket. "This building is cinderblock on three sides. I can't get a signal out."

I checked my bars, but he was right. "What about a back door?" I pointed to the illuminated exit sign behind him.

"It has an alarm. The moment I open it, it'll trigger lockdown. Emergency lights, sirens, the whole shebang. I was afraid to do anything that might set him off. I figured if I waited long enough, he'd just leave. I tried to get someone to go for help, but none of my customers took their receipt. None of them. What is wrong with these people?"

Removing my gun from my holster, I blew out a breath. I couldn't leave an armed killer inside a store with civilians. I had to stay here to protect them. "Sir, here's what I need you to do. Clear out the rest of your customers, then go out the back door, and call 9-1-1. Tell them the situation. Tell them the suspect in today's murder spree is inside your liquor store. Tell them a plainclothes officer is inside and to send immediate backup. Do you understand?"

"Murder spree?" He paled. "What are you going to do?"

"Make sure everyone remains breathing."

The bell above the door chimed. Dammit. More people had just entered. I had to prevent this psycho from opening fire. But I couldn't announce, or that'd be the first thing he'd do. I'd have to subdue him quickly and quietly, but that would be easier once we were alone. Making a move on him now would only lead to violence and potential casualties.

"Get rid of them. I need you to stay calm and act like everything is normal. Can you do that for me?" I asked.

He nodded and went back into the store. I stepped out of the storage room, but the shelves around the rear door were too tall for me to see over. The owner must have done that intentionally to conceal the storeroom and keep customers out, but it didn't provide any tactical advantages. If anything, it was a detriment. I checked my phone again for a signal.

I tried calling dispatch, but the call wouldn't connect. The owner wasn't kidding about the cinderblock. Dread filled me as another thought crept into my mind. Brad said the killers used a jammer. Was this their next target?

The liquor store owner handed the brown paper sack to his newest customers, and the two men left in a hurry. I moved toward the cooler doors, hoping to keep an eye on the suspect, but he had moved deeper down the aisle. From here, I could only glimpse his back. Average build and dark hair. He could have been the asshole who shot at me inside the subway station, but I wasn't positive.

The couple continued to bicker, and the suspect turned down the next aisle and out of my line of sight. "Why don't you get one of each? My treat. Tell the clerk to put it on my tab," I said to them.

"Seriously?" the guy asked.

"Yeah."

"Thanks, lady." He grabbed two different twelve packs.

His girlfriend smiled at me. "I thought we'd be here all night."

"Come on, Crista." He headed to the counter, and she followed after him.

I crossed to the other side of the store, but the man had moved down the next aisle, almost as if he knew to avoid me. Once the couple left, the owner headed toward the back. I moved to intercept the suspect, but the owner grabbed my arm. His eyes showed fear, and I backstepped until we were concealed behind the tall shelves.

"You need to go. Now." I didn't have time to ask how much money the liquor store had on the premises or why the killers would target this store. "Call for help as soon as you're safe. Don't stop for anyone." Since the killer had an accomplice, I didn't know if he had someone else waiting out back, but I hoped not. As it was, we were on a clock. Since the killer had been staking out the store for nearly an hour, we had to be getting close to go-time, and even if we weren't, the patrol car I called for would spook them. And when these guys spooked, they got trigger happy, or so I'd learned this morning.

"There's one more thing you should know," the owner said as he reached the emergency exit. "There's two of them now. A second guy wandered inside. I saw his reflection in the mirror. He went right to the man with the gun. They're whispering about something."

"Shit." I jerked my chin at the door. "Hurry. Go."

My heart hammered against my ribs. By now, backup should be close. As soon as the liquor store owner called 9-1-1, this location would become a priority. I just had to hold out until then. It'd be okay. Everything would be okay. I took a deep breath and gripped my gun. These bastards wouldn't harm anyone else. Not if I could help it.

A part of me thought about going out the front and waiting it out, but the moment the alarm sounded, I knew that was no longer an option. The emergency exit triggered an alarm, causing the regular lights to dim and the emergency flashing lights to turn on, along with the shrieking alarm claxons.

"Police. Freeze." I blinked against the flashing lights. Footsteps sounded against the tile floor, and a glass bottle shattered to my right. I aimed at the sound and reached for the LED flashlight hanging from my keychain. I clicked it on. "Throw down your weapons and come out with your hands up. If you surrender, you will not be harmed."

I edged to the side, keeping my back against the shelf as I approached the middle aisle. At first, I didn't see anything, but with the flashing lights it was hard to see. And then I heard whispers from across the room and to my left.

I moved toward the voices, surprised when the emergency lights suddenly shut off and the room was plunged into darkness. The only illumination came from the lights inside the glass refrigerated cases and a single neon sign hanging above one of the coolers. The shrill squeal of rubber soles against the tile floor alerted me to movement, and I swiveled toward it, catching a glimpse of a man in the beam of my flashlight.

He stood near the register, one hand on the control panel behind the counter. A moment later, the shrieking, repetitive warning beep stopped.

"Let me see your hands," I said, keeping one eye on him while I scanned the rest of the store for signs of his accomplice. He spun around to face me, a plastic Halloween mask covering his face. "I said put your hands up." He had dark hair too, just like the man who fired on me earlier.

"Is there a problem, officer?" the offender asked, his voice gravelly. "Shouldn't you be in uniform?"

"I'm not on duty."

He snickered. "I knew this place had a mess of first responders who liked to drop by." He turned his left wrist so he could see the time. "Aren't you a bit early? Shift's not over for another couple of hours. Was it a slow night?" He moved sideways, away from the register, and backed against the nearest shelf. "Do you want to come over here and frisk me?"

This felt like a trap. "Where's your friend?"

The guy laughed again. "You're all alike. Afraid. Pathetic." His words dripped disgust. "What the hell makes you think you're any better than anyone else?"

"Stop moving," I ordered.

"Make me." He grabbed one of the large bottles from behind him and held it in the air, as if he intended to throw it at me.

But I didn't move toward him. Instead, I took a step closer to the front door. They wouldn't get out this way, but now I had to worry about his accomplice escaping out the back. Where was my backup?

"No," he taunted, taking a step closer, "you won't make me. You're scared. You're alone and frightened. That's always when they attack. When no one else is around to see it or step in. When no one else can come to help. It's pathetic," he screamed, spittle flying from the opening in the plastic mask. "You coward."

"Sir, drop the bottle."

"Oh, this?" He looked at it as if he had no idea how it'd gotten into his hand. "Well, okay." It shattered on the floor.

"Who are they?" I asked, edging just slightly closer.

Before he could answer, another bottle shattered two aisles away. I kept my gun aimed at the first suspect but pointed my flashlight toward where the sound originated. Just as I did that, the bastard near the register knocked over a display, causing numerous bottles to crash to the floor. Glass and liquor shot out in all directions.

I turned to face him, pointing my gun in his face. "Hands on your head. Get on your knees. I won't ask twice."

He put his hands on his head and slowly knelt down, wincing as he did so. "Y'know, I got a bad knee."

"Interlock your fingers," I ordered, afraid to turn my back on him and even more afraid not to turn around to search for his friend. As soon as his fingers were laced together, I moved toward him, letting my flashlight dangle while I reached for my cuffs.

He wasn't armed, but the shop owner said the man had a gun. Was this his friend? It didn't make sense, but I'd get that sorted later. Right now, every instinct told me I was in trouble.

I just tightened the first bracelet and maneuvered his other arm around and clicked it in place when something knocked into me. My gun and flashlight slid across the floor, thrusting me into darkness.

TWENTY-FIVE

I dragged myself off the floor, blindly feeling for my weapon. I spotted the small cone of light rolling back and forth from my flashlight, but I couldn't get to it. Not with these bastards so close. I just had to hope if I couldn't see them, they couldn't see me.

"What's a matter, baby? Scared of the dark?" the one with the gravelly voice taunted.

"Stay where you are," I commanded.

His laugh was joined by that of another man. I felt behind me, finding a solid shelf. At least that would provide some protection and limit the direction of their attacks. The rattle of the handcuffs sounded at my ten o'clock. He was close. Too close.

"Don't move. On your knees." I kept my head on a swivel, glimpsing dim shadows cast by the neon sign near the coolers. I could make out the form of a man, but I couldn't be certain if he was getting closer. I needed a weapon, specifically my gun. Both of the men were taller and bigger than I was. They'd taken out security guards. I wasn't sure I'd stand a chance in a fair fight. And they sure as hell didn't fight fair. I tried to move silently toward the exit, and that's when I spotted his accomplice. They had boxed me in. They didn't come here to score. They came here to kill more people in uniform.

I resisted the urge to speak. I wasn't sure they could see me. I knew it was a trap. Why did I walk right into it?

"You realize you never asked us what we wanted," the gravelly voice said. "Tell me, baby, you're the same bitch from this morning, aren't you?"

I grabbed a bottle of wine off the shelf and held it by the neck while I desperately searched for my gun.

The gravelly voice chuckled. "I guess that means you already know what I want. Why don't you come over here and give it to me?"

A piece of glass crunched beneath my foot. I froze, but it was too late.

"Diego," the gravelly voice warned.

The accomplice darted forward, attempting to grab me. I swung the bottle, smashing it against his temple. I felt the jarring impact run up my arm and through my shoulder. The bottle broke due to the force and cut my palm. Diego didn't make a sound as he collapsed to the ground.

But before I even felt relief at having taken down one offender, the other one grabbed me from behind. His strong, thick arms encompassed my body and forced my arms down at my sides. For the briefest second, I thought I smelled menthol mixed in with the pungent smell of wine and spirits. How'd he get out of the cuffs?

"You're going to pay for that. I'm going to make it hurt the same way they hurt me. You're going to beg to die before I kill you. And then I'm going to laugh when I put a bullet through your brain." He knocked me sideways into one of the racks, knocking more bottles to the ground in the process.

I struggled and kicked, trying to get free. Lifting my legs, I threw off his center of gravity. He teetered to the side, and I thought about the way he winced when he knelt on the ground. He hadn't lied about an injured knee.

He tried to compensate for the sudden shift, and I drove the ball of my foot into his left kneecap. He howled, losing his hold on me and stumbling backward.

Spotting my gun, I dove for it, but he saw it first and knocked it out of the way. It slid beneath a shelf and disappeared into the darkness.

"You're gonna pay for that, bitch." He grabbed my leg and pulled my foot out from beneath me.

He was strong. I kicked him in the stomach or maybe his chest. I couldn't tell, but he held tighter, dragging me across the floor toward him. Shards of glass cut into my exposed skin, and my clothes became soaked with tequila and rum.

He pinned me beneath him, hitting me hard with his elbow before switching to his fists. He tightened one hand around my throat and squeezed. I pushed against his chin, trying to get away from him. I shoved his mask up a couple of inches, exposing a grizzled chin and a small scar, but that had no effect on the stranglehold he had on me. So I went for his throat. I hit him hard, and he reared back, making a wheezing sound. He coughed a few times, and I used that opportunity to slip out from beneath him.

I'd just gotten to my feet when he eked out, "Grab her."

Someone rammed into me from the side, knocking me into a shelf. Before I had time to recover, he launched his full weight at me. In the dark, all I could see were his hands spread out in front of him like Superman mid-flight, and then we crashed through the glass door of one of the coolers. Large shards crashed to the floor around me, and the sudden cold was a shock to my system, even as warmth ran down my face and neck.

My legs gave out, and I slid to the floor, one arm and shoulder wedged inside the refrigerator. My vision swam. Dark bubbles crowded out the tiny bits of light. I tried to push away from the door, getting snagged and caught. The tiny lightbulbs inside allowed me to see. Blood dripped from a few of the cans and pooled at the bottom. He must have been cut.

I tried to climb out of the broken door, my shoes sliding on the wet floor as pieces of glass scraped against the tile like pebbles on asphalt. Then two hands yanked me out of the cooler, and the world flipped upside down. I was barely aware of the laughter or the pressure easing from around my shoulder as they threw me to the ground. The pain came in waves as something warm and sticky spread down my back.

"What should we do with her?" one of the voices asked.

"I know what I came here to do," Gravelly Voice said. "But she's too much of a mess. It's time you prove yourself. Finish this."

"Look at her, man. She's done. Let's just go," the first voice insisted.

"Shut up." Gravelly Voice stomped toward me. "You said you'd do it. You already fucked up more times than I care to count. Now fuck her up."

My gun, where was it? I needed to find it. Pulling myself to my hands and knees, I barely made it a few inches toward the shelf before I fell back to the ground, dizzy and in agony. I couldn't breathe. My chest burned, and I struggled to suck in air. One of the men kicked me in the side, hard enough to flip me over, and I gasped, unable to scream.

Gravelly Voice crouched down over me as my chest heaved, and a gurgling sound came from deep within my throat. But I could barely hear it over my pounding heart. I tried not to panic, but I saw it in his eyes. He was going to kill me. He reached for the belt loops on my pants and tugged me a few inches closer. He yanked my badge free and scoffed at it. Then he forced my head to the side. "Beg," he whispered.

The smell of the broken liquor bottles nauseated me and burned my eyes. I gasped again, forcing the impeding darkness to momentarily dissipate. And that's when I spotted my gun. I stretched out, reaching for it beneath the shelf.

"We don't have time for that," the other one hissed. "Don't you hear the sirens? The police are coming."

"Again with the fucking sirens? What did I tell you about smoking that shit?" This time, a third voice joined the mix.

"You all right, Diego?" Gravelly Voice asked.

"Uh-huh."

"Then keep watch. The police will be here soon."

That's when I realized there were three of them. We had no way of knowing before. Now it made sense. The third uniform. The way they split up. Two with dark hair, one with light. I had to tell Brad. He needed to know.

Two of them crouched over me, but with the masks I couldn't tell them apart. One of them grabbed my chin and forced me to look at him. "How long?" he asked. I caught a glimpse of him in the dim lights. Dark hair beneath the Halloween mask, but he didn't have the gravelly voice. The one with the gravelly voice was in charge. This must be Diego. A welt the size of a plum stuck out from his temple where I hit him with the bottle. "How long for patrol to arrive?"

"Fuck you," I spat.

"Don't be stupid," Diego warned.

"Let's speed this up." Gravelly Voice forced a gun into the palm of the third man. I couldn't be sure, but I thought he might have been the blond. "Kill her or I'll kill you." Gravelly Voice stepped back and aimed at the back of his accomplice's head.

"Yeah, okay." The blond stared at me for a long time. I found his gaze disconcerting and vaguely familiar. He checked to make sure the weapon was loaded, flipped the safety, and aimed at me.

I stretched my arm farther beneath the shelf. Pain radiated down the side of my neck, across my collarbones, and along the muscles in my arm, but I had to get my gun. My breath came in frantic, short gasps. And no matter how hard I tried, I couldn't control my breathing.

He pressed the barrel against my temple, and I closed my eyes, unable to move or talk. My entire body had practically shut down since I'd gone through the cooler door, but I couldn't figure out why.

"Wait." Gravelly Voice crouched down. "I want to leave a message first." He towered over me. "Don't worry, bitch. Your friends are gonna join you soon enough. You won't burn in hell alone."

He ran his fingers against the side of my neck. I screamed, feeling as if he'd stabbed me with ice or burned me with a poker. Expelling that much air nearly knocked me out. I was drowning in the black bubbles. As a last ditch effort, I clawed more frantically beneath the shelving for my gun and managed to hook my middle finger inside the trigger guard.

I pulled it closer, finding it difficult to get my shoulder unwedged from beneath the shelf to draw on them.

Gravelly Voice stood up. "That's done. Now, blow her brains—"

"The cops are here. I see lights," Diego said. I couldn't see him, but his voice came from near the front door.

"Shoot her now," Gravelly Voice retreated, leaving the blond behind.

I stared up at him, my shallow gasps almost sounded like choked laughter, taunting him. But I couldn't help it. No matter how much I gasped, I couldn't get enough oxygen. "Please," I managed.

He stared at me. "I'm sorry."

I freed the gun from beneath the shelf and fired. I didn't even have the strength to aim, but the gunshot scared him. He bolted from beside me and ran for the front door.

I stared up at the ceiling, unable to see anything. Even the neon sign on the wall was nothing but a hazy blur. Everything dimmed. I felt cold, except for the burning in my neck. I sputtered, gagging now.

Two officers burst through the front door with guns at the ready and their flashlights aimed. I couldn't call to them, but they found me.

"Shit. It's DeMarco." One of them knelt down beside me. "Liv, hey, come on now. You have to hang on." Officer Roberts keyed his radio. "Officer down. I need an ambulance rolled to this location. Hurry." He rolled me onto my side, so I wouldn't choke. "Clear the building, Ainsley."

"Yes, sir." The other officer headed toward the back.

"Olive, don't you fucking die on me. I don't need that kind of shit raining down on my career." He took out a knife and sliced a strip off the bottom of my shirt, then he ripped it across and rolled it up. He pressed it against the side of my neck, tore off a second strip, and put it against the back of my neck.

"Clear," Officer Ainsley said.

"Good, get down here and help me," Roberts said. "See what you can find to hold this in place, and whatever you do, don't remove the glass. She'll bleed out if you do."

"She's going to bleed out anyway."

"Bite your tongue. This is Vince DeMarco's kid." Roberts kept his hand against my neck. "You hang on, Olive. You hear me?"

TWENTY-SIX

"Shit." Carter couldn't stop shaking. "Shit." He yanked the mask off his face, sucking in deep breaths. "Pull over."

Diego glanced at him from the rearview mirror. "Not yet. We're still too close."

"Oh god." Carter clutched his stomach and hurled.

"Son of a bitch." The third man turned around, waited for Carter to wipe his mouth, and slapped him across the face. Carter's cheek stung, and his eyes watered. "It's done." The third man stared at him. "Pull yourself together. She's dead, right?"

"Ye-yeah," Carter said.

The third man held out his hand. "Give me the gun before you blow your brains out."

Carter fumbled with it, accidentally ejecting the magazine. It dropped into the pool of sick, and he scooped it up, thumbing out one of the bullets before offering it to the third man. The third man reached back, wiped the magazine on Carter's shirt, and shoved it back into the gun.

"I wish I could have seen it," the third man said. "What was it like?" He grinned, the tip of his tongue snaking out to moisten his lips. "Did you feel that rush? The thrill? There's nothing like it."

Carter doubled-over and heaved uncontrollably.

"You're cleaning this when we get back," the third man said. "The car. The gun. All of it." He turned back around. "Pussy."

Diego glanced at the man in charge. "What the hell are we doing?"

"Taking back what's ours."

"I thought this was about a payday, a means to an end. What we just did, that put targets on our backs."

The third man laughed. "How naïve are you? They were already hunting us. Now they know we're hunting them right back."

Diego ran a hand through his hair, wincing when he brushed against the welt. He glanced down at his fingers. Blood. His DNA was in the system. They might identify him. Then again, after the cop came out of the fridge with the piece of glass stuck in her neck, it'd be hard to find any blood evidence in the store that didn't belong to her. She'd bled rivers. Frankly, he was surprised she'd stayed conscious as long as she had.

"Still," Diego glanced at Carter who had curled up on the back seat, clutching his stomach, "what did tonight accomplish? We almost got caught. I stayed in that store for almost an hour. The owner might be able to identify me, and he escaped."

"I know." The third man held up the detective's badge. "But we got what we came for. And Carter, here, finally became a man." He wrinkled his nose at the disgusting smell coming from the rear of the car. "Just remember, you killed a cop tonight. That's all they're going to care about. So if you even think about changing your mind or opening your big mouth, remember they want you dead or buried in some deep dark hole for the rest of your life."

"But what's a badge going to do for us?" Diego asked. "I thought you wanted to snag some police uniforms."

"This is better." The third man examined his prize. "I never thought we'd bag a detective. This," he flashed the badge at Diego, "comes with a lot more perks and opportunities. We're going to live like kings."

*   *   *

"Careful," a voice said as I was lifted off the ground. The motion made me sick, and I coughed up more blood. "We have to hurry." The EMTs slammed the rig doors closed. The one in the back checked the IV. "The lines are wide open," he called to his partner. "Notify the hospital to have an OR ready. They'll have to take her immediately into surgery."

"Do you think they wrote that using her blood?" another voice asked, but their conversation made no sense to me.

The words swirled around, getting lost in the agonizing abyss. My world went dark. My last thoughts were of my parents, Emma, and Brad. I had to hang on for them. I had to tell Brad.

By the time I opened my eyes again, I couldn't remember what happened. But terror flooded my senses. Someone wanted to hurt me. My head throbbed in time to my heartbeat. He was close. I remembered him hovering over me, staring at me. He had a gun. He was going to kill me.

I screamed and shoved myself backward. I had to get away from him. He was hiding in the dark. Where was my gun?

"Whoa, easy, Liv. Easy."

The room was a dingy white, and the lights were too bright. Everything spun and wobbled. But despite the brightness, the darkness encroached, threatening to black out the world. Not again. It hurt to breathe, but I couldn't stop gasping.

"Liv, look at me. You're safe. I got you." Brad took my hand and reached for my face. He stared into my eyes until I actually saw him and not the images floating around my subconscious. "I'm here. I'm right here."

"Brad?" I clutched his hand, realizing I was on the brink of passing out. "What happened?" Something was wrong with me. I just didn't know what.

He eased me back against the pillow. Concern furrowed his brow and etched lines around his eyes. "You don't remember?"

I squinted, hoping to recall details, but everything was a blur. I tried to force myself to think, and panic overtook my senses again. Somewhere in the room, something started beeping. My breathing bordered on hyperventilating.

"Liv, I won't let anyone hurt you. I'm not leaving your side. Not ever." The emotion in his voice scared me more than whatever memories were lurking just out of reach. His gaze flicked to something behind me, but I couldn't turn to see what it was. Instead, I clung to his arm like it was a lifeline. He grasped my hand in both of his, running one down the bandage along my forearm and holding my knuckles against his lips. "Everything's going to be okay. I promise. Shh. You're okay. You're okay." His breath warmed my fingers.

I winced with each breath, slowly calming as he shushed me. Once I had my faculties in order, I realized where I was. "Oh god, Emma's gonna kill me."

"Emma's going to be relieved you're okay." Brad lowered my hand to the bed when my eyes fluttered. "Just rest. I'm not going anywhere. You're safe now." I clung to his fingers, afraid if I let go I'd be alone in the dark again.

The next time I came to wasn't nearly as traumatic. For the first time since the attack, I felt like I could breathe. The constant slow beeping meant everything was normal. I was okay.

Turning my head to the side, I felt a pinch along the back of my neck, but it wasn't enough to worry about. My partner had one leg crossed over the other, his knee resting on the edge of the bed while I kept one of his hands prisoner beneath mine. When I loosened my grip, he opened his eyes and looked at me.

"Hey, are you okay?" he asked.

"You tell me. What did they do to me?"

"They rushed you into surgery. They did a decent patch job, but you know doctors. They love running tests. We're still waiting on a few of the results. Emma's been making sure they don't screw anything up. You know how she is." He offered a smile that didn't make it to his eyes. "CSU's still processing the scene and whatever evidence they were able to retrieve from you." He pressed his lips together. "What the hell were you thinking? Why didn't you call me?"

"Brad, please, not now."

He clenched his jaw and looked away. "What do you remember?"

"Nothing...everything. I don't know. It's a blur."

"Okay. None of that matters right now. The only thing that matters is you're going to be okay."

The door opened, followed by the overhead light coming on. I winced but forced my eyes to remain open. The doctor flipped through a few pages on the chart.

"It seems you've had quite an eventful night, Liv. How are you feeling?"

"Not great."

"I can imagine." He ran through a list of rudimentary questions. He marked something on the chart and took out a penlight. While he was checking my pupils, Emma trailed in behind him. She crossed her arms over her chest and leaned against the back wall, as far from me as she could get while still being in the same room. Nothing I'd been through tonight could compare to what was about to happen. "Are you in any pain?" the doctor asked.

"No, but I'm about to be."

He quirked an eyebrow and glanced behind him. "Ah, Nurse Emma." He glanced at her scrubs. "I thought you were taking a personal day."

"Uh-huh." She stared at me, the temperature in the room dropping a good twenty degrees.

"All right," the doctor turned back to me, "you need rest and plenty of fluids. I'll have someone change the IV bag. We'll keep an eye on your blood pressure and oxygen levels and see if we need to reassess." He walked out the door, and I spotted several cops waiting just outside my room.

"Bradley," Emma said, "Captain Grayson wants to speak to you."

He slipped his fingers out from beneath my palm. "I'll be right back, okay, Liv?"

"Hurry," I said.

He went past Emma, putting a reassuring hand on her shoulder. "Go easy."

Once we were alone, the hard façade cracked and Emma sniffed. She came closer to the bed and threw her arms around me. She hugged me as tightly as she dared, which seemed to have about as much strength behind it as a soggy tissue. "You promised me nothing like this would ever happen again."

"Em, I'm sorry." I thought I might cry, but Emma released me before I got too choked up. She dabbed at her eyes and climbed onto the bed.

"Scooch over." She ran her fingers through my hair, obsessed with brushing the tangles to one side. "We should have had a sleepover. I should have made you stay. Then none of this would have happened."

"Emma."

"No," she cut me off, "it's bad enough your parents wanted me to watch the house and the dog, but now I'm expected to make decisions about you. About your medical treatment. I'm not equipped to do that. What if you were brain dead? Would you have wanted me to pull the plug?"

"Well, maybe give it a day or two, just to make sure."

She raised her palm to smack me but thought better of it. "That's not funny. I was getting ready for work when I got the call. Since they couldn't get in contact with anyone else, they notified me you were in surgery. That I better get down here. That decisions might have to be made."

"You've been making decisions for me since we were sixteen. Obviously, I trust you. No one's better equipped to handle these kinds of situations." I watched the cops gathered outside my room through the opened blinds. Voletek offered a slight wave. Lt. Winston and Captain Grayson turned to see what was going on, but by then, Emma had poked me in the arm to get my attention.

"I don't want that kind of responsibility." She sighed. "Did Brad say when your parents are supposed to get here?"

"Oh god." I knew protocol. And I knew my father. He'd be the first call they made as soon as they found me. "Did they get through?"

She shrugged. "I tried calling a few times, but it always went to voicemail."

"Give me your phone." I grabbed it out of her hand and dialed. Voicemail. So I left a message. "Hey, Dad, it's me. I don't know what you've heard or the rumors that are flying around right now. I ended up on a bad call, but I'm okay. Just stay where you are. No reason you should cut your trip short, just call me back if you have any questions. I love you." Then I dialed my mom and left a much more positive and flowery message on her voicemail. Hopefully, I'd performed the proper damage control. But with any luck, they wouldn't have cell service until they disembarked from their cruise. I didn't want this to ruin their trip.

"You're being dumb." Emma tucked the phone away. "They'd want to be here. We could have lost you. Do you understand that?"

"Don't be so dramatic."

She climbed off the bed and glared at me. "I'm not." The door opened, but Brad remained in the doorway. "Tell her I'm not."

"You're not what?" Brad asked. For a moment, I thought my partner might make a run for it. But if he did, he'd look like a coward in front of his fellow detectives and the police brass.

"Being dramatic," Emma insisted. "Vince and Maria would want to be here."

"She's right," Brad said.

"No." I saw the guilt cross his features. He called them already. He told them to come home. "You have to call them back. They're going to panic. Tell them I'm okay. Tell them not to come. I just left voicemails, but it'd mean more coming from you."

"Yeah, all right. I'll take care of it." He ran a hand over his mouth. "You don't look so good, Liv. Are you tired? You should probably get some sleep. The doctor's pretty concerned about the blood loss. You shouldn't exert yourself too much."

Truthfully, I was exhausted. If I closed my eyes for more than three seconds, I'd be out like a light, but I also knew for Brad to ask that, the brass had questions. Sleep could wait. "It's okay. Send them in."

"Are you sure?"

"I'm sure."

I answered their questions until I couldn't anymore. And then I slept.

The next two days were a blur. I spent most of it passed out in a hospital bed. The few waking hours I had were spent with the police brass, IAD investigators, Voletek and Lisco. Brad hadn't left my side, aside from having to answer some questions and the occasional bathroom or shower break. Emma appeared to be fighting with him over who had priority to watch over me, but they kept the bickering to a minimum, which I appreciated.

"It must be nice to be so loved," Lt. Winston said. He reached for one of the cards in the nearest arrangement. "I got injured once. The entire unit pitched in and got me a balloon basket. What the hell was I supposed to do with that?" He laughed, noticing a similar arrangement on the other side of the room. "Never mind. It must be a homicide thing. Since you can't solve murders right not, here are some smiley face balloons." He ran a hand down his face. "Sheesh, if those don't make you want to get back to work, I don't know what will."

"Any progress on the case?" I asked.

Winston glanced from me to Brad. "Not yet, but we'll get these guys. At least they haven't killed anyone since the attempted murder of a police detective." He worked something loose from between his back teeth. "It goes without saying, but in case you need reminding, neither of you are allowed anywhere near this."

"But sir," Brad argued, "there's no reason I can't—"

"She's your partner. Don't tell me your judgment's not clouded. You know the rules. You're too close. Hell, the whole unit's too close, but we're going to see this through. Voletek and Lisco will handle it. I assigned everyone we got to it. Intelligence offered us a hand. We're going to find these assholes, and we're going to take them down." He looked back at me. "Are you still having a hard time remembering details?"

"I'm not sure. I just feel like I'm forgetting something."

He licked his lips. "Doctors said that happens with trauma. But it should come back. You spoke to the department counselor and that expert the FBI sent over. They think once you have time to process, you'll remember more details. Once you do, make sure to let me know. In the meantime, we'll drop by if we have questions. Who knows, maybe it'll help jog your memory."

"Yes, sir."

He gripped the rail at the end of the bed. "Feel better, DeMarco. And once you do, we're gonna have a chat about what you were doing alone in that liquor store in the first place."

"Yes, sir," I repeated, dreading the inevitable.

TWENTY-SEVEN

"Brad, go home."

He looked around my apartment. "You're one to talk. You should be at home."

"This is my home."

"You know what I mean." He turned down my bed. "For a moment there, I thought I was going to have to carry you up the steps. So lie down, or I'll end up scooping you off the floor."

"I'm okay."

"No, you're not. Nothing about this is okay." He backed away from the bed and rubbed his eyes. "Look, until Emma gets off work, you're stuck with me. So get used to it. I'm not going anywhere." He peered out the window at the patrol car who'd been assigned for my protection. "Winston should have assigned more than one unit. I don't like this. They haven't made a move since they attacked you, but by now, the news has broken. They must know you're still alive. We can't take any chances."

"What about the liquor store owner? They'll go

after him. He knows what they look like, at least one of them. I don't even know that."

"He's in protective custody."

I nodded, searching my dresser for clean clothes. Emma had brought me the clothes I was wearing, but now they smelled like a hospital. And that was one smell I wanted to shake.

"If he'd come forward when you first approached him, none of this would have happened." The anger burned in Brad's eyes. "We'd have these assholes or at least have some idea who they are. They wouldn't have gotten the drop on you. They wouldn't have hurt you."

"I know."

"He's nothing but a selfish prick." Brad fought to keep his rage in check, but sleep deprivation and a tense few days had decimated the more laidback qualities of his personality.

"He was scared."

"I don't give a shit." He swallowed and held up his palms. "Whatever."

"Are you all right?"

"Yeah, Liv. I'm great. So fucking great." He rubbed a hand down his face. "I'm just hungry and tired, probably the same as you. I'll see what I can scrounge up for lunch. Emma said she brought food and groceries over last night in preparation for today." He didn't wait for me to say anything before walking out of the room. I'd seen my partner at his worst, but this was something else. I didn't think I'd ever seen him like this. It scared me.

I was too nauseous to think about food. I could smell the hospital on me, specifically that disgusting stench that wafted up from the tray they'd left in my room. Eventually, Emma found someone to take it away, but the odor remained. And mixed with the lingering olfactory memory from all those broken liquor bottles, it was no wonder I didn't have much of an appetite.

The only thing I wanted to do was shower and get into something comfortable. Every part of my body ached, though I wasn't sure why. As soon as I entered the bathroom, I had my answer.

The sight of my reflection froze me in place. I hadn't seen the extent of the damage until now. My face was bruised, and one of my eyes was black from where Gravelly Voice had hit me. His fingers left marks on my neck.

I turned away from the mirror and struggled to get my top off. My shoulder hurt, and I grunted. Finally, I pulled it over my head to find my right shoulder bandaged. I'd been so out of it these last two days, I barely remembered Emma and the hospital staff changing the dressing.

Reluctantly, I turned back to the mirror, twisting to see the extensive bandages that covered my shoulder and the side of my neck. I ran my fingers gently against them, recalling bits and pieces of what happened once Officer Roberts arrived.

I felt dizzy and gripped the vanity. My ribs on the left side were purple from where one of the bastards had kicked me. An unexpected sob escaped, and I clamped a hand over my mouth.

Brad's footsteps sounded outside the door. "Liv, are you okay?"

"Uh-huh," I managed, squeezing my eyes closed. I couldn't lose it in front of him.

"Are you sure? Do you need help? I promise not to look."

I almost laughed.

"I can call Emma," he said.

"I'm okay."

"All right."

But I didn't hear his footsteps retreat.

I finished undressing and looked down at the bandages covering my arms and hands. Since I couldn't get most of them wet, showering was out of the question. Instead, I filled the sink and grabbed a washcloth. When I was as clean as I could get, I put on some yoga pants and a button-up shirt. Opening the door, I found Brad waiting on the other side.

"I'm heating soup. Do you want a salad or something else to go with it? I found a package of those wraps you like in the fridge."

"Just soup for me."

He looked like he wanted to argue. "Fine, but there are leftovers in the fridge in case you change your mind."

I sat down on the couch while Brad puttered around the kitchen. In the hospital, he promised he wouldn't leave me, and aside from the few times he'd been forced away by the hospital staff or police investigators, he had kept his word. Emma practically had to turn a fire hose on him to get him to go home and shower and change yesterday afternoon.

He finished in the kitchen and brought a tray out with my soup and a glass of water and placed it over my lap. Then he went back into the kitchen, grabbed a plate with several wraps, which he'd cut in half, and sat down beside me. When I finished the soup, he nudged one of the remaining wraps toward me.

I picked it up, too tired to argue. I got half of it down before my stomach protested, and I pushed it away. He moved the tray out of my way, but I couldn't get comfortable on the couch.

"Do you want some pain meds?" Brad looked at the clock. "You're about due."

"No, Emma's weird about that. She lost one parent

to cancer and the other to an overdose right after that. I don't want to cause her any more anxiety. I'll be okay without them. They make me fuzzy anyway. I'm sure the department isn't happy I've never been able to give them a sober statement."

"First of all, you're sober enough. I don't care what anyone says. Second, Emma's not here. And third, no one wants to see you in pain. So if you are, say something. You've been through enough. You don't have to soldier through any more."

"I'm okay for now."

"I should have been there."

"I know. It was stupid."

"You're damn right it was stupid. I don't want to think about what could have happened if Roberts and Ainsley hadn't arrived when they did. Why didn't you wait for me?"

"I'd been there before. I didn't think they'd go back. We didn't think 24/7 Spirits was a target. We thought it was a distraction, remember? I just wanted to follow up with the owner. I hoped after what happened in the subway station he'd be more forthcoming. I just... I didn't think it'd be dangerous."

"But it was. These guys are psychotic. They want to kill. First it was guards, now it's cops. We're partners. Partners have each other's back. Why didn't you let me have your back? Huh?"

"They had jammers. I couldn't call out."

"Why didn't you call me before that?"

"I did, but you didn't answer. I figured you were probably asleep or out drinking."

"I wasn't." He licked his lips. "I'm sorry. God, Liv, I'm so sorry. I should have answered. I should have stayed with you. You asked me to hang out that night. I should have. Then you wouldn't have been alone. They wouldn't have...we could have stopped them."

"That's not—"

"By the time anyone notified me, they'd already taken you into surgery. Roberts was waiting in the lobby. I don't think I've ever seen that much blood on a police uniform, and we've seen cops who've been killed in the line of duty. That was your blood." He looked away. "I could have stopped it. I fucked up."

"No, you didn't. And neither did I." I scooted closer, afraid Brad would pull away. He had so many issues when it came to losing colleagues. That night might have broken him more than it broke me. "It's not your fault."

"It doesn't matter. I'm supposed to have your back."

I leaned against his shoulder and hugged him, hurt, exhausted, and enraged by everything that had happened. His hand trembled for a moment before he hugged me back.

"Thank you for being here," I whispered.

He pressed his lips gently against my temple. "Don't die on me, Liv."

"I won't, but you have to make sure Emma doesn't pull the plug."

"What?" he asked, confused.

"Nothing. It's an inside joke." My shoulder throbbed from the sudden shift in position. Once the sharp stabbing turned into a dull ache, I climbed off the couch. "I'm going to lie down for a while. Try to get some sleep, okay? You look like shit."

"You're one to talk."

I stuck my tongue out at him. "And Ellie thinks you're charming. Clearly, she doesn't know you very well."

"I told you so." He watched me disappear into the bedroom. Then he stacked the pillows on the other end of the couch and settled down, so he could keep one eye on me and the other on the front door. He put his gun on the coffee table and scooted it closer, so it'd be within reach. And that's when I realized this wasn't over yet.

TWENTY-EIGHT

By the time I woke up, it had gotten dark out. Frankly, I couldn't be sure if it was morning or night. "Who turned my apartment into a flower shop?"

When I went to nap, there hadn't been any get well gifts in my house. The ones in my hospital room stayed in the hospital. Emma had them redistributed to those receiving long-term care. And now it looked like they'd come back to haunt me, and they'd brought their friends.

"You didn't hear the constant knocking at the door?" Brad asked. "They started around five and didn't quit until seven. The unit outside has had their hands full checking IDs. At one point, I thought we'd have to call for a bomb sniffing dog."

"Speaking of, I have to go check on Gunnie," Emma said. She and Brad had been in the midst of a conversation. Their voices woke me up, but I didn't want to tell them that. "You shouldn't be walking around, Liv. You're supposed to be resting," Emma said. "Were we too loud?"

"No, I'm just thirsty."

"That's because you need fluids." She gave Brad an annoyed look. "I told you that."

He held up his palms and backed away. He knew better than to argue with Emma.

"I can get my own water." I tossed an apologetic look at my partner.

"Drink this." She opened a bottle of coconut water and poured it into a covered stainless steel tumbler with matching straw. "It has electrolytes. Don't overdo it, but one a day might help. You can have water after you finish that."

"Why do I have to drink it out of a sippy cup?"

"Because you are going back to bed. And I don't want you to spill."

"I'm tired of being in bed." I was also just plain old tired, but that wouldn't help my argument.

"Fine. Couch," she pointed, "now."

"Do you talk to Gunnie like this? That would explain why he doesn't want to play with you and won't let you near his toys."

"No, I don't talk to him like this because he doesn't get himself hurt by doing stupid things."

My patience waned, but I bit my tongue. I already felt bad enough without having her pile more on me. So I took a seat on the couch, and Brad came over to stack some pillows up behind me so I could sit more comfortably. From the bags beneath his eyes, I knew he hadn't gotten any sleep. "You must be exhausted."

"I'm fine. Emma and I were deciding what to make for dinner. What would you like? You've barely eaten anything in days."

"I'm not hungry. Whatever you guys want is fine." I shifted on the couch, unable to get comfortable. "We could order in."

"I'll see what Maria has in the fridge that I haven't

grabbed yet," Emma said. "And you can talk while I'm gone." She went to the door. "Let her decide, Bradley. Don't force it. She needs her rest."

"What was that about?" I took another sip before reaching across to put the cup on the coffee table. Something snagged, and I winced. "Shit." I felt the bandage on my neck and checked my fingers for blood. "Tell me I didn't rip a stitch."

Brad brushed my hair to the side and carefully peeled the bandage away from my skin. "You're not bleeding."

"Good."

He pressed the tape back down. "Liv, there's been another attack. Voletek called earlier. He wants to stop by to discuss it and that night, but Emma's afraid it'll retraumatize you."

Worst case scenarios played through my mind. "What happened? How many people did these bastards kill?"

"I don't know. He didn't say. We're off the case." But I saw the lie in my partner's eyes.

"You're still working this behind Winston's back, aren't you?"

"I'll assist Voletek and Lisco any way I can. Unfortunately, Jake didn't get the chance to tell me what happened. He just said he needs to talk to you. To us. This was our case. Yours and mine. I'm not washing my hands of it until these bastards have been stopped. But you don't have to be a part of this." He stared into my eyes. "I'm not sure I want you to be a part of this. It's too dangerous."

"Don't pull that macho bullshit on me, Fennel. I'm not some damsel in distress, recent events notwithstanding. If I know something that can stop this from happening again, I want to help. I have to help. But not at the expense of tainting the case or sacrificing a conviction. When we catch them, I want these bastards to go away for life."

"I thought you might. I told Jake to drop by after shift. I hope that's okay. He walks the line, but he won't compromise the case. You can trust him to do the right thing. I'm just not sure IAD would see it like that, if they were to find out we're working this off the books with him."

"It's fine." Jake Voletek was Teflon, and so was I. "But we'll have to keep this from Emma." And that also meant I needed to stay away from the pain meds, which I'd been reconsidering since the moment I woke up.

I adjusted on the couch and closed my eyes. Brad turned on the TV, but the news didn't mention anything about the killers' latest attack. Brad's phone buzzed, and I opened my eyes to watch him read the text.

"Is that Jake?" I asked.

"No, Winters."

"Crap, I forgot about court. What day is it?"

"Tuesday."

"You were supposed to meet with him yesterday. Did you go?"

"I was with you all day." He typed out a reply and put his phone on the coffee table. "I'll get together with him tomorrow. I have court Thursday. I can't get out of it. Winters tried to delay the proceedings, but the defense wouldn't budge. And since they're willing to accept your affidavit into evidence and give up their right to cross, the judge didn't see any reason why we couldn't proceed."

"So I'm off the hook?"

Brad chuckled. "I see you found a way to get out of going to court, but don't do it again."

"Is Winters' case solid without me?"

"You'll be there in spirit, metaphorically speaking. But I can handle this. We've done enough of these. It's solid. So was the arrest. Actually, the defense was afraid your appearance," he waved his hand at my face, "would bias the jury in the prosecution's favor. I think he's glad you won't be there."

"But that offender didn't do this to me."

"No, but you know juries."

The phone buzzed again, and Brad reached over to read the message. "Winters wants me to tell you he hopes you feel better, and he promises we'll get these guys." Brad looked around the living room and pointed to a giant basket in the corner. "He sent that over. His card said something about not wanting you to miss breakfast."

"Ugh."

"You spent the night with Logan Winters." Brad crossed his arms over his chest and stared at me like he would a perp in interrogation. "That's why you smelled like cologne the other morning."

"Nothing happened. I had a headache, and he let me crash at his place."

"Likely story," Brad teased, growing concerned when I didn't argue. "Maybe Jake should hold off tonight. You just got home, and I'm not sure the doctors were too keen on releasing you. Everyone seems to forget you went through major surgery."

"They stitched up a scratch. It was no big deal."

"That's what you think." Brad exhaled, but the blood drained from his face. He turned back to the TV and flipped channels. We didn't speak again until Emma returned with dinner.

TWENTY-NINE

"I don't remember everything. Do you have a copy of the liquor store owner's report? He told me the suspect had been inside 24/7 Spirits for almost an hour by the time I showed up. But before we could clear out the customers, another man entered. It must have been two men since there were three of them, but I never saw them until it was too late." I reached for one of the files Voletek had brought. "One of them's blond. The other two have dark hair. They all wore those plastic Halloween masks. The clear plastic with the brightly colored makeup around the eyes, cheeks, and lips."

"Like this?" Voletek tapped on his phone a few times and showed me a photo from a store's website.

"Just like that."

"Okay, I just wanted to make sure. We've been running recent purchases, but we haven't had any luck. I don't think we will. Too many places sell these, both local and online. And they could have stocked up last Halloween or several Halloweens ago."

"Did you check with robbery?" I asked.

"No crew used this as their signature, but there are dozens of armed robberies and smash and grabs where the robbers wore these masks. We're checking into them and reinterviewing the previous victims to make sure we haven't missed anything."

"You think one of these crews has escalated to murder?"

"We won't know unless we check. But they're attacking cops now, so we're checking everything, no matter how miniscule," Jake said.

I reached for another file, hoping to find the liquor store owner's statement. Perhaps his description of one of the killers would jog my memory.

"You don't need to see that one." Brad snatched the file from me. "IAD would say you want to look at it just to keep your story straight. No reason to make them question you or what you remember. We've already had enough run-ins with them when we worked that last case for intelligence."

"Don't remind me, but this is different." All I knew was Brad didn't want me to see that file.

"IAD already verified her story. Liv acted above and beyond her duties. We have evidence, the calls to dispatch, and Officers Roberts' and Ainsley's reports. That's not a concern." Jake smiled at me. "Have I mentioned it's good to see you up and around."

"Thanks." I reached for one of the grain-free pastries he'd gotten from a Paleo bakery. "And thanks for not sending flowers."

"They can be overwhelming."

"Like this case," Brad mumbled. "Liv's supposed to be taking it easy. Maybe we should call it a night." He put the folder down beside Jake.

"What did Emma say to you before she left?" I asked. "Did she tell you to be a pain in my ass?"

Brad didn't even bother to acknowledge that I'd spoken. Instead, he stared at Jake, hoping to silently communicate something.

Jake handed me a copy of the owner's statement and took the file I had grabbed and tucked it beneath his elbow. "That's what you're looking for. He spoke to a sketch artist, but I don't know if that'll help."

"I never saw his face, just the back of him." I skimmed what the store owner said and studied the line drawing. "I just wanted to see what one of these bastards looks like."

"Might look like," Brad corrected. "If the security camera worked, we'd know for sure."

"If the security camera worked, the guy wouldn't have gone inside the store." And then a thought hit me. "Did the offenders do anything to the camera? Spray the lens or try to destroy it?"

"Nothing," Jake said.

"So they knew it didn't work." I leaned back in the chair, resisting the urge to rub my sore shoulder. Touching it only made the bruises and cuts hurt worse. "The one with the gravelly voice knew how to disarm the system. Once the alarm sounded, he went to the counter and turned off the alarm and the flashing lights. Or maybe the lights went out first." I rubbed the bridge of my nose, which was also sore. "I can't remember the order in which it happened."

"That's understandable." Jake got up from the table and poured himself a cup of coffee. "You said they were armed, but when you frisked one of them, he didn't have a gun. Are you sure you cuffed him?"

"Yeah." But now I wondered if I failed to fasten the second bracelet.

"We found your cuffs on the floor." Jake swallowed and stared into his mug. "He's the one you said hit you."

"He's the one who wanted to kill me – the one with the gravelly voice. He was in charge. He told me he'd make it hurt, that I'd beg him to kill me before it was over." I licked my lips, recalling the look in his eyes. "He meant it."

Brad pushed away from the table and circled the living room a few times, looking for something to hit. "I should have been there."

Jake leaned against the counter, looking anywhere but at me. "Anything else?"

"He has brown eyes," I said. "Dark brown."

Jake put down the mug. "Okay, that's something."

"I guess." I stared at the folder the men had taken from me and slid to the other side of the table. "I know he had a weapon. Actually, he had two." I squinted. "He gave one to the blond. He wanted him to shoot me, almost like a gang initiation. But if the blond man didn't do it, he was going to shoot him."

"What about the other guy?" Jake asked.

"I hit him with a bottle. I thought I knocked him out, but these guys are like cockroaches. Nothing can keep them down for long. He got up."

"That's Diego, right?" Brad asked.

I nodded.

"Did you find anything on the name?" Brad asked Jake. "You should have robbery cross-reference it with known crews and previous offenders."

"I did," Jake said.

Brad stopped pacing and put his hands on his hips. "And?"

"There are a lot of Diegos in the system."

"You're not doing it right. Did you cross-reference it to other cases with crews of three? If you enter the stats we have on the other two, you'd probably get a hit."

"I know what I'm doing," Jake said.

"I doubt that."

"Then get your ass down to the precinct and do some research. No one's stopping you," Jake said.

"Fellows," I snapped, and two sets of eyes turned to me, "this sucks. Don't make it worse."

"Sorry," Brad mumbled.

"Me too," Jake said. The three of us stared at the table for a few moments.

"All right, we need to reassess. We know they broke into Star Cleaners to steal LockBox uniforms, but they only got two. We assume they attempted to rob the truck and not the dispensary, but the money truck never showed. So they kidnapped the LockBox driver, stripped him, and killed him."

"They tortured him," Jake said. "The medical examiner noticed his fingers and toes had been broken, probably smashed with a hammer. Not a lot of blood, but a lot of pain."

"They didn't want to make a mess on the uniform," Brad said, which went along with what we'd already learned.

"They needed the third LockBox uniform," I said. "When they went into the subway station, they each had one."

"We're working under the assumption they intended to rob the station agent, possibly to increase their score from the dispensary," Jake said. "Footage from the subway tunnel showed two LockBox guards enter together. They each carried a duffel bag."

"Those are the two with the dark hair – Gravelly Voice and Diego."

"So where was Blondie?" Brad asked. "Did you find anything else on the footage?"

"Another guy in a LockBox uniform entered a few seconds after they did. He didn't go to the station agent. He went through the turnstiles and straight to the platform. The three were never together, so we couldn't be sure it wasn't a coincidence," Jake said.

"Except I'm guessing Blondie hopped the next train and attacked Officer Cruz in the out of order restroom," I said. "Do you think they sent him ahead to act as a diversion?"

"It's possible. We don't know. We don't know where Diego or Gravelly went after they killed the station agent. We're still assuming they took refuge in the tunnels, but our search was inconclusive," Jake said. "Nothing ever popped up."

"They could have taken off the uniforms and tossed them into the bags they carried," Brad said, "or they climbed up one of the service ladders. There's a million places they could have gone that we wouldn't have noticed if they went through the tunnels."

"And since we shut down the trains, they didn't have to worry about getting run over," I said. "Dammit." The back of my neck throbbed, and I put my head in my hands, hoping to ease the muscle tension.

"After the fiasco in the subway, they vanished," Jake said, "except they didn't stay gone for long. Fourteen hours later, these bastards had the gall to show their faces back at their favorite haunt, 24/7 Spirits." He flipped open the folder by his elbow and pulled out a few shots of the exterior and the neighborhood. "What's so special about that liquor store?"

"Nothing."

"Did you run the owner?" Brad asked. "He could be in on it. He left Liv inside. He waited until he was halfway out the door before telling her the asshole brought his friends in with him, and he kept her from leaving by telling her the offender had someone keeping watch out front."

"I couldn't have left anyway," I said. "Civilian lives were at risk."

"You could have walked outside, got in your car, and radioed for help. It's what you should have done," Brad argued.

I glared at him. "Bullshit. Bull. Shit."

"Her presence might have saved lives," Jake said.

But Brad just stared at him. "No one else was at risk, Voletek. You know that as well as I do. They went there for one purpose. You wanted to bring Liv back into this, so are you going to tell her what's going on? Or are you going to make me do it?"

No one had told me much of anything about that night or what happened today. Jake cleared his throat, clearly uncomfortable. "It doesn't matter. What matters is Liv's safe."

"She's not going to be safe until we catch these assholes." Brad came back to the table and flipped the chair backward before sitting down. "We recovered your gun from the scene. And your cuffs. But these chuckleheads took your badge."

"Okay," I said, not following along.

"They took Officer Cruz's badge too," Jake said. "We know they like to play dress-up. Today, we got a call from the company that supplies police uniforms. Three men assaulted the delivery truck driver and stole a box of uniforms off the truck. We believe the reason they were staking out 24/7 Spirits was to get the jump on a few first responders. The owner says he has several regulars who show up every day right after they get off graveyard."

"They plan on impersonating cops," Brad said. "We just don't know why."

"And they plan on using my badge to do it," I said.

"It appears that way." Jake sighed. "Unless this is some kind of gang initiation thing, like you suggested, in which case, the badges might be trophies."

"That wouldn't explain stealing the uniforms off a truck or the lengths they've gone to dress the part before making a score." I tried to think through the details. "They still want a big payday. They must. And killing, especially cops or people in uniform, is just a bonus. They must have realized as soon as the armored truck heist went south, that we'd provide added security to LockBox and other high value targets in the area. For all we know, the botched robbery might have been intentional so we'd play right into their hands." I looked from one man to the other. "What are we guarding that'd be worth going to this much trouble?"

"I have no idea," Jake said. "I hoped you heard them say something."

I tried to think back. "Most of that night's a blur."

"Understandable." Jake drained his coffee cup. "I just thought I'd ask."

He put his mug in the dishwasher, and I stood, reaching for the folder he'd kept me from reading. The sudden shift in position made me lightheaded, and I teetered. Brad was on his feet in a second, grabbing my arm and pulling me against him before I could collapse.

"Whoa, Liv." He waited until I regained my balance before he sat me back down in the chair. "That's enough for tonight. You need to rest, or Emma's gonna kill us all."

"You okay?" Jake asked.

"Get her some water," Brad said.

Jake refilled the stainless steel tumbler I'd been saddled with and put it down beside me. "Are you okay?" he asked again.

"I'm fine." But I hated having my colleagues take care of me.

"Her blood pressure's wonky." Brad glanced at the cuff Emma had brought home, along with a pulse oximeter and a few other diagnostic tools. I grabbed his arm before he decided to play doctor. That would probably make Jake the nurse. If I wasn't the patient, it might have been entertaining or the plot of one of Emma's smuttier daydreams.

"Before you have me hauled out of here in a body bag," I pointed to the folder, "I want to see what you're hiding from me. I'm not buying your story, gentlemen."

"Liv, now's not the time. Not after that episode," Brad said.

"He's right, princess."

I glared at Jake. "What did I tell you about calling me that?"

"Well, you did almost faint. That's a very princess-like thing to do."

"Voletek," I growled, "let me see it."

"It's mostly crime scene photos." Jake and Brad exchanged a look.

"I have a right to know what happened to me. Please." I held out my hand, unwilling to take no for an answer.

Brad blew out a breath. It was clear he didn't think this was a good idea, but he nodded, and Jake handed over the folder.

THIRTY

"I wish I'd been there to protect you." Brad swallowed uncomfortably but forced himself to look at the photos with me. He slipped his hand underneath the table to hide the tremor from our fellow homicide detective.

"That's not your job," I said.

"Yes, it is. I'm your partner. I won't let you down again. I've done it too many times already."

Jake circled the table. "We didn't pull any prints from the security panel. The camera hadn't been tampered with. With all the broken bottles and disturbed shelves, it's hard to tell exactly what went down, besides one hell of a fight. You sure can hold your own."

"That's what makes me a DeMarco."

"Roberts found you here. Your gun was here. Only one bullet was missing, and we found it lodged here." Jake spread a few of the photos out and pointed to a spot near the bottom of the counter. "Your statement goes along with our findings. You shot once, and it scared them away."

"I hit Diego with a bottle." I shuffled the photos

around. "We were near the front door. Somewhere around here."

"Okay." Jake handed Brad the evidence list. "Forensics said they found two blood samples that didn't belong to Liv."

"One was right here." Brad pointed to a close-up of a broken piece of glass. "That's not wine. That's blood."

"Did we get DNA?" I asked. "Or was it too degraded by the alcohol?"

"It's still processing," Brad said. "At least it was the last I heard."

"Ellie?" I asked.

Brad shook his head. "No. Winston had me removed from everything. She won't call me with any updates."

"Son of a bitch." I understood why, but I didn't like it. "This was our case. We've been dealing with it since the call came in. You should be on top of this." I met Jake's eyes. "No offense."

He held up his palms. "None taken, and for the record, I concur. The LT's a stickler. You're one of ours. He should be willing to compromise and take help from wherever he can get it."

"What about Captain Grayson?" Brad asked. "Liv's his goddaughter. I'm sure he's got everyone from our old unit on this."

"I'm sure he does." Jake rubbed the scruff on his face. As usual, he looked like he should be working the streets instead of hanging out behind a desk. "But Lisco and I were assigned this. So it's our show, I guess. Except I want this stopped as soon as possible, which is why I came here."

"That's because I'm the best," I teased.

Jake winked. "I bet you are."

Brad cleared his throat. "Anyway, we need to find

what connects the unsubs to that liquor store. The owner said he's seen the killer before. But he didn't go into details. Is the killer a frequent flyer?"

"I don't know," Jake said.

"Didn't you speak to him?" I asked.

"Yeah, but you met the guy. He's not what you'd call cooperative."

"Yeah." But no matter how I thought about it, I kept reaching the same conclusion. "There's no way the unsubs would have known I'd be there. Gravelly Voice was surprised. He asked me if I was the bitch from the subway." A flash of something important ran through my mind, but it was gone before I could latch on to it.

"So he recognized you," Brad said. From the look on his face, I didn't want to know what he was thinking. "You definitely need protection." He reached for his phone. "If Winston won't assign another unit, I bet Grayson will."

"Stop." I put my hand over his phone. "Why are you so worried?" But as usual, my partner ignored my question and did what he wanted. He went into the living room and spoke in hushed tones. "What's his deal?" I asked, realizing Brad had only left my side when other police officers had been right outside.

"You know, Brad. He's loyal."

"Try overprotective."

Jake laughed. "In a past life, I bet he was a German shepherd or a pit bull. Either way, he saw the crime scene photos and flipped out a little. He demanded Winston take action, but when the lieutenant was a little slow on the uptake, Brad pulled the pin. He requested personal leave."

"And hasn't left my side since."

Jake removed the last photo from the folder. This one had been facing the other way, so I couldn't see it.

Slowly, he turned it over, resting one hand on the back of my chair, as if I might need to have someone close by. Scrawled on the floor in my blood was a message:

She's the first cop to die, but she won't be the last.

"Jesus." I grasped the folder in my hands, noting the pool of blood that covered the floor like a bucket of spilled paint. That was my blood. The room spun, and I sucked in a breath. A memory of the gravelly voice making threats, saying he knew what he wanted to do if he had more time, if I hadn't made such a mess, now made sense. I remembered when he grabbed my belt loops and dragged me toward him. A shiver went through me, and Jake closed the folder.

"If they realize you're alive, they might make another attempt. That's what your partner's worried about."

"Have they killed anyone else?" I asked.

"Not yet. We've been vigilant. No one goes anywhere alone. Two units to every call. It's a miracle they didn't kill the truck driver today."

"What did he have to say about the attack?"

"A man with a Halloween mask jumped him when he went to make the delivery. He got out of the truck, opened the back, heard a noise, turned, and got clubbed. If they hit him any harder, we would have been scooping his brains off the asphalt."

I cringed, causing Jake to regret his words.

"But they didn't," he assured me.

Brad hung up the phone and returned to the table. "Grayson said he'll make the request, but he's certain the higher brass will approve."

I opened my mouth to protest, but one look from Brad silenced me. I'd give him this one because now I understood why he was so concerned. But I was a cop. I could handle myself. And if those men came back, they'd regret it.

"I think that's enough for tonight," Jake said. "You've given me some great starting points. I'm going to see if I can find any Diegos who live within walking distance of 24/7 Spirits. Maybe we'll get lucky. I'll have Lisco check to see if there's anything the police have access to that no one else does. It could lead us somewhere. In the meantime, we're keeping an eye out for your badge in case it turns up at another crime scene or in a pawn shop. If these bastards try to use it somewhere, we'll hear about it. But in the meantime, I need you to get some rest. I'll drop by tomorrow after work and we'll hammer out more of these details. Who knows what we might have learned by then?"

"Thanks, Jake," I said.

Brad got up to walk him out. They stood just outside my apartment for ten minutes, but I couldn't hear what they were saying. More than likely, it had to do with me and aspects of the case they didn't want me to know about. If I hadn't been so tired, I would have gone into the hallway and given them a piece of my mind. Instead, I took my water, changed back into my pajamas, got into bed, and called Emma.

"Do you want me to come back?" Emma asked.

"No," I said, "Brad's staying the night. And I only have one couch. I don't want either of you to have to sleep on the floor."

"I could always bunk with you," Emma offered. "You remember, like summer camp. Girls in one cabin, boys in the other."

"You snore."

"Fine, but I'll be over first thing in the morning. Make sure the cops outside add me to the list. I don't want to have to run through another twenty questions and get cavity searched just to see you."

"They didn't really do that."

"No, but I think they wanted to. Good night, Liv. And just remember, if you don't feel well or something happens, go straight to the hospital and call me on the way, okay?"

"Fine."

"I'm serious." Emma let out a sigh. "I don't like not being there. You should be staying at your parents' house. There are plenty of extra rooms. I'm here. Gunnie's here. Bradley could sleep in the guest room or on the couch or whatever."

"Not tonight," I said.

"Tomorrow."

"Maybe." I wished her a good night and hung up.

THIRTY-ONE

Something wet pressed against the side of my hand. It wasn't exactly cold or warm, just wet. Not blood, I thought, though that had been the only thing on my mind since I went to bed. That and the crime scene photos. I hated when Brad was right. He didn't want me to see them. One of these days maybe I'd learn to listen to my partner.

The wet thing slid beneath my hand and pressed up against my palm, followed by a low whine. Surely, I didn't make that noise.

Forcing my eyelids open, I watched Gunnie nudge my hand with his wet nose, intent on slipping his head beneath my palm so I would pet him.

"What are you doing here?"

He gave up on his quest and stood on his hind legs, with his front paws on the edge of the bed, and barked once.

"Emma," I mumbled, interpreting his bark. After all, if he could talk, that's what he would have said. He nudged me again. "Fine, I'll get up."

I swung my legs over the side of the bed and waited for the room to stop spinning before I attempted to stand. It was freezing, so I grabbed a zippered sweatshirt from the drawer, got cleaned up, and went into the kitchen. Everything hurt, especially my neck and shoulder which burned nonstop.

Brad glanced in my direction as I stumbled toward the table. "You didn't sleep well." He had bags beneath the bags.

"Neither did you."

"I was busy."

"Doing what?" I peered into the living room. "Where'd you get the giant whiteboard?"

"The office supply store has two hour delivery."

"In the middle of the night?"

"No, but they opened at six. And since I ordered around two, I guess I was their first stop."

"And the files?" I asked.

"Copies. Jake dropped them off on his way to work, but if anyone asks, we didn't get them from him."

I pantomimed zipping my lip and tossing away the key. Over the course of the night, Brad had recreated our murder board with all the updated intel from each of the five crime scenes. He flipped the board around to show me the profiles he'd been working on for our three suspects.

"I'm gonna need coffee first," I said.

"Emma said you better eat breakfast and don't forget to take your antibiotics. She wanted to change your bandages before she left, but since you were asleep, she left me in charge."

"Eh, they're okay." I ran a hand over the one at the side of my neck and winced.

"That's not okay." He abandoned the work he'd been doing and grabbed the supplies. "It doesn't look infected." He took a few snapshots with his phone.

"Are you adding that to the file?" I pointed to his work in progress.

"No, Em made me promise to send her photos since she couldn't check on you herself." He pressed a clean bandage against my skin, and I made the same noise Gunnie had earlier. "Hold this," he said. And I held it so he could tape it.

"I could have done that myself."

"I'd like to see you do the one on your shoulder yourself."

"You're enjoying this, aren't you?"

"Not even a little."

I unzipped my sweatshirt and shrugged out of it. Brad let my bra strap hang off my shoulder while he patched up what he could.

"No wonder you couldn't sleep. That must hurt like a son of a bitch." He put the tape down and carefully readjusted my bra strap so it wouldn't dig into the bandage or my bruises. Then he helped me get my sweatshirt back on.

"You tell anyone about this, and I'll kick your ass," I teased.

He cleaned off the table, tossed the gloves he wore into the trash, and washed his hands. Then he poured me a cup of coffee and took the skillet off the warming burner and put the contents on a plate. While I ate, Gunnie stared at me, licking his chops every time I took a bite.

"What's he doing here?" I pointed my fork at the dog.

"Emma brought him over. She said you'd want the company."

"But I have you."

Brad laughed. "That's what I said." His phone beeped, and he picked it up. "I swear she has this place bugged." He handed me the device, so I could read her message. She said the wounds looked clean and appeared to be healing, followed by a long list of things Brad should watch out for and do should any problems arise.

I handed him back his phone and finished eating. "What are you doing?" I asked. "This isn't you. You follow orders. The LT reassigned you to another case, and according to Voletek, you basically told your commanding officer to shove it."

"Don't believe everything you hear." He cleared away my dishes. "I thought we agreed last night that someone has to stop these guys."

"Voletek and Lisco can handle it."

"I told you, Liv, you don't have to do this. I'll take care of it."

"I don't want you to get in trouble."

"Then I'm gonna have to request a new partner."

Rolling my eyes, I took my cup and went into the living room and stared at the notations on the board. "We need a map."

Brad pointed to the back of my front door.

"Smart ass," I mumbled.

We knew the order in which things happened. The killers were taking things step by step, as if each move was part of a masterplan. Unfortunately, they were playing chess while we were playing checkers. They wanted to take down our king, except I had no idea who or what was the king. This had to be about a score.

"What happened with Moonlight Security?" I asked.

"Nothing. Lisco spoke to the CEO. Apparently, they default the security codes to street addresses, but since Star Cleaners didn't have a four-figure street number, they used the name of the business. They do that with every system they install, but they tell the owners to change the codes. Apparently, Mr. Lee didn't pay attention."

"That means anyone who worked for Moonlight Security could have gained access, in addition to the employees at Star Cleaners."

"Everyone from Star Cleaners checked out, remember? And Lisco ran down everyone currently employed by Moonlight Security, but every regular and part-time security guard alibied out for Gardner's murder. I don't know about the employees they let go, but no one had a sheet. They did extensive background checks before hiring, the same as LockBox."

"Are you sure we checked everyone?"

"As far as I know. What are you thinking?"

"Gravelly Voice knew exactly where the panel was to deactivate the security system in 24/7 Spirits. He went straight for it. He didn't try to attack me. He wanted to turn off the system before it drew anyone's attention."

"Moonlight didn't install the security system at 24/7 Spirits," Brad said. "That system came from one of the nationwide chains. It was a one and done. Just lights and sound. It doesn't connect to any service. The liquor store owner thought that'd be enough of a theft deterrent on its own."

"Yeah, just like the freaking surveillance camera." I dropped onto the couch. "None of this makes any sense. Could Gravelly Voice have been a previous liquor store employee?"

"Wouldn't the owner have recognized him?"

"Maybe he wasn't the guy staking out the store for an hour."

"All right, I'll have someone check records on previous employees since the only people who work there now are the owner and Shelly something or other." Brad picked up his phone and shot off a message, even though I was certain the guys in homicide had already done it. Then Brad spun the whiteboard over to where he'd created a flow chart showing the places these bastards hit, the victims they left in their wake, and the items they stole. A big square with a question mark remained at the end of the chart. "They might be reacting to changing conditions and intel."

"Meaning?"

"Okay, so they hit Star Cleaners to get the uniforms because they had a hundred million dollar goal in mind, except the armored truck broke down. So they decided to improvise. There's three of them and dissension in the ranks. The mess they made outside the dispensary wasn't methodical like Star Cleaners."

"They made a mess there too."

Brad swallowed as images of Gardner's body resurfaced. "Whatever their new plan is, they needed a third uniform. They could have waited for the truck, possibly taken all three guards at once, and attracted less attention. Or they could have waited until the two guards went inside and then just took out the driver while they were disguised. I'd say that would have been the best plan. The safest. Easiest."

"You think one of them got greedy."

"Or panicked. Or they had something else in mind."

"Maybe they didn't know the truck was coming," I said. "It was delayed for over an hour. They could have thought they missed it."

"Then why didn't they wait and try another day?" Brad asked.

"Greed. Impatience."

"Or they're afraid we're getting too close."

"Which would mean someone we questioned or something we found leads straight to them." I bit my lip, hit by the nagging feeling I was forgetting something. "So they had to keep moving. But that means they don't have a plan."

"I think they have a plan, but it's changing and evolving as they go."

"That's not much of a plan," I argued.

"No, but for whatever the reason, they robbed the dispensary. Perhaps they thought the pickup was greater than it was. And when they didn't get a ton of money, they changed the play on the fly and decided they needed a third uniform, so they abducted Rook."

I put my head in my hands and let out a frustrated growl, which resulted in Gunnie enthusiastically wagging his tail at me. Apparently, I spoke dog. "Okay, here's what I don't understand. They strip and kill the LockBox driver, which gave them three LockBox uniforms. Why shift tactics and steal badges and police uniforms?"

Brad pointed a marker at me. "They must need both."

"For what?"

"Your guess is as good as mine."

We spent most of the afternoon researching overlap locations, but there weren't many. Police were only present at prominent locations or areas where the public gathered. The LockBox armored trucks had specific routes and locations. They varied by the day and week in order to prevent psychos from getting any funny ideas.

"They tortured Lindsey Rook, the armored truck driver. We need to know what he knew," I said.

"The transcripts from the LockBox interviews are on the police servers."

I grabbed my laptop and readjusted on the couch, placing a pillow beneath my bruised side to keep from aggravating it while I kept the pressure off my shoulder and neck. Then I logged in and searched for the data. While I read, Brad researched possible targets. Oddly enough, this was almost exactly where we left off several days ago.

"It can't be a government site," Brad declared. "LockBox doesn't have any contracts with the city. The only thing I can say is the offenders know the police are covering LockBox's ass, which might explain why they wanted to have police uniforms handy."

"Why did they go down to the subway?" I asked. The transcripts hadn't provided much. At full capacity, each armored truck could hold almost half a billion dollars, but they didn't collect that much on any route. The hundred million was the largest amount any of their trucks carried. Once they hit close to that amount, they'd take the money to the depository.

"To escape."

"They had a getaway vehicle. They could have dumped the body anywhere and drove off. They went there for a reason. LockBox doesn't have any government contracts, so it's no wonder the station agent didn't react well when they demanded she hand over the money from her booth."

"Assuming that's what they demanded." Brad reached for a map of the subway tunnels and hung it beneath the city map. Then he marked the subway lines and stations on the regular map with a red pen. "The witness didn't hear what they said."

"So why do you think they approached the station agent and then killed her if it wasn't for money? I know she doesn't exactly have millions in the booth with her, just a regular cash drawer, but still, they took $250 from the dry cleaner's. Money's money to them."

Brad thought for a moment. "It's not like the old

G.K. Parks

days where you had the ticket booths and all the collected fares. Everything's electronic and automated. The station agent is basically customer service and in charge of handling emergencies." The thought hit us at the same time. "Station agents direct evacuations and have all the emergency exits and escape routes from the tunnels mapped out."

"This is about orchestrating the perfect getaway," I said.

"And they did, didn't they?" Brad cocked an eyebrow at me. "But that was a dry run. They want to use the tunnels to pull off the real thing." He turned back to the map and his list of possible targets. "Wherever they plan to strike must be close to the subway or one of the access tunnels."

"Or they plan on hitting one of the hubs. The combination of high-end shops and subway access would make it ideal, if they could find a way to escape without getting stopped at the next station." I scanned the transcript again. LockBox had contracts with most of the high-end shops at several of the hubs, even some of the shops at the Oculus. "They could jack the truck, empty it out, and use one of the emergency evacuation plans to escape."

"Or one of the old tunnels that's no longer in use." He jerked his chin at my computer. "Any idea how much one of the LockBox trucks would have by the time they reached the end of the line?"

"It varies based on the day, but at least fifty, possibly seventy-five million."

"That has to be it. But how exactly would the killers cart it away?"

"I don't know. Maybe they would drop the locked boxes down one of the manhole covers and recover them later."

"If they pick the wrong manhole, it'd end up in the

- 241 -

sewers or washed out to sea," Brad said.

"Maybe that's why they wanted to speak to the station agent." Unfortunately, we didn't know if they had taken anything from her booth or if they'd gotten additional intel. "Unfortunately, this is nothing more than speculation. We have no proof. We have nothing, except loads of farfetched conjecture."

Brad shrugged. "On the bright side, that's not our problem. That's Voletek's."

THIRTY-TWO

"How long are we supposed to wait?" Diego asked. "She cut me. Eventually, the cops are going to connect me to the liquor store."

"You didn't murder her." Carter rocked back and forth on the edge of the double bed. "I did."

"I was there. It doesn't matter if I pulled the trigger or not, it's felony murder. And she's a cop. They won't care who killed her. They'll come for all of us." Diego turned to the third man. "We need to grab as much cash as we can and go. The longer we wait, the more likely it is they'll find us."

The third man hung the last uniform on a hanger and closed the closet door. "We wait as long as it takes. The news hasn't mentioned anything about it, which means the cops are still investigating. They probably don't have any idea what's going on. If they did, they'd be asking for people to call in tips or they'd already have your face plastered on every wanted poster in the state."

"I need a drink." Diego opened the mini fridge and

took out a bottle of bourbon. He wanted whiskey, but this would do for now. "Just tell me again when we're moving on the truck."

"We have to wait. It should arrive on schedule. So we stick to the schedule. Changing the play is what got us into trouble in the first place." The third man glared at his two accomplices. "If things had gone down the way they were supposed to, we wouldn't be in this predicament."

"That's not my fault," Carter said. "I had nothing to do with that."

The third man stormed toward him. "You keep saying that. It makes me think you got something to hide."

"I-I don't." Carter swallowed the bile that rose in his throat, but that wasn't enough. He got up and ran into the bathroom where he proceeded to heave.

"Jesus," the third man shook his head, "what is wrong with that guy? He needs to grow a pair."

"This isn't his life," Diego said. "He's not like us. We shouldn't have involved him."

"You're the one who said he could handle it. That he deserved to be a part of this."

Diego downed a shot. "Hey, man, if it weren't for him, we wouldn't have gotten any of that intel. We wouldn't have known about the night watchman or the uniforms or the trucks. His hard work is what got us to this point. He deserved to get a piece for providing us the intel."

"His intel is why we're in this fucking mess."

"Is this a mess? Or is this what you wanted all along?" Diego poured another shot and knocked it back. "Admit it, you got off on watching that cop bleed out."

"So? What's your point?"

"Do you even care about the cash? That's why I'm

doing this and why Carter agreed to go along with the plan. But you promised him no one would get hurt."

"And you knew that was bullshit from the start."

"Yeah, but," Diego shook his head, "you're enjoying it a bit too much."

"They deserve to pay. You know what they did to me. It's about time I get even."

*   *   *

"Liv?"

"Hmm?" I opened one eye, surprised to find Gunnie curled up in a ball on the couch beside me.

"I have to sleep there. I don't need a dog on my bed," Brad said.

I moved my arm from where it had been resting on top of the puppy and winced. "But he's the perfect size to keep the pressure off my shoulder and neck. Plus, it's my couch. You really should go home and get some sleep in an actual bed."

"Like you're doing?"

I sat up, and Gunnie let out a little grunt, wiggling his body backward to lie in the warm spot my shift in position created. "I wasn't sleeping. I was just resting my eyes."

"And drooling on my pillow."

"Sorry." I wiped the corner of my mouth and flipped the top pillow over to hide the evidence. "I'll get you a new pillowcase."

He waved his hand dismissively at it. "At least it was your drool and not the dog's."

"Did anything pan out on our theory?" I stared at the whiteboard, but Brad had flipped it back to the profiles. "What did Voletek say?"

"He and Lisco reached the same conclusion, but they don't have proof either. We have to ID these bastards. Until we know who they are, we have no way of knowing when or where they might strike."

"Or why." I sunk back onto the pillow and stared at the board. "Gravelly Voice made it sound personal. He wanted to hurt me because he'd been hurt."

"Do you think he's a victim of police brutality?"

"It's possible."

Brad sat on my coffee table and leaned forward, studying the board. "Blondie's the weak link. He's not a criminal. At least he wasn't before the team hooked up, or he's new and never worked with this crew before. Either way, Gravelly Voice doesn't trust him. He wouldn't have forced him to try to kill a cop if he did."

"If Roberts and Ainsley didn't arrive when they did, we probably wouldn't be having this conversation. That's what distracted Gravelly Voice, and then I fired off a shot and they bolted." I closed my eyes, seeing the blond-haired man stare at me. I'm sorry. I recognized that voice. I just couldn't place it. "Shit."

"What is it?"

Before I could answer, the phone rang.

"DNA analysis came back on one of the samples," Detective Lisco said when I answered. "Diego Eisner. Does the name mean anything to you?"

"Diego Eisner." I caught Brad's eye. "He attacked me?"

"It looks that way," she said. "The lab just got a hit off the blood we found on the broken wine bottle. He has a record. He served five years for armed robbery. He got paroled eighteen months ago. According to his PO, Diego appears to have been rehabilitated. Well, that was before he went on this high stakes crime spree."

"High risk, high reward," I said.

"Ain't that the truth." Lisco hesitated. "I just

thought you'd want to know."

"Yeah, thanks. Are you bringing him in?"

"Ink's drying now."

I went to the computer and typed in his name, narrowed my search to the city, and waited. "Great," I said absently. "Have you made any progress identifying the other two men?"

"Not yet. Voletek's hoping Diego will give up his accomplices for a deal. Since our boy's been through the system a few times, he ought to know how this works. I bet he'll talk with the proper incentive." She lowered her voice. "By the way, have you seen Fennel?"

"I'm looking right at him."

She let out a sigh. "Okay, good."

That caught my attention. "Why? What's wrong?"

"Nothing's wrong. I just wondered what he was up to. I wanted to make sure he was staying out of the investigation."

"Of course," I said. "We both are."

She chuckled. "Yeah, right. Just know, we'll handle this, DeMarco. If we need you, we'll call. And remember, that goes both ways. You remember something, make sure you let me know."

"Absolutely." I put down the phone to find Brad had already written Diego's full name on the board and had confiscated my computer to continue running a search. "They IDed one of them."

"I heard," Brad said, lost in the research. "Why was Lisco asking about me?"

"I'm not sure." I scooped his tablet off the table and brought up Diego Eisner's photo. I never would have been able to ID him with the Halloween mask, but he fit the bill.

He mumbled something under his breath. "I'm gonna make sure Lisco gave Mac the heads up. Is

Voletek bringing Diego in now?"

"Someone is," I said while Brad shot off a text. While I searched the internet and social media for Diego Eisner, it hit me. I realized why the blond man's voice was so familiar. "Shit. The bastard who nearly shot me . is Michael Tolliver's roommate. Carter something." My brows scrunched together while I concentrated on recalling his last name. "Moore. Carter Moore."

Brad started dialing before he even asked, "Are you sure?"

"Almost positive."

"That's good enough for me." He relayed the news while he paced in front of the board. "Yeah, you should bring him in too. Bring them all in. The roommate. Everyone. Scoop up the whole bachelor party if you have to." Brad disconnected and tapped the phone against his chin a few times. "What about Michael Tolliver? Was he there too? Is he the one with the gravelly voice?"

"No, Gravelly Voice has a bad knee. He's the one who must have been using the CBD and menthol. He probably kept an eye on Gardner. He's probably also the one who killed him."

"Tolliver doesn't have bad knees." Brad knelt down beside me, so I could see the computer screen. "Carter Moore." He checked the police database first. "He doesn't have a record. No priors. Nothing. Dammit."

"What?"

"They smoke pot."

"So does forty percent of the population or something like that." I didn't know the statistics, but it was common enough. But I saw where his mind had gone. "The dispensary."

"Assuming Carter Moore or Michael Tolliver obtained their stash legally, they could have gotten it from the dispensary that was targeted. And Tolliver works at Star Cleaners."

"You checked Tolliver's alibi. He's not involved."

"No, but his roommate is. We just don't know if Tolliver is assisting or if his roommate obtained the intel unintentionally. Even if Tolliver didn't tell Carter a damn thing about work or the security code or the uniforms, Carter could have overheard Tolliver talking to Gardner when they were playing video games. And if Gardner was talking to his buddies about work or bitching about guarding the dispensary, Carter could have gotten even more intel. And if that's where he went for his stash, he could have seen it firsthand." Brad keyed in another search.

We had requested a warrant to access the dispensary's records, but it never came through. The judge thought our request was nothing more than a fishing expedition, and given the nature of the shop, an attempt to harass people with medical conditions.

"We knocked right on their fucking door. That's how they knew we were on to them," I said. "That's why they panicked and moved on the dispensary even when the truck didn't show up. Shit. By following up on a lead, we tipped them off."

"That's what I said."

"Yeah, well, shit."

Brad climbed to his feet, automatically checking his belt for his gun and cuffs. I knew my partner. He wanted to make the arrest, except he was barred.

"Voletek will get him."

"Yeah." Brad paced back and forth, his hands tucked in his back pockets while he stared at the data on the board. "How did we miss this?"

"We checked. They alibied out. Wait," I sat up, forcing Gunnie to return to the floor, and grabbed the computer, "they alibied out. Carter Moore attended the bachelor party. It can't be him. I must be mistaken." But my gut said I wasn't. I searched Carter's social media page, finding him tagged in only two photos from the night in question. One of the photos was a group shot of the men when they first arrived, and it was taken in the parking lot. I knew it was early in the evening since everyone looked sober. The second photo was taken inside, but I didn't spot the girl from the cake. The cake came an hour after they arrived, though I wasn't clear why they needed a girl to pop out of a cake for a bachelor party, but that wasn't something I needed to waste my brain power on.

"Are these the only photos he's in?" Brad asked.

"I think so."

"Son of a bitch. He took them just to make it look like he had an alibi. He must have slipped away without anyone noticing."

"We have to be sure." I checked Michael Tolliver's photos and the ones his friends posted of the event. Apparently, the few who were concerned about getting in trouble with work or their spouses weren't tagged, but Michael had given us a list of names. None of them had records. And even the ones who weren't tagged popped up in dozens of photos.

"We never did a deep dive on Carter." Brad cursed. "I should have. I told you I'd check with the strip club." He dialed the rideshare driver he'd previously questioned and asked a dozen questions about the men. By now, I was certain the driver had forgotten most of the details, but when Brad hung up, I could see the answer on his face. "He doesn't remember driving a blond guy home."

"Carter's our guy. Well, one of them." I sucked in a breath. "He apologized at the apartment. I remember thinking it was weird, like he wanted to tell us something but couldn't. Do you remember that? I thought it was guilt over the weed and being high while we questioned him. I didn't realize there was more to it."

"Neither did I."

"Our cop instincts suck. What's worse is he apologized to me in the liquor store. He didn't want to kill me, but he didn't think he had a choice. If we can bring him in, I think we can flip him. Diego stayed cool and detached, but Carter was a mess. He'll break."

"That's why Gravelly Voice wanted him to pull the trigger. He needed him to commit such a heinous act that we wouldn't consider giving Carter a deal or would refuse to believe anything he said."

"Do you think that's why Carter attacked Officer Cruz? Because he was forced to?"

"Possibly, or because he thought it'd be better to knock out a cop than to kill one."

While we waited to hear back from the precinct, Brad and I searched every database and social media platform we could think of in order to find a connection between Diego Eisner and Carter Moore. But as far as I could tell, none existed.

Brad picked up his phone a few dozen times, blew into his fist, and stared at the board from his spot on my coffee table. I slumped back onto the pillows and reread his notations a hundred times. Since we weren't at work, Brad picked up Gunnie's tennis ball and tossed it in the air.

Immediately, the puppy sat up from where he'd been lying on the floor next to me and watched the ball sail toward the ceiling. Two tosses later, he went over to Brad and wagged his tail.

"Sorry, buddy." Brad gently tossed the ball down the hall, and Gunnie chased after it, returning a few seconds later. He dropped it at Brad's feet, and my partner tossed it again.

I turned the computer back on, typing with one hand so I wouldn't have to get up. Carter didn't have much of a social media presence. Then again, neither did Diego. "Did Mac tell you how long it'd take for her to do a deep dive?"

"She said she'd get right on it and let us know, unless Lisco or the LT intercepts her first."

"She'll still call you back." I tapped my finger against the side of the laptop. "What if we cross-reference Diego and Carter with Moonlight Security and LockBox. We might find something."

"I doubt it. We know Carter's name didn't pop when we checked, and Diego has a record. They don't hire felons, remember?"

"Right." I tried to think of another way to figure out why these men committed these crimes and who their ringleader could be. "What about an address search?" I opened a tab and brought up the map. Then I entered Diego's home and work address into it. I repeated the process with Carter's apartment number and the addresses for his two jobs. They had to intersect somewhere, but where?

"Find something I missed?"

"Nope." I rubbed my eyes, glad that the yellowish-green bruises no longer hurt. "But Carter and Diego have to link together."

"Not necessarily. Gravelly Voice could be the connection. Diego and Carter might not have anything in common."

"Then why wouldn't Gravelly Voice trust Carter?" I asked.

Brad tossed the tennis ball again. "I don't know." But his mind was elsewhere. "We found two blood samples in the liquor store that didn't match you. One has to be Diego. He's the one you hit with the bottle."

"I'm not following."

"The other sample was beside the broken glass door to the cooler. That would make it...?"

"Carter's blood, I think. It happened so fast, but it must have been him." So much of it was a blur, probably from the adrenaline, the injury, and the lack of proper lighting.

"That doesn't help us ID the ringleader." Brad went to the board. "You're sure our unsub disarmed the security system? It wasn't Carter or Diego who did it?"

"No, it's the unknown third party. When I told him to put his hands on his head and get on the ground, that's when I found out he had a bad knee. We've been over this. He wore that stupid Halloween mask and gloves. I cuffed him, but he got out of them somehow."

"And you're certain he wasn't armed?"

"I patted him down. I didn't find a gun. But he had one, after he got the cuffs off. Well, two, but it's possible he got the second one from Diego."

"And you're positive the guy you cuffed and the one who wanted Carter to shoot you is the same man?"

"Same voice. Same build. It has to be the same man." I glared at Brad's back. "What? You think there's four of them now?"

"No, but I think he's done this before. He knows how it goes. He's more likely to get shot if he's holding a gun when you approach him. He knows if you found a weapon on him during the pat down, you'd confiscate it. And he knew damn well you'd restrain him with your cuffs." Brad glanced at me. "I'm surprised you had them with you. I thought you weren't expecting trouble."

"Dad taught me to be prepared."

"But the unsub didn't expect to encounter you. He

expected to run into officers who just finished working graveyard. They would still have their gear, unless they left it in their lockers."

"Okay, so?"

"So he knew if he was restrained it would be with actual cuffs, not zip ties. I think he had a handcuff key. Or one of his friends did." Brad turned back to the board. "This isn't the unsub's first rodeo. Based on the store layout and what you said about him studying the shelves, he could have hidden the gun anywhere, waited for the lights to go out and for you to be distracted, and then he retrieved it."

"Okay, Tex."

"I'm serious, Liv. Whoever this guy is, he must have a record. The crap he was sputtering, that would explain it. At least some of it." He reached for his tablet. "The worst part about this is no one we've investigated has a record. LockBox, Moonlight, and Star Cleaners refuse to hire felons."

"The same's true of the dispensary. So where did this guy come from, and how did these three cross paths and end up deciding on these targets?"

"Those are good questions. We should ask these bastards that as soon as they're brought in." Brad checked the time again. "Voletek should have called by now. How long does it take to get an arrest warrant signed?"

"It's not just the warrant." But the wait seemed interminable to me too. "They have to find Diego and Carter, bring them in, and book them. That takes time."

I pulled up everything we had on Carter Moore. His family history didn't show much. His parents were divorced. No reports of abuse or neglect. He graduated high school, went on to get his associate's degree from the city college, and then he worked at various retail and fast food places. Currently, he had two jobs. One at a bookstore and the other at a supermarket. He could have crossed paths with the other two men in his crew at any time or place. But I had no idea where or when it might have happened or even why.

"I hate this," Brad said. "Maybe I should head to the precinct to see what's going on." He crossed to the window to make sure the patrol units were stationed outside. But before he could make up his mind, the phone rang.

THIRTY-THREE

"We can't find them," Voletek said.

Brad circled, glaring at his phone. He clenched his fists, fighting to control himself. "What do you mean you can't find them?"

"Diego's gone. His apartment's the size of a closet. He cleared it out. We checked at the mattress factory where he works, but no one's seen him since he finished his shift on Friday. He didn't call in sick or request time off. He just didn't show up," Voletek said.

"What about pinging his phone?" I asked.

"It's off. We're monitoring it, in the event he turns it back on."

"What about the GPS in his car? If he has one of those roadside assistance things, we might be able to track it," Brad said.

"Sorry, man. Diego doesn't own a car. We flagged his credit cards, so if he buys something, we'll be able to swoop in and pick him up. In the meantime, I'll go through his financials to determine where he hangs out. Then we'll ask around. Someone has to know something." Voletek sighed. "Liv, are you listening?"

"Yeah, Jake, I'm here."

"We're gonna get them. I promise."

"What about Carter Moore?" Brad asked. "Any leads on his whereabouts?"

"Michael Tolliver said Carter left before he got up this morning. We went by his work, but he wasn't there. According to his boss, he wasn't on the schedule for today."

"He has two jobs," I said. "The supermarket and the bookstore."

"Right, I know. He wasn't scheduled to work at either one. His boss at the bookstore said Carter was acting weird last week. Sweaty, pale, vomiting, so he sent him home last Thursday and told him to take a few days off to get better."

"Thursday, that's the day before Jonathan Gardner was killed." I looked at Brad. "Carter knew what was going to happen. He must have gone to Star Cleaners that night. If he was that messed up about it, why didn't he call in a tip?"

"You have an awful lot of faith in someone who left you to bleed out on the floor, who nearly blew your brains all over the place." Brad stared out the window, his cheek twitching.

"Michael said Carter's supposed to pick up dinner for them tonight. If he doesn't show by seven, we'll have his roommate reach out and leave a voicemail. Until we know what's what, we'll keep Michael Tolliver on ice in case he's involved." Voletek sighed. "He looks clean. Patrol is bringing in the rest of the bachelor party for questioning. We'll hold everyone as long as we can. You already spoke to them, didn't you?"

"Yeah," Brad said. "But we didn't know enough at the time. Liv might need to hear their voices. She could ID the ringleader that way."

"Do you want me to come in?" I asked.

"No," Voletek said, "I'll make sure something gets recorded. Right now, just focus on getting better. The LT authorized us to stay on this, so I won't be dropping by tonight. But I will call if something pops."

"You better." Brad disconnected and let out a frustrated growl. "I can't believe Voletek's not doing more to get Carter."

"Wasn't that a movie?"

Brad stopped what he was doing and eyed me over the laptop lid. "Not the time, DeMarco." He put my computer down. "They should be combing the streets."

"They will."

"Fuck." His outburst scared Gunnie, who crawled beneath the coffee table. "If they've gone to ground, we might not find them."

"They can't leave. They haven't made a big enough score." Even though I said it, I didn't know if it was true.

"Yeah, well, if Voletek can't find them, I will."

I didn't want to know what he meant by that. "Let's get back to building a profile. There might be something in Diego's history that would indicate where he'd go."

"He's got a sheet. Two counts of armed robbery. But there's a notation about a stint in juvie. His juvenile record was probably sealed since I'm not seeing many details. The first time he got tried as an adult, he pled and got some kind of sweetheart deal. The last time he did this, he served time. But he's been out a year and a half. As far as we know, he's been keeping his nose clean. He's holding down a job in a mattress factory. So what changed?"

I ran through the usual possibilities, but as far as

we could tell, none of them applied to Diego. "And he's never been violent before?"

"Just threatened violence, but never resorted to it." Brad read the details on Diego's previous convictions. "He never had a crew before either. It was just him." He snorted. "Turns out he knocked over a liquor store."

"24/7 Spirits?" I asked.

"No."

I went to the map. "So what's Diego's deal with 24/7 Spirits?"

"If he takes the bus home from work, he would pass 24/7 Spirits," Brad said.

"So that could be his liquor store of choice, depending on the nearest bus stop."

"There's one half a block from that liquor store to the northeast." Brad read off the cross streets.

Just as I moved closer to the door to mark it, a knock sounded from the other side. I jumped back, a yelp escaping from my lips.

"Liv, get back." Brad came up beside me. He palmed his gun and approached the side of the door. The knock sounded again. "Who is it?" Brad gestured for me to get into cover.

"It's Logan." The ADA waited a moment. "C'mon, Fennel, open the damn door. We have an appointment. You can't skip out on me again."

Cautiously, Brad opened the door. Logan Winters stood on the other side with his messenger bag slung across his chest, the files practically spilling out. The officer in the hallway gave Brad a nod. "All right, counselor, I guess I can let you inside."

Logan entered, spotting me immediately. "Hey, I'm sorry to barge in on you. How are you feeling? You look good."

"I look bruised and tired."

"But you still look good." Logan pointed to the gift basket. "I'm glad you got it."

"I meant to call and thank you."

"Don't even worry about it. I'm just glad you're okay." He turned, seeing the mess Brad and I had made out of my living room. "What's going on? Did I interrupt something?"

"Nothing," I said.

Gunnie snuck up behind Logan and let out a high-pitched bark, causing the ADA to jump. It served him right for startling me, and I couldn't help but laugh. The puppy had my back.

Logan knelt down. "Who's this guy?"

"That's Gunnie. I'm dogsitting until my parents get back from vacation."

Logan ruffled the dog's ears and stood up. "Captain DeMarco doesn't know what happened yet?"

"No," I glanced at Brad, who busied himself with clearing off the coffee table, "I don't think they have cell service, and once they get it, I hate to think how he and my mom are going to react."

"Parents will be parents." Logan shrugged. "At least you're okay."

"Yeah."

He watched my partner push the board into the corner of the room. "Where should we set up?"

"Right here's fine." Brad pointed to the coffee table.

Logan put his bag on the floor and took out the files. While he did that, I returned to the map. Based on the bus schedule, Diego could have gotten off the bus, bought whatever, and caught the next bus when it arrived twenty minutes later.

"I'm gonna call Voletek and have him pass along a few questions to ask the liquor store owner. If Diego was a regular, the owner might know him," I said.

"That's assuming he feels like cooperating," Brad

said.

I bit my lip and stared at the map. "Even if he doesn't, Lisco and Voletek are running Diego's financials. If he ever paid with plastic, we'll find the charges and place him inside."

"We don't need to place him at the liquor store, Liv," Brad reminded me. "We already have DNA evidence. He was there. He attacked you. He can refute it all he wants, but we got him. We just have to find him and ID the third guy."

THIRTY-FOUR

"Hold still, Liv." Emma disinfected the area around my stitches, causing me to hiss, then she taped the plastic over them. "There." She made sure the plastic on my shoulder was in place and gave the exposed cuts on my hands and arms a cursory look. "Those aren't severe enough to worry about. Just make sure you keep them clean. We should probably bandage them up again once you're dry, just so your clothes or sheets don't rub off the scabs."

"Yeah, okay. Whatever." Now everything stung and throbbed.

"Hey, are you all right?"

"Not really." I saw the concerned look on my friend's face. "We're getting close, but not close enough."

"Does that have anything to do with why the assistant district attorney is in your living room?"

"No, that's for a different case. I was supposed to be testifying in court this week."

"Don't tell me you still have to go?" Emma turned

around to face the door, and I slipped out of my clothes and stepped into the shower.

Once I pulled the curtain closed, I said, "No, but Brad does."

"And soldier boy couldn't have gone over these details somewhere else?"

"He's staying close."

"Why?"

I didn't say anything, hoping she'd think I didn't hear her question over the running water. After much pain and cursing that came with trying to shampoo my hair with only one hand, I rinsed off as best I could, wrapped a towel around me, and stepped out of the shower. She checked my stitches to make sure nothing got wet that wasn't supposed to and then took the hairdryer into my bedroom. Once I was dressed, I joined her.

"So that's Logan?" She patted a spot on the bed, and I eased onto it. "He's not what I pictured."

"What did you picture?"

She turned the hairdryer on low and took the brush from my hand. "I'm not sure. Maybe one of those ambulance chasers we see on the backs of buses or doing those cheesy TV commercials late at night. You know the ones with the bald guys wearing ill-fitting suits or young, thin, pimply guys with oversized glasses and bad hair."

"Em, I never described him like that."

"You never described his looks at all." She pulled the brush through my hair, and I gasped when it came in contact with my injured shoulder. The constant stinging turned into white-hot pain. She cringed. "Sorry." She shifted the way she brushed from straight down to sweeping my hair toward the left.

"Stop, Em." Even that slight motion pulled at my neck, and my eyes watered. It felt like I'd just been stabbed, and for a moment, I was back in the liquor store, on the floor, staring up at the ceiling, choking on my own blood, and struggling to breathe.

Immediately, she turned off the hairdryer and dropped the brush. "Liv?" She checked the wounds, but the stitches remained intact. I trembled, and she gently ran a hand up and down my spine. "Talk to me. Are you okay? Can you breathe?"

I swallowed, nodding.

"You're shaking."

"I'm okay." I took a few deep breaths. "It just pulled, and that didn't feel so good." But I could see it in Emma's eyes that she didn't believe that was the entire story. "By the way, you're fired as my hairdresser."

"I never wanted the job anyway."

"Good."

"Do I still get a tip?" she teased as she grabbed her bag from my dresser and came back with fresh bandages and medical tape.

"Nope, and I'm not paying for the service either. If this was any other establishment, I'd ask to speak to the manager." I winked at her, hiding my discomfort behind a few jokes.

"You should come back to the house tonight. Brad and Logan have turned this place into a man-cave. Have you seen the whiteboard they put in the living room or the stuff they taped on the door?"

"Yeah."

"Do they really need all of that for court?"

"I guess they're practicing going over the exhibits," I said, hoping she wouldn't realize I was lying. I'd spent years perfecting the skill undercover, but Emma was practically my sister. We'd been inseparable since age sixteen. But my answer satisfied her. "Plus, I have two patrol units monitoring the apartment. They already did a perimeter check. They're used to my neighbors. I don't want to complicate matters for them."

"Then why don't you tell Brad to go home and I'll stay here with the guard pup?" She jerked her chin toward Gunnie, who'd fallen asleep in my laundry basket after his dinner and walk.

"Brad can go home anytime he wants. I didn't ask him to stay."

"But he's staying anyway."

"He's my partner."

"Right." Emma looked skeptical. "What does his girlfriend think about this?"

"Carrie's not his girlfriend."

"Well, what does his friend with benefits think about this?"

"There's nothing to think about. He's watching my back."

"From where I'm sitting, he needs to do a better job."

I sighed, and Emma gave me a hug. "Don't forget to take your antibiotics before bed. I brought over another bottle of OTC painkillers in case you're running low. Just try to take it easy on them. They come with risks too."

"I know."

"Have you heard from your parents?"

"Not yet. At first, I was relieved, but now I'm a little worried. Is that weird?"

"I'll admit it's strange not talking to your mom every day. But I don't think you have reason to worry. They're across the world on a cruise ship in the middle of the ocean."

"Those sound like reasons to worry."

"Don't. I'm sure you're right about their cell phones. You know they'd have knocked down your door by now if they'd heard what had happened. And if something happened on the cruise, it'd be all over the news. They're fine. Just out of cell range. Enjoy the reprieve while it lasts."

"Yeah, I'll try."

She scooted Gunnie out of the laundry basket and clipped on his leash, making an exaggerated grunt as she pulled him toward the door. She poked her head into the living room. "Good night, Mr. Assistant District Attorney."

Logan turned to her. "It's Logan. And it was nice meeting you."

She nodded at him before turning the evil eye on my partner. "The emergency contacts are on the fridge. You know what to do in case of anything."

"Yes, ma'am," Brad said. "You're off tomorrow, right? So you can stay with Liv."

"Yep."

"Okay," Brad said. "Night, Emma."

"Night."

I opened the door and waved goodbye to Emma and Gunnie while one of the two officers out front offered to help her to her car. She turned back to me. "Now that's what I call serving and protecting."

Returning to the living room, I took a seat on the end of the sofa and leaned against the stacked pillows. "All right, what did you want me to go over with you?" I asked.

Logan handed me a copy of my sworn statement. "Since I can't exactly ask you about any of this in front of the jury, I'll be asking your partner about it. So I just want to make sure I have everything down." He glanced at Fennel. "Would you mind giving us a few minutes? I don't want to risk tainting your testimony."

"Not a problem. I need to make some calls anyway." Brad went into my bedroom and closed the door.

"Do I want to know what's going on?" Logan pointed the end of his pen at the whiteboard hidden in the corner. "The police department has certain policies for a reason. Since you're the daughter of a decorated police captain, you're well aware what those reasons are."

"We're not doing anything."

Logan snorted. "I don't blame you. These guys killed six people. They attacked another cop. They hurt you. I get it. Believe me, I do. And as soon as the police department brings my office a strong case, we will file every charge that'll stick and make sure these guys pay for what they've done. That being said, whatever you and Fennel are doing is only going to hurt that."

"We're not doing anything."

"Who took over the case?"

"Lisco and Voletek."

Logan thought for a few moments. "It'll be airtight. They do good work. Trust them to handle this."

I held up my palms. "Yeah, no problem."

Fifteen minutes later, Logan finished asking me the same things we'd gone over Friday night. Then he packed up his belongings, wished me well, and told Brad he'd see him at the courthouse tomorrow at ten. After he drove away, I went into the kitchen and reached for the prescription pill bottles.

"What did Voletek say?" I asked.

Brad took a seat at the table. "They're still looking."

"We need to ID the man with the gravelly voice." I swallowed the antibiotics and peeled a banana while eyeing the prescription painkillers. Whatever Emma had done to clean my wounds made me want to crawl out of my skin, and the incident with the brush hadn't helped matters. But I left the pills on the counter and reached for the alternative instead. I swallowed two of those, ignoring the concern in Brad's eyes. He always knew when something was wrong with me. "Before Logan showed up, I thought we were on to something."

"Then let's retrace our steps and figure out what that was."

THIRTY-FIVE

"We need access to prison records," I said. "Diego and the third man might have served time together."

"Well, we're not going to find out tonight." Brad rubbed his eyes. "It's late. You need to sleep. And so do I. After court tomorrow, I'll drop by the precinct and see what kind of progress has been made." He blew out a breath. "Surveillance vans are sitting on every known location we have for Diego and Carter, but neither has surfaced. Voletek thinks they must be together, probably with their third."

"Unless they disappeared. Did their photos and identities go out?"

"They haven't been made public yet. The brass thinks that will force them to act. Voletek didn't go into the details, but he and Lisco tore apart our suspects' apartments. I'm guessing they found something related to their next target. The units outside told me officers were called back to work to guard the metro plazas. It looks like our assumption was correct."

"Do we know the timetable for their next strike?"

"Not that I'm aware. Voletek said he'd keep us looped in, but he's doing a crappy job. But that will be tomorrow's problem. You have enough to deal with tonight." Brad held out a hand to help me off the couch. "Do you wanna tell me what's wrong?"

"Nothing a little sleep can't fix." I turned in the doorway to the bedroom, watching Brad make his bed and position his firearm. "You are allowed to go home, you know."

He snorted, settling onto his makeshift bed. "Really, Liv? You want me to drive home at this time of night when there are all sorts of lunatics and drunks out there? That doesn't seem particularly safe."

"I think you'll be okay."

"I can't take any chances. I'm key to Logan's case. Without me, it might fall apart. It's best I stay here where you can protect me."

"Wiseass. And for the record, I don't need protecting."

"I never said you did. But I might."

For the next few hours I twisted and turned, hoping to find a position that didn't result in sharp, stabbing pain. Eventually, I gave up and tried to ignore it. But that didn't work either. When I realized my teeth were clenched and my muscles were tensed, I shifted again, letting out a frustrated whine. I wondered if this was why babies cried when they couldn't sleep, minus the stitches.

I forced my jaw to go slack. But I couldn't get my body to relax. I turned again, going back to three pillows instead of two, but that only made it worse. I slid the third pillow beneath my shoulder, but that didn't help. I got rid of all but one pillow and tried to lie on my stomach, but that hurt almost as much as lying on my back.

"Liv," Brad stood in the doorway with my pill bottle and a glass of water, "I don't care what Emma says. You're on sick leave, you have a prescription, and if it causes some kind of problem at work, I'm sure your dad knows a good FOP rep you can talk to. But you're going to take one of these, or I'm gonna end up downing the entire bottle. I can't take seeing you in pain."

"Don't say things like that."

"It was a joke."

"A bad one."

He moved to my bedside and turned on the lamp. He read the directions and checked the time. "It's been six hours since you took that other crap. It should be fine." He shook one tablet into his hand and held it out. "You seemed better earlier. What happened?"

"An unfortunate incident with the hairbrush." I swallowed the pill and put the water on my nightstand. "I just can't get comfortable."

"I noticed." He eyed the mess I'd made. "The problem is you're not at the right angle."

"Well, Gunnie went home with Emma."

"Let me see what I can do." He rearranged the pillows a few times. "Unfortunately, I have some experience with this. You have to keep the injury in a neutral position, which is complicated since you were cut from behind your ear down to your shoulder blade." He eyed the pillows, annoyed that they wouldn't cooperate. "Do you want to try sleeping like a horse?"

"How do they sleep?"

"Standing up."

"Ha ha."

"How is it you've been sleeping just fine these last

few days?" Brad asked.

"I haven't, but I've been too tired to care." And I was way too tired to be having this conversation. The only thing I wanted was for it to stop hurting long enough so I could go to sleep. "Damn."

"What?"

"I just realized what you meant when you said you just wanted it all to stop." But that hadn't been physical torment; that had been emotional.

"Hey." Brad sat on the bed beside me. "That was one bad night and one mistake I don't plan on repeating. Jokes aside, I'm not going to swallow a bottle of pills or drink my way to the bottom of a bottle. Well, not a brand new bottle. Lesson learned." He brushed my hair to the side and made sure I wasn't bleeding through the bandages. "Do you want to lie on the couch? Do you think that'll help?"

"You just want the bed."

"Is that an invitation?" He slid in beside me. "You need a recliner. It'd probably give you the proper angle to sleep."

"Oh god, do not order furniture. I don't want to wake up to find more crap in my living room."

He maneuvered around me, taking a pillow and propping it against his chest. "Then pretend I'm a piece of furniture."

"Brad," I protested.

"Just give it a try. I can't make up for what happened, but I want to do something to make this better."

"It's not your fault. It's theirs. You know that."

"It doesn't matter. I should have been there. If you still worked undercover, I would have made sure to keep my phone close. This transfer was supposed to keep you out of harm's way. But I royally screwed up. I promise it'll never happen again."

"You can't blame yourself. I called late. You were probably asleep."

"I was with Carrie."

I nudged him playfully in the ribs. "Twice in two days. I thought you had a rule about that."

"We broke it off, so we thought we'd take the weekend and end things on a high note."

I pulled away, stunned. "What happened?"

"Lie down, Liv." He stroked the bandage wrapped around my hand. "She met someone else and wants to give it a real shot."

"I'm sorry."

"Don't be. I knew what it was. We were just having fun. I was a placeholder or a seat warmer."

"Bad metaphor."

"That's not how I meant it." The deep velvety chuckle washed over me, and I realized that was my favorite sound in the entire world. "But that's why I didn't hear your call, why I didn't hang out with you that night." He licked his lips. "I should have been with you instead."

"Don't be ridiculous. You're entitled to a life outside of work."

"It's complicated. You know that." He adjusted so he could look at me. "But there's nowhere else I'd rather be than with you. On duty or off, it doesn't matter. I won't make that mistake again." He ran a hand gently against my cheek. "We should get some sleep. I have to be sharp for court tomorrow. Are you feeling any better yet?"

I nodded, unsure what to say. After a few minutes, the pills kicked in enough to take the edge off, and I found a comfortable position. For the next few hours there was nothing but blissful oblivion, which ended too quickly when Brad's alarm clock went off.

THIRTY-SIX

Emma looked up from her spot at the table. "You don't look so good, Liv. Come, sit down. Do you have a headache?"

"I don't know."

"What do you mean you don't know?" She pressed the back of her hand against my forehead, biting her lip and frowning.

"Em," I shrugged away from her, "I'm fine."

But she didn't believe me and checked my vitals. "Well, you appear to be okay."

"That's what I said." I put my head in my hands. "I didn't sleep well." I turned to find Brad manning the stove. "How'd you sleep?"

"Better than I should have." He turned to face me. "Does your neck still hurt?"

"It's not great."

"Shoulder too?" he asked.

"I'll be okay."

Emma washed her hands and removed the bandage at my neck. "It looks like everything's healing. The internal stitches should melt away in a few more days." She turned to Brad. "You don't look so good either. What did you two do after I left? I thought you were going to make sure Liv took it easy. I hope you didn't have her up all night working on some stupid case. She's supposed to be resting, Bradley."

"Em," I warned, "leave him alone."

Brad gripped the counter, internally debating with himself for a moment before speaking. "I'm not the reason she looks like that. I didn't aggravate Liv's injury and guilt-trip her into not taking her medicine. But I guess that's okay since you don't have to listen to her groan and whimper all night."

"Liv, what's he talking about?"

"Nothing."

Emma swallowed. "The hairbrush. Shit. I thought you said you were okay."

"I guess not."

Emma examined the wounds again. "I'm sorry, Liv. This never should have happened."

Brad's cheek twitched, and he turned back to the stove. This was eating him up inside, and no matter what I said, it wouldn't make a damn bit of difference. He knew the truth, but until the bastards were in custody, my partner would continue to blame himself.

Emma replaced that bandage with a fresh one. "On a scale of one to ten, what's your pain level?"

"I don't know. A five."

She gave me a look. "Which would translate to an eight." She reached for the prescription bottle. "Take these as directed. Less if you can handle it, but only if you can handle it." She gave Brad a look. "Happy?"

"Nope." He finished making breakfast burritos, rolled them up, and put them on plates. He put one down in front of me and the other in front of Emma. He wrapped a napkin around his. "I gotta get ready for court. I'll be back tonight. If anything pops up, Voletek knows to call you. I'll try to get a progress report and see what I can find out."

"Okay." I gave him an encouraging smile. "Have fun testifying."

He snorted. "Yeah, right."

He disappeared out the front door, and I locked it behind him. I stared at the maps taped to the back of my door for a moment, wondering when these killers would strike again. Ballistics indicated two shooters. That meant we had two killers. Diego Eisner and Gravelly Voice. Up until now, I believed Carter Moore hadn't killed anyone, but that would change. The ringleader would make sure of it. Their next hit would come with a body count. They might plan a perfect escape, but they weren't planning a perfect crime. The man in charge liked to kill. He proved it with Jonathan Gardner, and based on the message he wrote in my blood, he now wanted to kill cops.

When I didn't return to the table, Emma stepped into the hallway. "Liv, I didn't know. You could have called me last night or made a run to the hospital to get things checked out. If I'd known you were in that much pain—"

"Don't worry about it." I took the maps off the door and spread them out on the coffee table. I didn't tell Emma what I was doing and left the whiteboard turned to the profiles so she wouldn't realize what case I was working on. As far as she knew, these were the facts Logan had wanted Brad to expound on for court today. "You didn't mean to hurt me." But someone did. And I had to do everything in my power to make sure he didn't hurt or kill someone else.

"You need to eat, especially with those pills." She brought my plate into the living room. "How much sleep did you get last night?"

"Not enough, but I can't lie down right now. It helps to focus on something else."

"What are you focusing on? What is this?" She sat down on the couch, and Gunnie jumped up beside her.

"It's a clusterfuck of a case." I reached for the burrito and took a bite. It'd be next to impossible to work with Emma watching my every move, but I knew they'd strike soon. It'd been too long. They stole the police uniforms for a reason. The last time they stole a uniform, they used it the next morning. They weren't going to wait on this. "Do you mind turning on the TV?"

She searched for the remote while I finished breakfast. "What channel?"

"Flip through the locals. I want to see if there's any news."

She stopped on the tail-end of a local morning show, getting distracted by a cooking demonstration. That worked for me. While she and Gunnie watched a woman whisk eggs and chop chives, I sat down at the end of the couch and turned on my computer.

Diego Eisner, I typed his name into the corrections database. Once I had his prisoner number and release date, I grabbed my phone and sent a text to Mac. She called me a few minutes later.

"Hey, Liv, how are you feeling?"

"Okay. Where do we stand?" I asked while Emma watched me out of the corner of her eye. "Any progress on that pet project?"

"I haven't come up with anything. The guys in homicide have been breathing down my neck for answers. The deep dive on Carter Moore didn't turn up anything. He hasn't turned his phone back on. The phone company gave us access to his records, but I haven't found anything in his texts or calls."

"No calls from unregistered numbers or burners?" I asked.

"No. The only people who call him are work, family, or his roommate."

"Nothing else?"

"A few telemarketers, but I ran them too. I got a list of everyone who played video games with your first vic and Michael Tolliver. We ran through them and cross-referenced them to our persons of interest but nothing popped." She lowered her voice. "Detective Voletek thinks Carter hooked up with the crew in the real world and they only communicate in person."

"But we believe Carter gained info on Star Cleaners from listening to his roommate and Gardner play video games. Has that changed? Did Tolliver say anything?"

"As far as I know, that's still the working theory. Tolliver's been nothing but cooperative. He's had an alibi for three of the crimes."

"What about our other suspect?"

"Diego Eisner?"

"Yeah, unless you got a third ID."

"Sorry."

"Okay, so tell me about Diego."

"I really shouldn't."

That meant there was something to tell. "Why not?" I reached for my glass and drained it, so I'd have an excuse to go into the kitchen. Once I was out of Emma's earshot, I said, "I know he has a sheet. He served time for armed robbery. More than likely, he's one of the two shooters. We think he must have hooked up with the ringleader while in prison, but we're not sure. I haven't been able to get a look at his prison records. Brad said he had a juvie record that was sealed. Do you know if anything's in the works to get that unsealed?"

"Voletek's working on that. We should know more soon."

"But you already know, don't you?" Before Mac came to work at the PD, she'd been a hacker and a damn good one.

"He used to run with a crew during his misspent youth. From what I've found, most of them are dead or incarcerated. Two are still alive and walking free."

"Names?"

She hesitated. "You can't touch this, Liv. I don't want to tempt you."

"Is there something worth touching?"

"If there is, promise me you'll let Voletek touch it."

"Fine, but make sure you warn Jake that afterward he might have to go through sensitivity training or face sexual harassment charges."

She laughed. "Will do." She lowered her voice "Aubrey Shaw and Mitchell Blake."

"Well, Aubrey's out, assuming she's a she. What about Mitchell?"

"He teaches sixth grade math. No known criminal activity since reaching adulthood. But I'm sure Voletek will follow up with both of them once he officially gets their names."

"Anything else I should know?"

"You shouldn't even know this."

"Do we know when the crew might strike again or what their target is?"

"Lisco found marked subway maps in Diego's apartment, along with a map that had the LockBox pickup routes marked. She assumed he obtained that information from the driver they killed."

"Most likely."

"Only one route corresponded to the markings we found on the map of the subway system. We can't be certain, but we think that's the target."

From what I recalled, LockBox altered its routes every day. "When's LockBox supposed to run that route?"

"Tomorrow night."

THIRTY-SEVEN

The sound of knocking drew my attention away from the computer screen. I blinked a few times to clear my blurry vision and stood up. My vision clouded even more, and I grabbed the arm of the couch and waited for it to clear.

"Liv, sit down. I got this." Emma shooed Gunnie away from the front door and peered through the peephole.

"Who is it?" I asked.

"A cop with a gift basket." She unlocked the door.

"Hey, DeMarco," a member of the protection detail said, "we intercepted this suspicious looking package. It was delivered to your desk at the precinct. Someone's got expensive taste." He glanced into my apartment. "Where do you want it?"

"I'll take it." Emma held out her hands.

"It's heavy."

"Just put it on the chair, Frank." I pointed to the spot beside the front door. "Hey, do you guys want some coffee and muffins?"

"That'd be great."

"Help yourself to the stack of pastry boxes. They came yesterday, so they might be a little stale."

"I'm sure they're fine, just as long as the coffee's fresh."

"It's from this morning." I turned to Emma. "Can you fill up that big thermos with whatever's left in the pot?"

"No problem." She smiled at Frank while he stuffed one of the mini muffins into his mouth and knelt down to pet Gunnie who'd been sniffing his shoe.

"How you doing, DeMarco? You staying out of trouble?"

"Nope," I said.

He laughed. "Just like your old man."

Emma returned with the thermos. He tucked it under his arm and grabbed the pastry boxes. "When you guys need a refill, just bring back the thermos," Emma said.

"Thanks, ladies. I appreciate it."

Emma locked the door and poked around at the newest gift basket. "Who's sending you expensive chocolates, cognac, and a get well bouquet?"

At the mention of chocolates and cognac, my stomach dropped. Brad should have finished in court a few hours ago, but I hadn't heard from him. I thought it was strange but figured he was bogged down at the precinct or went home to get some sleep. "Is there a card?" If my partner did what I think he did, I'd kill him.

Emma sifted through the packaging, removing the two boxes of gourmet artisan chocolate and the $200 bottle of liquor. Then she lifted the flower arrangement out of the basket. Bright blue, purple, and white flowers spread in every direction. She put the crystal vase on the table and handed me the card.

I would have hand-delivered it but figured you'd have me arrested. I know how much you enjoy doing that. Feel better, Detective.

"Who sent it?" Emma studied the chocolates before picking up the cognac. "Do you have a lover I don't know about?"

"Axel Kincaid." I put the card down and reached for my phone.

"The nightclub owner?"

"Uh-huh." I drummed my fingers against the table. "You better answer your damn phone, Fennel."

"How do you know him?"

"I arrested him."

She gave me a look. "Okay, so why is he sending you a gift basket?"

"That's what I'd like to know." On the third ring, Brad picked up. "What did you do?"

"Liv, is everything okay?" Brad asked.

"You tell me. I just got a get well gift from Axel Kincaid."

"Huh, that's weird." Brad ignored my accusatory tone. "Look, I gotta jump off here. Jake and I are in the middle of something. He thinks the crew's set to move on their next target tomorrow night. So we need to focus on this, but I should be back in a couple of hours. We can talk then."

I stared at the end call message and let out a frustrated growl.

Emma held out the box. "Chocolate?"

"Ugh."

She lifted the lid, stopping momentarily to eye me. "You don't think these are poisoned, do you?"

"No, if Axel wanted me dead, he'd shoot me. He wouldn't send a three hundred dollar gift basket just to get rid of me."

"More like five." Emma picked up one of the dark

chocolate pieces and took a bite.

"I thought you were opposed to processed sugar."

"It's organic. Soy and dairy free." She cocked an eyebrow. "For someone you arrested, he seems to know a lot about you. Isn't that dangerous?"

"Yes, but that's what happens when you spend six months undercover to make a bust and it turns out he's been flipped by the Feds."

"So he's a CI?"

"I don't know what he is. But he's untouchable, at least for now." I glanced at the basket. He didn't even sign his name. And since the protection detail accepted the delivery, I couldn't refuse it. "This better not be construed as a bribe." I just wondered what deal my partner had made with the devil.

THIRTY-EIGHT

I jerked upright, regretting the movement instantly. My computer had gone into sleep mode, just like I had. I rubbed the grit from my eyes. Falling asleep while researching Diego Eisner's associates shouldn't have happened. I glanced at the pill bottle. This was why I wasn't supposed to operate heavy machinery. Thankfully, my computer only weighed a couple of pounds.

Closing the lid, I turned my attention to the figure across the room. Brad quietly tapped away at his tablet while updating the notes on our whiteboard. He put the tablet down and puffed out his cheeks while he stared at our progress.

"Where's Emma?" I asked.

He turned, offering me a choir boy smile. "She took Gunnie out for a walk." He grabbed a gift bag from the floor and held it out to me. "I got you something."

"Brad—"

"Open it." He moved closer, waiting for me to pull the stuffed animal out of the bag. It was a plush

German shepherd, lying on its side, wearing a little police vest and badge. It had a fluffy brown and black tail and a sewn on smile. Top Cop was embroidered on the back of its vest.

"Gunnie's going to think this is for him."

"Don't worry. I got him something too." He pointed to a chew toy on the floor. "It has a hidden compartment to hold a treat. He has to figure out how to get it out. He's been gnawing on it since I arrived. I thought that'd be better than a squeaky toy."

"I'd kill you if you got him a squeaky toy."

"That's what I figured."

"Fair warning, I might kill you anyway." I stared down at the stuffed animal, which Brad had bought just so I wouldn't be mad at him. "I don't accept bribes. At least not on purpose."

"It's not a bribe. Last night you complained you couldn't get comfortable because Gunnie had gone home. I know you were joking, but I thought it might help to elevate your arm and keep some of the pressure off your shoulder and neck. Plus, I'm the only idiot who hasn't gotten you something since the attack. Winters pointed that out to me last night. As your partner, I should have been first in line. My bad." Brad took the plush dog out of my hand and placed it on the couch beside me. "See, it's almost the same size as Gunnie. And he's a cop, just like you. I thought it was perfect."

"It is." I swallowed. "Thank you. But I'd like to know what happened today. You went to Kincaid, didn't you?"

Brad folded the gift bag and placed it flat on the table. "I did what had to be done."

"What does that mean? Axel's a killer. You said so yourself."

"It's never been proven."

"You and I watched him shoot someone."

"In self-defense," Brad muttered.

"That's not how you interpreted it when it happened."

"Things change, Liv."

"How? Did you get stupid all of a sudden?" I blinked, regretting my words. "Why would you go to Axel for help? You can't stand the guy."

A dark cloud settled over him. "I'll do whatever it takes to keep these bastards from hurting you or anyone else again. Jake found out Diego Eisner used to run with a crew."

"They boosted cars."

Brad's gaze flicked to me. "So you know why I went to Axel."

"That was almost ten years ago."

"True, but Kincaid knows things. The players. The targets. In case you haven't realized this yet, we don't have much to go on. If he can point us in the right direction, we can stop this."

"Fine, but you're the one who always tells me we can't trust him."

"This isn't about trust. I made a promise to you, and I plan to keep it. I'd rather beg Kincaid for help than gamble with your life or anyone else's."

"Does Jake know?"

"No. The brass wants this intel locked down tight. The stores in the plaza have been warned to watch out for suspicious activity and to look out for men matching the descriptions we have. LockBox is the only other entity that knows the extent of what's going on, and even they only know about the potential risk."

"If Axel blabs, what will that do to your career?"

"It's a calculated risk. And one I have no problem taking." Brad rubbed his face. "But he won't blab."

"Probably not, but he might blackmail you."

"So be it."

I pointed to the fancy gift basket. "In that case, that's your bribe. Not mine."

"Come on, don't be like that."

I sat up, resting my elbows on my knees and holding my head in my hands. "I never thought I'd see the day where you went to Kincaid for help."

"He's helped us in the past. This isn't any different."

But after our last encounter, Brad's already negative opinion of the car thief turned club owner had decreased further. I just wondered how many lines my partner would cross or the compromises he'd make to nail these bastards. "Don't lose who you are or what you stand for. I don't want to lose you."

He stared into my eyes. "You know me, Liv. You might be the only person who does. I know where the line is. Don't ever doubt that."

"At least tell me Axel gave you something solid."

"He's going to ask around and see what he can find out. In the meantime," Brad returned to the whiteboard, "Jake thinks he's on to something. We went over the prison records. Three weeks ago, Diego's cellmate was released from prison. He has a record of violence. Everything from assault and battery to voluntary manslaughter. The prosecutor pursued murder charges, but the jury didn't go for it. They convicted under the lesser sentence."

"What's his name?"

"Brandon Tarelli." Fennel handed me the tablet. "While you were getting your beauty rest, I was digging into him. He's a former military contractor, who went to work for a security firm before he let his anger issues get out of line."

"Not regular military?"

"No, but that would explain the training and his

knowledge of disarming security systems. Jake's hoping to get his hands on a recording for you to listen to."

"That would help." I eyed Tarelli's mugshot. He was older than I imagined, but he'd been in prison for quite some time.

"He had his hip and knee replaced in prison after a fight broke out and an overzealous guard went a little crazy with the baton."

"That fits the bill." I stared at Tarelli's mugshot and tried to imagine what he'd look like wearing a plastic Halloween mask. "But I'm not sure."

"Well, it's a mugshot. Not even a good one. The guy looks like a madman with frizzed out hair and gnarly teeth."

"Do we know where he is now?"

"We went by his last known address, but it's been boarded up."

"Has he checked in with his parole officer. He could be in a halfway house or something."

"No dice. Tarelli doesn't have a PO. He didn't get an early release. He ran out the clock."

"So he served a full term."

"What do you expect with that kind of behavior?"

I skimmed the page. He fought often with other inmates, had been found with contraband, and had generally done whatever it took to make his stay even less pleasant. "I'm surprised they didn't tack more time on to his sentence."

"Me too, but I'm guessing after the beating he took, the state didn't want to accidentally open a can of worms."

"What about before his arrest?"

"Jake's checking with Tarelli's ex-wife and whatever family he's got left to see if anyone has seen or heard from him. According to prison records, the only person who ever visited was his lawyer, and that stopped once his appeal was denied."

"Does Axel know him?"

"No, according to Mr. Fancy Pants, he wouldn't associate with anyone like that."

I read Tarelli's record again. "I doubt they ever traveled in the same circles. This guy's nothing but a bully and a barroom brawler." One glaringly obvious omission struck me. "He's not a thief."

"Kincaid?"

"No, he's definitely a thief. But Tarelli's not." I held out the tablet for Brad to reread.

"That would explain why so many people have gotten killed. Tarelli's out, and now he wants revenge."

Brad didn't say it, but I knew what he was thinking. A guy like Tarelli would have no qualms about writing a threatening message in a slain cop's blood. And I couldn't argue with that kind of logic.

THIRTY-NINE

The police are on the way. Get out now. Tarelli read the text one more time. This wasn't good. It's not what he planned. But this unexpected turn of events could work in his favor. He intended to kill Carter anyway. This would save him the trouble and hopefully lead the police on a wild goose chase. Then he could enact his actual plan. By the time anyone figured out what was really happening, it'd be too late. He smiled. This would be fun.

"I'm gonna grab a burger. I'll be back in a few minutes. Don't go anywhere."

"Hey, can you get me a soda?" Carter asked. "My stomach's not feeling so good."

"Really, I hadn't noticed." Tarelli rolled his eyes.

"Dude, I can't help it. You make me nervous. This," Carter waved his hand around the room, "makes me nervous. Diego too. That's why he went on a whiskey run."

"I don't care how nervous you get. You stay here. I mean it. You better be here when I get back or else you'll have plenty of reasons to toss your cookies."

Carter held up his palms. "Where the hell would I even go?"

"Good." Tarelli collected a few things, tucked a gun into the holster at the small of his back, and stuck the second one into the opened cardboard box. He picked it up, making sure he had everything he needed for his plan. The subway maps and LockBox uniforms were nothing more than a misdirect, but he knew once the police banged down the doors and found all of this, they'd be convinced. And that's exactly what he needed. This might be the best thing that had happened since watching the cop writhe on the floor. He found himself smiling.

"Why are you taking the box? Don't we need those?"

"I'm putting it in the trunk. It'll make it easier for us to grab when it's go-time. Why are you questioning me?"

"Whatever, man." Carter waited for the door to close before adding, "Psycho." Cautiously, he crossed the room and peered out the curtain. Once the car pulled away, Carter went to the door and turned the knob. If he wanted to escape, now was his chance, but he just couldn't do it. He knew if he did, Tarelli would hunt him down and kill him. And after seeing how much he enjoyed shooting the night watchman and torturing that poor police detective, Carter didn't want to know what types of agony he'd face if he fled. So he stayed and waited.

*   *   *

Every time I closed my eyes, I found myself back in the liquor store. The murder in his eyes chilled me to the bone. I shivered uncontrollably, unsure if that was from the blood loss or fear. "Who are you?" I screamed.

The notepad fell to the floor with a thunk, and I opened my eyes. "Em?" I called.

"She left three hours ago," Brad said. "She didn't want to wake you." He yawned. "What's wrong?"

"Take those away from me. Every time I take one, I pass out."

He picked up the bottle and put it on the end table out of my reach. He yawned again and stretched. "So what woke you up?"

"A nightmare."

He nodded, bleary-eyed. "Is that why you don't want to risk going back to sleep?"

I hadn't actually thought about it. I was too determined to reconcile Brandon Tarelli's mugshot with my memory of the third man to think about my rapidly beating heart or the cold sweat dripping down my back. "I don't want to sleep when the clock's ticking. What if we're wrong about the target?"

Brad picked up the notebook, piled everything onto the table, and offered me his hand. "Then we'll figure it out tomorrow. You need to sleep. You haven't recovered yet, and you won't unless you get enough rest. Give the bed another try, and if that doesn't work, we'll trade. Okay?" He looked exhausted.

I sighed, knowing he was right. There was nothing we could do. This wasn't even our show. It was Voletek's. "Okay." I picked up the plush toy, laughing to myself. "We'll see how this works. But I normally don't sleep with cops."

"Unless it's me," he teased.

"That's because you're special."

"So are you." A strange look came over his face. "Sweet dreams."

I went down the hall and climbed into bed, too

tired to change out of my clothes. The moment my head hit the pillow, I was out. And I didn't wake again until the phone rang.

From my bedroom, I could hear Brad's voice. During the course of the night, a patrol unit pulled over a car with expired tags. When they ran the plates, they found it had been reported stolen a few hours earlier. Diego Eisner was behind the wheel.

"Did they find anything in the car?" Brad asked. "Really? A motel room?" He paused. "Uh-huh."

I got out of bed, grabbed some clothes, and went into the bathroom. Through the wall I could still hear him.

"What about the other one?" Brad waited for a response. "But you found Carter?" Another pause. "Okay, I'll tell Liv."

By the time Brad hung up, I had finished in the bathroom. "What's going on?" I asked.

"Patrol made a stop last night. They arrested Diego Eisner leaving a liquor store and they found a motel key in his wallet which led to Carter Moore. They didn't get eyes on the third man, but the motel clerk recognized Tarelli's mugshot. He's been renting the room for the last three weeks."

"Since his release."

"It looks that way. Tarelli paid up for the rest of the month in cash the same day he robbed Star Cleaners."

"He probably used the money from the drawer."

"Voletek and Lisco found the LockBox uniforms and the empty cash boxes from the dispensary in the motel room. They didn't find any cash though, except whatever Diego and Carter had in their wallets, which didn't sound like much. Voletek thinks Tarelli must have everything with him. He might not trust his accomplices."

"Did they find anything else?"

"Not really."

"Guns?" I asked.

"No. Tarelli must have those too, unless Diego and Carter ditched them when they spotted the patrol unit. Voletek thinks Tarelli still plans to go through with this even though we have his crew in custody." Brad stepped past me and toward the bathroom. "Grab some breakfast and get ready to go. Lt. Winston wants to conduct a lineup to cover his ass. So every witness we have is being brought in to point out whoever they recognize, and the LT wants you to make an ID too."

"I never saw them."

"I know, but you heard their voices. You already know who they are. So all you have to do is ID them."

Blowing out a breath, I went into the kitchen, dumped some fruits and veggies into the blender and made us breakfast to go. Then I filled our travel mugs and took a seat at the table and stared into the living room. The profiles on the board stared back at me. Why wasn't Tarelli there? Was he tipped off?

"Ready?" Brad asked.

"Just one sec." I went into my bedroom and grabbed my backup piece from my nightstand drawer, checked the safety, and tucked it into my purse. "I guess."

"Expecting trouble?"

"Yeah, from Winston."

Brad laughed. "I wouldn't doubt it."

I followed my partner out to his car. The protection detail would escort us to the precinct and await orders there. I hated having them babysit me, but there was nothing I could do about it. Not while Brandon Tarelli remained at large.

When I walked through the doors to homicide, several sets of eyes turned to me, quickly followed by several "welcome back"s and "how are you feeling"s. During the commotion, Lt. Winston appeared in the conference room doorway with his arms folded over his chest.

"Everyone, get back to work. We have a killer to find." Winston waved me over. "DeMarco, glad to see you up and about. Now get in here." He glared at my partner. "You too, Fennel."

"He's mad at you," I whispered.

"He's mad at both of us," Brad replied. "It's a good thing I have you to protect me."

I fought to conceal my grin. "Shut up."

Winston paced near the table, his attention split between the files and the data on the board. "Close the door." He didn't even bother to look up at us. "I take it you're aware of what's been going on, DeMarco."

"Just bits and pieces, sir."

"You're recovering from a life-threatening injury sustained while on the job. You shouldn't be aware of any of this, but given the circumstances, I understand you have a vested interest. No one who wears a uniform could fault you for wanting to know the men responsible have been taken into custody. However, you are prohibited from working on this case. You aren't a detective. You're a victim. And right now, I need you to be a witness. Only five people have survived their encounters with these men, and you're one of them."

"Sir?"

"Normally, I would have let them sweat it out in holding before moving forward. But in case you haven't heard," he scowled at Voletek, who pretended not to notice, "we're on a time crunch. We believe the killer plans to strike again in less than twelve hours. We need as much information as we can get on what he plans to rob and who he might want to kill. So we're moving quickly on this. I know you haven't been cleared for duty. But I'm not asking you to be a cop."

"What are you asking me?"

"The delivery truck driver, the liquor store owner, and the woman from the subway station are already here. We've been conducting lineups. Only one witness has positively identified one of the men. I need you to do better than that."

"I don't know if I can." I'd seen Diego's photo and I'd met Carter. Defense council would have a field day with this one.

"You're a cop. What you say carries more weight, the same's true of Officer Cruz."

"I didn't see them, sir. You read my statement."

Winston nodded, shifting the papers around on the table. "But you said you could recognize their voices. It's the only way to keep it unbiased. Cruz wasn't much help. Diego we have dead to rights because of the DNA evidence found at the scene. But the other one, he's gonna walk if you don't do something."

"Can't you compel Carter Moore to turn over a blood sample?" Brad asked.

"Easier said than done," Winston muttered.

"I got this, sir," I said.

"Good, and once we have grounds to hold him, Voletek and Lisco are going to need you and Fennel to assist on breaking him." The lieutenant focused on my partner. "You said Carter's the weak link. That he'd give up the other two. You better be right about that."

"He apologized to us," Brad said. "When we spoke to him the morning we questioned his roommate, Carter Moore apologized. He has a conscience. Seeing Liv will make him feel guilty. He'll crack." At least that had been my theory, and the one Brad must have shared with Voletek and Lisco.

Winston pressed his lips together. "One step at a

time." But he didn't like this. Police work needed to be clean, and this case was anything but. "All right, DeMarco. Officer Roberts will escort you to the waiting area. Once everything's set, you'll be asked to ID the offenders from the lineup. We're doing it blind. They won't see you, and you won't see them. Voice recognition only. And if you're not sure..." He didn't finish that statement. I wasn't sure if he wanted me to lie, but I wasn't that kind of cop.

FORTY

"Number four," I faced the wall, my back to the glass, "that's him."

"You're positive? You barely heard him speak. At the time, you were suffering from shock brought about by extreme blood loss."

"I'm positive." I turned to defense council. "You don't forget the man who planned to put a bullet in your head after he shoved you through a glass door." And based on the attorney's protest, I knew I picked the right guy.

"Roberts, take number four into the interrogation room to get comfortable." The officer conducting the lineup pressed the intercom and had the room cleared.

Roberts exited, waiting at the door to escort Carter Moore to his own private suite. I remained in the closed room, just so the suspect wouldn't see me. Winston might want to use my presence as an element of surprise. Another officer escorted the defense attorney out of the room, so he could confer with his client, who had just gone from being in the wrong place at the wrong time to facing serious charges.

"Was a lineup really necessary?" the officer asked, glancing in my direction. "You're a homicide detective. You told us who attacked you before we even arrested him. This was a waste." He rolled his eyes. "Just another hoop IAD wants us to jump through."

"I know, but we're doing things by the book. Every T is getting crossed. The DA's office doesn't want to risk anything jeopardizing this case. Not with these stakes."

Officer Roberts returned a few minutes later. "You ready, DeMarco? I'm supposed to escort you back to homicide."

"Sure." I nodded to the officer and followed Roberts out of the room. "Hey, I didn't get a chance to say it earlier, but thank you."

Roberts didn't even slow on the stairs. "You're a cop. You bleed blue, just like me."

"Yeah, but you saved my life. I can't thank you enough."

Roberts grunted. We'd crossed paths several times over the years, but he never liked me much. At first, I thought it had to do with my father, but Brad thought it was because Roberts had a misogynistic streak, like a lot of men in the department. "I was just doing my job, DeMarco. And if you'd done yours better, you might not have been in that situation. But you're okay. And it looks like we'll get these guys, so I guess it all worked out. Just remember, patrol does a lot more than run errands and fetch your coffee."

I never asked patrol to bring me coffee, but I let that slide. "Regardless, I owe you."

He shook his head. "Your partner already thanked me with a bottle of something aged, brown, and fairly expensive." He stopped at the door to homicide. "Just be careful out there. I don't like going to cop funerals."

Brad waited for me near his desk. "Heard you did good down there."

"Yep."

"You okay?"

"Why wouldn't I be?"

"Y'never know." He jerked his chin toward the conference room. "Voletek and Lisco want to go over everything that happened at 24/7 Spirits again. They're hoping they can use your firsthand account to play on Carter Moore's emotions. If that doesn't fly, they'll take a crack at Diego Eisner."

"What are you doing?"

"Trying to stay off the LT's shit list."

"I think it's too late for that."

"You better get in there unless you want to join me as persona non grata."

After going over everything for what felt like the millionth time, Detectives Voletek and Lisco entered the interrogation room. Lt. Winston stood beside me on the other side of the two way glass while we watched them go over the information and potential charges with Carter and his council. I kept my eyes glued to what was happening inside the interrogation room, but Winston hadn't even bothered to face the glass. Instead, he just stared at me.

"You feel like having a conversation, DeMarco? Because I'd love to know what you were doing at that liquor store while off duty at that time of night."

"I couldn't sleep."

He sipped his coffee. "How'd you know they'd be there?"

"I didn't."

"But they were. And I have a hard time believing that was purely coincidental."

"Of course it wasn't coincidental," I fought to hold my tone in check, "sir. Diego Eisner's been there before. I'd bet my badge on it. That's his preferred location. I just don't know why."

"According to the liquor store owner, our suspect is not a regular. He only recalls seeing him once before, and that's from the morning in question."

"No, he's been there before."

"How do you know that, DeMarco? Where's your proof?"

"I don't have any."

"And yet you were so convinced of this fact that you drove there in the middle of the night to question the store owner again."

"I was right, wasn't I? Diego was there. They were all there, lieutenant."

"But how did you know that?"

"I didn't. If I did, I would have waited for backup. I might have even called in tactical." I looked away from the window, realizing Winston really didn't understand. "They used Jonathan Gardner's credit card at that liquor store a few minutes after they killed him. It had to be significant. It's the only thing they've done that hasn't made sense. Everything else has gone from point A to point B. But that was just a random unconnected event. Why do it?"

"So why did they do it?"

"I don't know. Originally, Fennel and I thought it might have been to confuse us or the timeline surrounding Gardner's murder. But that never quite fit. After what happened," I touched the bandage on my neck, realizing I hadn't changed it this morning, "and the threat Tarelli left and the theft of the police uniforms, I think he wanted to get his hands on some cops when they got off shift. I think that might have been the goal."

"But since he couldn't get his hands on any first responders that day, he bought a bottle of hooch to celebrate?"

"I guess."

"Which he?" Winston asked. "Tarelli's the brains behind this. He's the violent killer, right? But Diego's the one who we found at a different liquor store last night. And the owner of 24/7 Spirits identified Diego as the man who bought the bottle of Jack and threatened his life. So what am I missing here? Do we have it wrong? Are you sure Tarelli has the bloodlust and not Diego?"

"The man who wanted me dead didn't sound like Diego Eisner. He had a gravelly voice and a bad knee. Diego has neither." I turned back to the glass. "Did you drug test them?"

"Carter came back positive for marijuana. Alcohol too."

"And Diego?"

"Alcohol."

"Nothing else?"

"No."

"That might be it."

"What's it?"

I shook my head and left the observation room. "Brad," I went to my desk, finding the computer off and a dozen or so get well cards stacked in the center, "you wanted to know where that CBD oil came from. Did you ever find out?"

"It wasn't a prescription. The proportions were off. Ellie thinks it might have been a homemade concoction." He lowered his voice. "Emma's pharmacist friend said the same thing."

"Thanks." I turned to head back to the observation room, shaking off the unexpected dizziness. You're still not 100%, the voice in my head reminded me. But I was on to something.

When I returned to the observation room, I found Lt. Winston waiting for me. "Well?" he asked.

"Diego and Tarelli were cellmates. That's how they hooked up."

"Brilliant deduction," he said sarcastically.

"Carter doesn't connect to Diego. He connects to Tarelli. I'm not sure where or how, but I'm guessing Carter's fondness for pot and Tarelli's use of CBD oil is how they met. It's possible Tarelli picked some up in the grocery store where Carter works. It's also possible they initially crossed paths at the dispensary. Since CBD doesn't have THC, it's legal in most places and doesn't require a prescription."

"Which means there'd be no record if they sold it to Tarelli. And that might explain why they had to kill the shop owner. Good job, DeMarco. Let's see if your assumptions pay off." Winston turned on his heel and entered the interrogation room.

I leaned against the table and watched the lieutenant take over. Within minutes, he convinced Carter Moore that we knew more than we did and it was just a matter of time before we could prove it. And while Carter tried to wait it out, the man who masterminded the entire thing would continue with his plan, kill more people, and escape to some tropical island with his ill-gotten gains.

"You attacked two cops," Winston said. "You put them both in the hospital. One of them nearly went to the morgue. You spoke to her. Twice, if I'm not mistaken. Both times you apologized, but sorry's not going to cut it. Right now, you're the only one we can prove has been violent. We have two cops who've pointed the finger right at you. So unless you give us something to indicate you aren't behind this entire thing, like you insisted by apologizing to the detective you almost murdered, I'd say we're done here. I'm sure your buddy, Diego, will have a lot more to say. He's been inside. He doesn't want to go back. He'll deal. And all it's going to take is for him to point the finger at you and it's game over."

Carter swallowed, his leg jittering up and down as sweat dripped down his temple. I almost felt bad for the guy. Almost.

The defense attorney came back with an argument of his own about wanting to see the evidence and the list of potential charges Carter might be facing, but Carter would have none of that. Despite the warning to remain silent and not incriminate himself, Carter's conscience won out.

"Brandon Tarelli. That's who you want. That's the guy who wanted me to shoot that cop lady. He," Carter swallowed, "he said he'd kill me if I didn't do it. He put a gun right to the back of my head."

"That changes things," his attorney said. "My client was acting under duress. Forced to participate while fearing for his life."

"Save the arguments. We're not in court yet," Winston warned. "But we'll take that into consideration." He placed his palms on the table and stared at Carter. "Where's Tarelli now?"

"I...I don't know," Carter whimpered, rocking slowly from side to side. "He said we had to stay together. He didn't trust me. He wanted to kill me." Carter jerked his chin up and pointed at his neck. "He tried to choke me, but Diego stopped him. Diego stopped him when Brandon tried to shoot me too."

Lisco put her hands on her thighs and leaned over to get a better look. At least someone in the interrogation room had the decency to pretend to care. "So you and Diego are friends?"

"Sort of. We've been hanging out a lot lately. Ever since we met."

"When was that?" she asked.

"I don't know. Like two weeks ago. I ran into Brandon Tarelli at the dispensary when I was filling my prescription. I have anxiety." Carter looked Winston in the eye for the first time since he entered. "Seriously, you can ask my doctor."

"We might." Winston wouldn't even give an inch. "So you met Brandon there."

"Yeah, he heard me joking around with Mr. D."

"Mr. D.?" Voletek stepped in. "You mean the man who ran the dispensary? The one who was murdered just outside his shop?"

Carter bit his lip, tears forming in his eyes. "Yeah. You gotta believe me. I didn't know that was going to happen. Brandon never said anything about hurting anyone, just like the security guard in the dry cleaner's. I didn't know about that either. Everything just went to shit real fast. I didn't know what to do. I just...I didn't want to die."

"All right," Winston said, "start at the beginning."

The attorney glared at the homicide lieutenant. "I want it put on record that my client is cooperating and that he was an unwilling participant in these crimes."

"Let's hear his story first before we start pinning medals on his chest," Winston retorted.

"Brandon followed me out of the dispensary and struck up a conversation while I was waiting for my rideshare to pick me up. He asked what blend I liked the best and how long I'd been going to that dispensary. I guess I must have told him that me and Mr. D. went way back." He got a little choked up. "I don't know. I've had a lot of weird conversations with people at that shop, so I didn't think too much about it. Then while we were talking, Diego shows up. Somehow, we just ended up hanging out at a bar and talking most of the day."

"About what?" Winston asked.

"The dispensary mostly. I had some crazy stories that Mr. D. had told me or that I'd heard from Mike's friend."

"Michael Tolliver, your roommate?" Voletek asked.

Carter looked around. "I don't want to get him in trouble. He doesn't know anything about any of this. He's a good guy. Leave him alone."

For the next half hour, Carter spilled his guts on the things he'd overheard Michael Tolliver and Jonathan Gardner saying about the night watchman gigs. And Carter had shared all of that with Brandon Tarelli and Diego Eisner. That must have been when Tarelli came up with his scheme to rob the armored truck. Based on Carter's story, it sounded like Tarelli might have planned to knock over the all-cash business but decided it'd be more lucrative to go for the truck instead. But since Carter possessed most of the intel needed, Tarelli invited him to join them. Since the pothead could barely scrape by on his two minimum wage jobs, he probably didn't need that much convincing.

"Brandon swore to me no one would get hurt. These were supposed to be victimless crimes. We go in, get some uniforms, then unload the back of the truck, and walk away. It was supposed to be easy money. But none of it went the way it was supposed to. When he killed the security guard at the dry cleaner's I knew I had to get away from him, but he made us stick together. It's like he knew."

"So when did he leave?" Winston asked.

"He left maybe fifteen minutes before you showed up. Diego wanted to get a drink. So he went to pick up some booze. Before he got back, Brandon said he needed to run an errand and he'd be right back. He told me not to go anywhere." Carter bit his lip. "By the time I worked up the courage to make a break for it, you guys busted in."

"Voletek," Winston jerked his chin at the door, "see if you can get some corroboration." Voletek slipped out of the room and went across to the other interrogation room. I remained where I was, watching Winston continue the interview. "We know he has police uniforms. What is he planning to do with them?"

"Don't answer that," the attorney warned.

"If he doesn't answer, Diego will." Winston waited. "And Diego didn't slice open my star detective's throat with a glass door."

"No, it's okay. I don't want anyone else to get hurt. I'm sorry that happened. Is she okay?" Carter asked.

"She should be fine," Lisco said. "But whoever Tarelli goes after next won't be. You know that. You know what he's capable of doing. You've seen it firsthand. Help us save someone's life."

"We were supposed to take out the armored transport tonight. He said it'd be filled with cash. All we had to do was dress the part, open the doors, and walk away. Brandon had the subway routes mapped out. We were going to split our shares and split up. I'd never have to see him again."

Winston shoved a pad and pen in front of Carter. "We need the location and time. Every detail you know."

And while Carter wrote everything down, Voletek convinced Diego Eisner to give up the same information in the next room. Tarelli planned to hit the LockBox armored truck when it arrived at metro plaza and escape on the subway.

"Do you think he'll go through with it without a crew?" Voletek asked once we reassembled in the conference room.

"He has everything he needs," Lisco said. "He won't be able to haul off as much, but he won't have to share it either."

"All right, let's get tactical on that truck, snipers in the area, and plainclothes officers covering every shop, exit, and entrance. This guy isn't killing anyone else, and he sure as hell isn't getting away." Winston dismissed the room, leaving Brad and me to see ourselves out.

Brad sighed. "I guess that's that. Are you ready to go home?"

"They're wrong."

Brad studied my expression. "The uniforms," he said. "Tarelli has the wrong uniform, unless this has been his plan all along. Maybe he figures he'll be able to slip in and out without anyone noticing if he's dressed like a cop."

"No, he didn't count on his team getting caught. And he didn't steal the police uniforms in order to rob a LockBox truck. He already had LockBox uniforms, and he left those behind. He has something else in mind." I reached for the copy of Carter Moore's statement and confession. "He said Tarelli wanted to hit the armored transport, not truck."

"He could have misspoken."

I peered into the bullpen, but everyone was already moving on this. "We better make sure."

FORTY-ONE

"What kind of armored transports do we have in the area?" I asked. "What about prison transfers?"

Brad shook his head. "Nothing close to us."

I looked at Brandon Tarelli's prison record. From what I gathered, he didn't make many friends in prison, aside from Diego. Okay, so this wasn't a prison break. "Federal?"

"I don't know. The Reserve does transport a lot of old money to get destroyed."

"It also delivers new money to get distributed." I thought for a moment. "It's not uncommon to have uniforms assist in securing the area."

"That's a possibility. I'll make some calls."

While my partner did that, I tried to come up with other possible targets. The bastard took my badge, either as a trophy or an access card. So what could I access that would be worth stealing?

"Hey, did they put an alert out if someone uses my badge number?" I asked Brad.

"That's the first thing they should have done, but since I've been with you, I'm not sure."

"All right, I'll check with Mac and then head down to forensics and see if maybe there's some evidence we haven't considered. It's possible they found something else in the motel room that Winston failed to share with us."

"Okay." He watched me climb out of the chair. "Are you sure you should be moving around so much?"

"I'm fine. I'll let you know when I'm not, or you'll find me curled up on the floor or napping in the stairwell."

My first stop was to see Mac. The department had alerts set up to find my badge and Officer Cruz's. So far, no one had tried to impersonate either one of us, and if they had, the civilians hadn't reported it, not that they would know to do that.

"Winston has a strike team on standby, I thought we were just waiting to scoop up the guy," Mac said.

"We are, but something doesn't feel right."

"Armored transport and armored truck are synonymous."

"Yeah, but he left the LockBox uniforms behind at the motel."

"How did he even know officers were coming to get him?" Mac asked.

"I'm guessing Diego sent him a message when he spotted a patrol car in the rearview mirror."

"Possibly. We didn't get a ping on his registered phone, but he might have had a burner he tossed before he got pulled over."

"That's the only thing that makes sense to me."

"So if Tarelli had time to grab the police uniforms, he should have had time to grab the LockBox uniforms too." She drummed her fingers on the desk while she thought. "I don't know. It could be anything."

"That's why I'm on my way to the lab. Cross your fingers that they have something useful to tell me."

On my way, I passed a few unis and fellow detectives. I just reached for the door handle to the lab when a gravelly voice sounded from the other end of the hallway. "Sure, no problem."

Ice ran through my veins. I knew that voice. It had haunted my dreams these last few days. I peered down the hallway, but I couldn't pinpoint the source. Too many other officers were in the way. Some were standing around talking. Others were headed somewhere. He has a bad knee, I reminded myself. But I didn't see anyone with a limp.

Grabbing my phone, I dialed my partner. "I think he's here."

"Who?" Brad asked.

"Tarelli. I swear I just heard his voice."

"Where are you?"

I told him while I slipped my hand into my bag and headed toward where I thought the voice had originated.

"All right, Liv. I'll get the building locked down, and we'll do a sweep. I'll have the emergency notification system text every cop in the building to be on alert for Tarelli. Just don't do anything stupid. I mean it."

But I couldn't let this bastard get away. I moved down the corridor, passing doors as I went. Why would he come to the police station? What could we possibly have here that would be worth stealing? Or did he just come to kill as many cops as he could? If that were the case, he would have opened fire already. So he must have had a goal in mind. I checked the evidence room, but everything was locked up tight.

"Did someone just come in here or leave?" I asked.

"No," the officer behind the counter said.

"Thanks." I stepped away from the counter and went back out the door. Evidence could be valuable, but that wasn't Tarelli's target. So what was? My phone let out two quick beeps, signifying the alert. My partner was on top of this, but now Tarelli had to scramble. And I knew he was armed.

At the end of the hallway was a stairwell that led downstairs to the parking garage. Since it was the only place I hadn't looked, I took a breath and headed down to the main parking level. Parked near the elevator was a police transport. The armored exterior shined beneath the fluorescent lights.

It was so obvious, we missed it. The transport came like clockwork to take the evidence from our lockup and move it to the evidence warehouse for safe keeping. Anything could be inside, from drugs to guns to stacks of money and jewels. Whatever we found at a crime scene was confiscated and held until it was cleared and released or destroyed. This must be the payday he was waiting for.

I crept around the truck, finding it empty. The rear door was open, and I peeked in, but no one was inside. The officers must be on their way to collect the evidence. From there, they'd bring it down to the garage and load the truck. Tarelli must be lying in wait for them. If he was smart, he wouldn't make his move until they loaded the truck. Then he'd probably take them out and drive away. The officer at the gate would see the police uniform and think nothing of raising the gate and letting him out. Tarelli would walk away with a major score and leave a few dead cops in his wake. It was everything he wanted and more, but I wasn't going to let him get it.

I texted Brad an update on the situation and moved to the freight elevator. They'd have to use the elevator to move the pallets down from evidence, so Tarelli might be inside or he could still be upstairs, assisting the police in wheeling down his prize.

The doors opened, but the elevator was empty. Letting out a sigh, I turned around just in time to see a police baton swinging toward my face. I threw myself to the ground and rolled out of the way of a second swing. I removed my gun from my bag as I fought to gain my footing and get up. The adrenaline surge kept the dizziness away.

Surprise etched the asshole's face. "I thought you were dead."

"Guess you were wrong." I aimed at him. He wore a standard patrol uniform, complete with hat and sunglasses. The brim concealed most of his features. He was clean-cut and fresh-faced. But his voice gave him away. "It's over, Tarelli. Drop the weapon and put your hands on your head."

He lowered the baton slowly to the ground, but he looked from side to side. Rows of vehicles divided up the parking garage. "Are you going to cuff me again?"

Thoughts of that night raced through my mind. Movement at the periphery caught my eye, and I glanced in that direction, expecting someone to jump out at me. But it was just the elevator doors closing.

However, in that split second, Tarelli broke to the side and darted between two parked cars. Now I couldn't see him.

"Give up. You're just making this worse for yourself," I warned.

He laughed, that awful sound I had heard while I lay in utter agony inside the liquor store. And then shots rang out. I dove to the side, sliding beneath a guardrail and rolling onto my knees beside a parked car. It might have been the captain's car. I wasn't sure, nor did I care. I steadied my aim on the hood of the vehicle and waited. The moment Brandon Tarelli's head popped into sight I fired.

"Missed." He used the parked cars as protection while I fired another three rounds straight at him. "Try again."

But I resisted the urge to fire. He wanted me to expel my entire clip, but I didn't have a good angle or a clear shot. My cell phone had fallen to the ground beside the elevator, along with the rest of the spilled items from my purse, so calling for backup was out of the question.

A metallic thud sounded somewhere deep in the garage. Was he alone? I didn't know. And I couldn't see him. Was he planning on sneaking up behind me again?

Suddenly the lights went out, replaced by the red emergency lighting. Not again, I thought.

Going against every bit of training that had been programmed into me, I calculated the distance to the stairwell, slid beneath the guardrail, and ran as fast as I could for the door. "Hurry," I screamed. "Tarelli's down here."

Before I made it up the steps, he was on me. He grabbed my hair and pulled me backward. I stumbled, twisting out of his grip and tripping on the steps. Turning, I squeezed the trigger again, grazing him. He howled, pinning my arm and banging it against the wall until my gun clattered to the floor.

"You fucking bitch." He pressed his palm into his shoulder, pulling his hand away to find it red with blood. "I'm gonna paint the walls with you." He removed the Glock from his police-issued holster and aimed.

I kicked him, knocking the gun from his hand. He stumbled backward down the steps and collided with the doorframe. He reached for my fallen gun, and I launched myself at him. We landed hard on the ground, rolling back into the parking garage. My injured shoulder collided with the concrete, and the sudden onslaught made me release him.

He climbed to his feet, scooping up the baton he'd been forced to discard. "I'm gonna make this hurt, just like they hurt me."

"Who hurt you?" I slid backward along the floor, desperate to get to my weapon.

"The guards. Officers. Men with their pathetic uniforms. They thought they were so much better. But they were just scared. You get one alone, and he'd practically piss himself." He gave me an ugly smile. "Just like you, right now. Scared. Alone. Afraid. You know I'm going to kill you. That you're going to die. That's why you want to hurt me. But I'm going to hurt you first. Show you what it's like."

The clang of the baton echoed through the garage.

"It won't matter. We know who you are. You can't hide. You're going back. You might as well smile pretty for the camera. It's right behind you."

Automatically, he glanced over his shoulder, and I kicked him in the sternum, sending him sprawling backward. I raced toward my gun, but he grabbed my ankle. I hit the ground hard.

White-hot pain went through me, sending a cascade of fire through my neck and shoulder. For a moment, I thought I'd black out. My instincts took over, and I kicked my free leg backward, forcing him to let go. I flipped over to face him, but I couldn't find my footing to get off the ground so I scrambled backward, digging my heels into the concrete and pushing off to put as much distance between us as possible. I had to get to the stairwell and get my gun.

He laughed, lifting the baton and moving toward me. He cleared the distance between us in no time. At that moment, I reached my gun, aimed, and fired.

Tarelli's eyes went wide, and he looked down, watching the blood blossom across his chest. Another shot rang out from above me, followed by two more from behind. All four bullets hit him center mass, and then Brad stepped between me and my fallen attacker. He held his gun in both hands and stared down at the man.

"Liv, are you okay?"

"Uh-huh." I climbed to my feet, still aiming at the killer.

Half a dozen police officers barreled down the stairs while another four stepped out of the freight elevator. Officer Roberts gave me a look. "Didn't I tell you to be more careful, DeMarco?"

While officers secured the scene, cuffed Tarelli, and attended to him while we waited for the paramedics to arrive, Brad took the gun from my shaking hand, passed it off to an officer, and hugged me tightly. "Are you sure you're okay?" He pulled away, eyeing my neck. "Sit down." He made sure the stairwell was clear and peeled the bandage away from my skin. "I think you ripped a stitch." He hollered into the parking garage, "Someone get me a first aid kit."

"What the hell took you so long?" I teased, gasping and trembling from too much adrenaline.

He gave me a lopsided grin. "Really? You're gonna be a ballbuster now? Didn't I tell you not to do anything stupid?"

"Here, Detective," one of the officers said. He gave us a look. "You both shot that prick. I'm sorry, but you know the rules."

"Yeah, just give me a minute to patch up my partner." Brad handed the waiting cop his firearm and opened the first aid kit. He took out some gauze and pressed it against my neck. "Keep pressure on it."

My fingertips brushed against his, and I felt the

tremor. "Are you okay?"

"Right as rain. How 'bout you?" He withdrew his hand from beneath mine. "Does anything else hurt?"

"My shoulder."

He checked the back of my shirt, finding it damp and sticky. He reached into the first aid kit and pulled out more gauze and some tape. "Liv's going to need a ride to the hospital."

Mac bounded down the steps, having heard the commotion. The entire precinct must be buzzing by now. "I'll take her," she volunteered, "unless you want to wait for an ambulance."

"No, I'm okay." I stood, glad that Brad steadied me when the floor suddenly pitched.

"You sure?" he asked.

"Positive." I let out a breath. "We got him."

"Yes. We did." He nodded to one of the cops who'd fired from the freight elevator.

"I'm just thankful it's finally over," I said.

"That makes two of us." Brad brushed my hair out of my face. "Go get stitched up. I'll meet you at the hospital later."

FORTY-TWO

"How long are you going to be out?" Dad asked. When the cruise ship docked at port, he'd gotten several dozen messages and called me immediately.

"A couple of weeks, but I'll be stuck behind a desk for a while. Something about my red blood cell count."

"But you're sure you're okay, honey?"

"I'm fine, Dad." I held the device farther away from my face so he could see more of me. "Just a few stitches. Nothing to worry about. Like I said, everyone overreacted."

"For a former UC, you should be better at lying."

"I'm fine. Now you sound like Mom."

"Your mother wanted to hop the first flight back. I thought she'd jump ship and swim to you." She smacked him, and he rubbed his shoulder. "Ouch."

"Are you sure you don't need us to come home, Olive?" Mom asked, leaning closer to my dad so I could see her too.

"I'm okay. I'm at home, hanging out on the couch and watching TV with Gunnie."

"What about food?" Mom asked. "Do you have anything to eat?"

"She's an adult, Maria," my dad scolded.

"I got it covered. Emma brought over the freezer meals you made, and Brad's on his way with pizza."

"Okay, but if you need anything, you let us know," Mom repeated for the hundredth time.

"Yeah, I will. I love you. Enjoy the rest of your trip." I disconnected and tossed the phone onto the table and sighed. Gunnie turned and looked at me. "Don't give me that look. They're your parents too."

A few minutes later, Brad let himself in to my apartment, carrying a cauliflower crust pizza. He put the box on the table, grabbed a hard cider from my fridge, and sat down on the opposite end of the couch.

"So what's the verdict?" I asked.

"Investigation's over. Everyone's been cleared. Not that we had any doubts. Brandon Tarelli was a piece of work. It turns out he'd launched several abuse claims in prison, but his lawyer never made much progress on them. The injuries Tarelli sustained were thought to be the result of prison fights and necessary force needed to break up the riots he caused. Based on the things he said to you and his two accomplices, I don't think that's what happened. I'm not sure if they'll launch an investigation into the prison and the guards in question, but I think they might."

"Prison made him worse."

"Perhaps, or it just made him angrier."

"What about Carter and Diego?"

"They'll both serve time. Diego killed someone, but the DA's willing to consider the factors involved. They might take a plea for manslaughter. Carter's an accessory, but there's mitigating circumstances. I'm sure they'll both face robbery and conspiracy charges, but other than that, you'd have to ask Logan Winters what the DA wants to do."

"How are you?"

He snorted. "Winston's pissed. He's angry we made him look bad, so he's blaming us for this mess. Apparently, we should have shared this intel with him, Voletek, and Lisco before they ran off with the strike team."

"We didn't know anything for sure. And something tells me he wouldn't have listened anyway."

"That's not really the point." Brad popped the top and took a sip. "Is Emma still mad at me?"

"Emma's always mad at you."

"To be honest, I'm enjoying the silent treatment."

"You know, since Tarelli's dead, you don't have to spend all your off hours hanging around here."

"Are you kicking me out? I came to the rescue, DeMarco. You should be grateful."

"I am." I reached for a slice of pizza, my gaze stopping on the bottle of cognac. "You want to crack that open?"

"I thought you weren't willing to accept bribes, especially from Axel Kincaid."

"I'm not. I also can't drink with my pills. But you are obviously in need of some libations." I pointed to the bottle in his hand. "And I don't have anything else in the house to offer you."

Brad drained the cider, unwilling to let it go to waste, and reached for the cognac. "That's the first time Kincaid hasn't come through with something for you. I guess that means this isn't a bribe. It's just a get well gift."

"Or he didn't have any intel on Tarelli, which makes sense. Tarelli didn't have much of a plan when he got out of prison aside from getting revenge on everybody in uniform and stealing as much money as possible. Everything just fell into place when he happened to overhear Carter Moore talking to the dispensary owner. And since Tarelli had a limited crew, Kincaid never heard a thing. Axel may be connected, but he's not a mind reader."

"I still don't get how Tarelli knew about the evidence transport. He had it timed perfectly, and he managed to get into the precinct and down to the parking garage without issue."

"Another problem for another day," I said.

Brad pointed at the box of chocolates. "Which means you shouldn't let those go to waste either."

"Maybe we'll have them for dessert."

"Oh, I get to stay for dessert?" His lip quirked up on the side. "I thought you were kicking me out."

"I'm not kicking you out. I just don't want what happened to me to keep you from having a life outside of work. Outside of us."

He put the bottle of cognac down. "What if this is what I want? You and me. This. What's wrong with that?"

"There's nothing wrong with it. But you deserve more."

"So do you, but I don't see you jumping at any of the offers coming your way."

I shrugged. "I'm good with this for now."

"Me too."

DON'T MISS FATAL MISTAKE, THE NEXT
NOVEL IN THE THRILLING DETECTIVE LIV
DEMARCO SERIES.

ABOUT THE AUTHOR

G.K. Parks is the author of the Alexis Parker series. The first novel, *Likely Suspects,* tells the story of Alexis' first foray into the private sector.

G.K. Parks received a Bachelor of Arts in Political Science and History. After spending some time in law school, G.K. changed paths and earned a Master of Arts in Criminology/Criminal Justice. Now all that education is being put to use creating a fictional world based upon years of study and research.

You can find additional information on G.K. Parks and the Alexis Parker series by visiting our website at
www.alexisparkerseries.com

Made in the USA
Monee, IL
26 October 2022

16579134R00194